# THE MYSTERY OF HAVERFORD HOUSE

# THE MYSTERY OF HAVERFORD HOUSE

Rachel Burton

An Aria Book

First published in the UK in 2024 by Head of Zeus

First published in the UK in 2024 by Head of Zeus Ltd,
part of Bloomsbury Publishing Plc

9 7 5 3 1 2 4 6 8

A catalogue record for this book is available from the British Library.

ISBN (PB): 9781803287287
ISBN (E): 9781803287263

Cover design: Leah Jacobs-Gordon

Typeset by Siliconchips Services Ltd UK

Printed and bound in Great Britain by
CPI Group (UK) Ltd, Croydon CR0 4YY

Head of Zeus Ltd
First Floor East
5–8 Hardwick Street
London EC1R 4RG

WWW.HEADOFZEUS.COM

For Simon

'O time, thou must untangle this, not I.
It is too hard a knot for me t'untie.'

William Shakespeare, *Twelfth Night*, Act 2, Scene 2

*Whether I shall turn out to be the hero of my own life,
or whether that station will be held by anybody else,
these pages must show.*

Charles Dickens, *David Copperfield*

# Part One

# BEGINNING

Central Park West, New York City – August 2003

*T*he *writer places her hands on her desk and breathes slowly. She looks out of the window towards Central Park and remembers all the times she has sat here before, watching the park change, season after season, year after year.*

*She is old now, almost too old. She is still able to look after herself – she has that dignity at least – but her books she dictates into a machine and her assistant Emily types them up for her. She looks at the Olivetti typewriter that still has pride of place on her desk, even though her hands are too arthritic to use it anymore. What would she do without Emily?*

*She wonders how many more books she has in her. This current one is her fortieth and the eleventh in the Inspector Monroe series. She doesn't sell quite as well as she did in her prime, but who does? The trend is turning towards a more psychological approach to crime than she is used to – examining the 'why' rather than the 'how'. But does it matter? She has more money than Croesus these days, as an*

3

old friend of hers used to say, more money than she has any use for, and no family to give it away to. Emily will become a very rich woman one day.

Today the writer finds herself thinking of England again. She hasn't been back for more decades than she cares to remember, more decades than either of her husbands lived for. She thinks of England more and more these days but today it was the article in The New York Times that started her off. A story about an old house that she used to know, a mystery that was never solved, and a discovery made last month in the grounds of the house during building works.

She smooths the pages of the newspaper, which still lies open in front of her, with her gnarled hands. Some days she can imagine she is still young, that the years haven't passed by so quickly, that she hasn't lost so much. But she only has to look down at her hands to remember. Where did the time go? When she looks in the mirror she barely recognises herself.

She glances at the newspaper again, but she has read it so many times that she knows it almost by heart. The name of the house will stay with her until the day she dies.

She could stay quiet of course, she could die holding on to the secret.

Or she could be brave and go back to England one last time, to put things to rights.

# I

Haverford House, Yorkshire – June 1928

The wooden stairs creak under my boots as I follow Mrs Derbyshire up towards the servants' quarters. The stairway smells musty and I grip the box containing my meagre belongings a little tighter. It is the same box that belonged to my mother when she worked here. My stomach contracts. I've never been away from home before. I've never slept anywhere other than the little room next to my mother's. What will it feel like to sleep somewhere else? What if I can't sleep at all?

'You'll be sharing a room with Polly,' Mrs Derbyshire says as we reach the top landing. I wonder who Polly is, what she is like, and whether she will like me.

Mrs Derbyshire seems stern and a little frightening at first. Everything seems frightening today and I'm not one for being easily frightened. I've never shared a room before – it has always been just me and my mother at home. I don't have any brothers or sisters, and although my room is tiny, it is my own. I'm trying to pull myself together a little when the housekeeper turns towards me and smiles kindly. Her face changes when she does, like a ray of sunlight breaking through rainclouds. My mother has already told me about Mrs Derbyshire, told me that her bark is worse than her bite.

'I know it's hard at first,' she says. 'I can still remember what it was like when I first left my parents' home to come to work here, even after all these years. You'll settle in soon enough – you'll see.'

Cheered a little by Mrs Derbyshire's words I look around the room that is to be mine. It is sparsely furnished, even more sparsely than the room I'd had at home – two single metal-framed beds with thin mattresses, a cupboard with a water pitcher on top of it, and a chest of drawers.

'The bed on the left will be yours,' Mrs Derbyshire says. 'And the bottom drawer of the chest.'

I nod, still clutching my mother's box in front of me as Mrs Derbyshire smiles again.

'Don't look so terrified, girl. We don't bite.' She pauses for a moment. 'How is your mother?' she asks. So she does know who I am then.

I nod again, my mouth dry. What is wrong with me? 'She's very well thank you, Mrs Derbyshire,' I manage in a strangled sort of voice.

Mrs Derbyshire presses her lips together as though drawing a line under any sort of reminiscence and I realise that it would not be the done thing to ask what it was like when my mother worked here.

'Now, there's a freshly pressed uniform for you there on the chest. When you're changed you can come down and meet the rest of the staff.' The housekeeper indicates the stairway we have just walked up – my way back down

6

to the kitchens without passing through the house itself. I am burning to see the house that my mother has spoken of so often but assume I am not to get a guided tour. I try to remember my place, like my mother told me to. I try to remember why I have to do this. I need to earn my living and find my way in the world.

After Mrs Derbyshire has left, the heels of her sensible black boots clunking back down the creaky stairs, the large bunch of housekeys jangling at her belt, I place my box on the narrow iron bed that will be mine for the foreseeable future. I wonder again what Polly will be like as I slowly undo the buckles and take out my few belongings – underthings, woollen stockings, a few other clothes, and one very precious item that I stow away in the bottom drawer wrapped in a scratchy blanket taken from home that I hope my mother won't miss. I couldn't be without this big grey book that I inherited from my father, even if I probably won't have much time to read it. I won't be separated from Shakespeare's *Complete Works* even if it does seem a strange thing for a housemaid to cherish.

Before I change into my uniform – a grey dress, made of material that looks almost as scratchy as the blanket, a white apron and cap – I look out of the window at the blue patch of sky I can see. A flock of birds flutter past and I envy them their freedom, wondering where they are going. My room, like all the servants' rooms, is in the eaves of the house, but if I crane my neck I can see the sunlight glinting off the famous Haverford Lake. Beyond it lies the village I have come from, the village I grew up in. I wish, just for a moment, I too were a bird that could fly over the lake and back to my home.

But life has changed as I always knew it would. I must stop dreaming now – dreaming about a life other than this, one that does not have me following in my mother's footsteps. I have known that Haverford House will be my future for most of my life and now that time has come.

I'm sixteen years old and it's time to grow up.

## 2

Haverford House, Yorkshire – June 2003

'Would one of these rooms have belonged to Annie Bishop?' an American accent asked from the back of the group. They didn't often get Americans on the tours. Americans always seemed to prefer to visit York or Harrogate rather than an old Georgian house in the middle of nowhere.

'Yes,' Viola replied. 'Annie would have slept up here although we don't have any records as to who slept in which room.'

'Would she have shared a room?' somebody else asked, slightly out of breath from the climb up to the servants' quarters.

'From what we know Annie was sixteen when she started as a housemaid so she would almost certainly have shared a room with one of the other maids. But later on, once she was a lady's maid, she may well have earned the privilege of her own room – not that that counted for much. If you take a look you'll see how small and bare the rooms were. We've kept them almost exactly as they would have been in the 1920s and 30s.'

'Not much room to keep any of your stuff,' a woman in a pink cardigan said, peering into the room.

Her friend nudged her. 'They wouldn't have had any stuff, silly,' she said. 'They were servants.'

'It must have been awful,' a young girl was saying to her mother. 'She was the same age as me when she started working here. I can't imagine.'

Viola felt herself wanting to stand up for the ghosts of the people who used to work here at Haverford House. She loved her job and the people she met on the tours. But she also loved the house and the people who used to work here, the people who had kept this house running decade after decade. She could still feel their presence in the very walls.

'It would actually have been seen as a very good opportunity at the time,' she said, smiling at the girl. 'Annie's mother would likely have been very proud of her.'

'Would she have still been able to see her mum?'

Viola nodded. 'She would have had an afternoon off each week and her mother lived in the village so she'd have still been able to go home for tea once a week.'

'It's not much is it?' the girl said, looking miserable.

'She wouldn't have expected any more. Times were very different.' Viola stuck to her usual platitudes and swallowed down the words she really wanted to say about privilege and poverty, about class divisions and women's rights.

'And Annie Bishop really just disappeared one day?' the woman in the pink cardigan asked, her voice loud in the corridor outside the servants' rooms. Viola was glad of the question, changing the subject from a complicated social history to one of her own particular favourite subjects.

'That's right. On the night of a house party at Haverford at the end of August 1933, when Annie was twenty-one, she packed up her few belongings, wrote what has become a rather famous letter, which she left with her employer, and was never seen again. Nobody ever found out what happened to her.'

'Someone was arrested weren't they?'

'A man staying at the house was questioned by the police,' Viola gently corrected, 'but there was no evidence to charge him and...'

'So they say,' the woman in the pink cardigan interrupted. 'But it's always the boyfriend isn't it. Just in this case the boyfriend was rich enough to pay off the police.' The rest of the group began to nod and mutter among themselves.

It was always the way. The story of the disappearance of Annie Bishop was synonymous with Haverford House and the village of Cranmere and – in one of its various incantations – had become local legend, as famous as the day the king came to the village. Visitors came from all over the country and, occasionally, even other countries, to see where Annie Bishop had spent her last years, her last days, and to give voice to their own theories about what happened to her. People disappeared all the time, both then and now, but there was something about the story of Annie Bishop and the letter she left behind that had captured the imagination of people from all over the world. The version of the story that had taken hold most strongly was that Annie had been murdered by person or persons unknown, and that the police inquiry had been bungled.

People love an unsolved murder, and Viola's story of Annie Bishop's ghost that still haunted Haverford House played on this. She never gave anything away though, preferring the people on her tours to come to their own conclusions.

Viola had felt an affinity to Annie from the moment she'd first heard her story – a woman who, like herself, had wanted something more than what she felt was on offer and had taken an opportunity that had, somehow, gone wrong. She didn't know what had happened on the night of 25 August 1933, the night Annie disappeared, but she often wished that she did. Was the woman in the pink cardigan right? Had Thomas Everard, the man questioned but not charged for the maid's murder, had something to do with her disappearance and then paid off the police to stop asking questions? Had someone else got to Annie first? Or was it something else – an accident for example, a case of being in the wrong place at the wrong time?

Nobody had ever discovered the reason Annie Bishop failed to leave for America with Thomas Everard on that fateful night. All Viola or any of the Haverford tourists had were stories and conjecture. Whether or not it was murder, Viola had always wondered if the case would have been left open like that had Annie been a member of the upper classes, rather than just a lady's maid.

And it was this that often made Viola wonder if Annie had ever left the grounds of Haverford at all that night. If she had, surely she would have made herself known later, when she knew that everyone had been looking for her and the police had been involved. Over the years she had become more and more convinced that Annie was somewhere here at Haverford. But where?

Viola's colleagues at Haverford House and her friends in

the village laughed gently at her convictions. 'She just left for a better life,' they'd say. 'You only pretend not to believe that something terrible happened because it brings in more revenue for the house, which is fair enough.'

That was partly true of course. Bringing in revenue for Haverford House was Viola's job after all, but there was more to it. She had been fascinated from the moment she first read the story of the old house in Yorkshire and the strange disappearance of one of its maids a few years before the Second World War. It had been reading that story that had made her apply for the job at Haverford House in the first place and the reason she'd packed her bag so suddenly and instinctively to leave London for Yorkshire.

One of the reasons anyway. But she didn't allow herself to think about the other reasons very often.

'There's a New York connection to the story of Annie Bishop isn't there?' asked the American man at the back of the group. 'I'd be interested to hear more about that.'

Before Viola had a chance to respond a little girl of about seven or eight turned to her. 'When can we go and see the dollhouses?' she asked.

'Well, the dollhouses are in the nursery. Shall we head there now and I can tell you the story of Annie Bishop on the way?'

Haverford was famous for more than just the disappearance of a lady's maid. While the legend was a draw, it wasn't the only thing that brought visitors out into rural Yorkshire for the day. The grounds were exquisite and the garden tours very popular, the ballroom ceiling was something to behold and even the café passed muster. The coffee cake, in Viola's opinion, was the best she'd ever tasted. But Annie Bishop's story certainly got people through the doors, especially when embellished by Viola into a potential murder mystery. There were old houses all over the country that were having to be sold off because they were no longer viable to run, either as private estates or as tourist attractions. Visitor numbers were waning but Viola was determined that would not happen to Haverford.

Because where else would she go if she wasn't here?

'Thank you so much for that,' the American man said to her at the end of the tour. 'I really enjoyed it.'

'I'm glad,' Viola replied looking up at him. He was very handsome – dark hair, blue eyes and those all-American whiter than white teeth. 'We don't get many Americans visiting us and I certainly haven't had anyone ask about Thomas Everard in a while.' Interest in what happened to Annie Bishop was dropping off. Viola knew that, but this year was the seventieth anniversary of her disappearance and Viola was determined to make something of it.

'What about Australians?'

'I'm sorry?' Viola looked up at him.

'Your accent,' he replied. 'I just thought I detected a little Antipodean lilt.'

Viola smiled. 'Yes, I'm from New South Wales but I've been in England a very long time.'

'Chase Matthews,' the American said, holding out a strong, tanned hand.

'Viola Hendricks,' she replied taking the proffered hand and noticing a spark of electricity when her skin touched his.

'Viola like the play?' Chase asked.

'*Twelfth Night* you mean?'

Chase nodded. 'The play Thomas Everard was putting on here at Haverford House the summer your Annie Bishop disappeared.'

'You seem to know a lot about Thomas Everard.' Viola hadn't meant it to sound so accusatory. She simply wasn't used to people taking such an interest in the history of the house. Especially once the tour was over. 'But in answer to your question, yes. My mother named me after the character in *Twelfth Night*. It was her favourite play.'

'Do you have a brother called Sebastian?' Chase smiled his very white smile.

'Funnily enough, yes.'

'Really? I was only joking!'

Viola looked away, hoping to change the subject. There were times when she didn't want to talk about her brother – it was always the same when people found out who he was, so she remained non-committal. Chase, clearly picking up on this, changed the course of the conversation instead.

'So tell me, Viola Hendricks. Do you think that he did it?'

'Thomas Everard, you mean?'

'Yes. Do you think he killed Annie Bishop?'

'He was questioned several times,' Viola replied, warming to one of her favourite subjects. 'But there was never enough evidence to charge him. It's always been a bit of a mystery.'

'But what do you think?'

Viola hesitated. She rarely gave away her own ideas. 'I don't think he did it,' she said eventually. 'I think he was meant to meet her that night and for some reason she didn't turn up. But then people point out that it's always the boyfriend and I wonder if I'm giving Mr Everard too much credit.'

'Like the woman in pink on the tour today?'

'Yes,' Viola said. 'To be fair her theory makes more sense but I don't know…'

'You think someone else did it?'

'Maybe or, well, isn't it more likely she had an accident somewhere on the grounds and…'

'And her ghost still haunts the estate.' Chase smiled, his eyes wide in mock horror.

Viola laughed. 'You never know.'

Chase nudged her. 'Perhaps I'll need to stow away one night and see what goes bump in the night after closing time.'

'We've actually had people try to do that,' Viola said as she started to round up the straggling visitors and herd them towards the gift shop before closing time. 'A group tried to hide in the house before we locked up for the night once last summer. They claimed to be professional ghost hunters writing a paper on the paranormal and investigating the mysterious sound of dusting in the library. Luckily we found them and escorted them off the premises but I do wonder if we should do some after-hours ghost hunts in the autumn as there's clearly a market for it.' She was always thinking up new ways of getting visitors through the gates and making the house turn a profit. She wished she could be a bit more successful at it. If enthusiasm paid the bills, she'd have nothing to worry about.

'Well, I'd be up for it if you did!' Chase stood next to her and suddenly Viola felt her mouth go dry, as though she didn't really know what to say.

He ducked his head. 'I'd better be going, Viola Hendricks,' he said. 'I'm staying in the village for a few days so I hope to see you around.'

It wasn't until he'd left that she thought Chase Matthews might have been flirting with her and she remembered that flicker of feeling when her hand had touched his.

It had been so long that she'd almost forgotten how it felt.

# 3

Haverford House, Yorkshire – July 1928

I have much to learn at first, so it is over a month before I get my first afternoon off and am able to go back into the village to visit my mother. It feels as though I've been away much longer, as though I can barely remember my life before I was a housemaid. I have been surprised by how quickly I've settled in, how easy it's been to slip into Mrs Derbyshire's routines, to sleep away from home, to share a bedroom. Mostly I am so tired from my long days and my duties that I am sound asleep as soon as my head hits the pillow.

As I walk down the hill towards the village I turn back to look at the big house that is now my home. I have grown up in the shadow of Haverford my whole life. Everyone in Cranmere has and most of us rely on it for our wages – whether we work in the house or the grounds or rent land as tenant farmers or sell our produce to Mrs Derbyshire and the kitchen staff. Cranmere is a village situated in a valley and surrounded by hills. The hill that Haverford House stands on is not the highest, but it does mean that every day, from the village, we see the grand Georgian house looking down on us. There is a metaphor in that, I think.

I earn six shillings and sixpence a week, most of which I send back to my mother. The rest I keep in my bottom drawer alongside my other treasured possessions, saving up for a rainy day. Because you never know what might happen these days, as Mrs Derbyshire is always telling us.

Something else Mrs Derbyshire is always telling us is what a small staff Haverford House has now in comparison to the old days. There are twelve of us in all and that seems like a huge crowd of people to be surrounded by every day to me, who is used to spending time only with my mother. I've had a hard time remembering all the names and the hierarchies, but I'm getting there. In charge of us all is Mr Prentice the butler – he's tall and thin with a hooked nose and a permanently frazzled expression. Then there's James the footman who is two years older than me with blonde floppy hair and absolutely no sense of a work ethic at all. Cook (whose name is Mrs Jones but we always just call her 'Cook') runs the kitchen along with two women who come in every day from the village to help and Lucy the scullery maid. Poor Lucy is at the very bottom of the pecking order and is small and pasty-looking. I try to make sure I say hello to her every day because she does seem to be taken for granted. Mrs Derbyshire is directly in charge of the housemaids but there are only two of us now – me and Polly who I share a room with. Polly is beautiful with green eyes and thick, wavy red hair that is always escaping from her cap. She is a housemaid too but in rank she is above me because even though we are the same age, she has been here two years already, since she was fourteen. We get along most of the time, I suppose.

That makes nine of us. Then there are three who I have yet to meet. Mr Williams, Lord Haverford's valet; Carruthers, who is lady's maid to His Lordship's two daughters; and His Lordship's new chauffeur whom nobody has met yet. All Mrs Derbyshire knows about him is that his name is Doug Andrews and he comes from Edinburgh. Mr Prentice doesn't seem impressed by the chauffer's Scottish heritage as he sniffs disapprovingly whenever Andrews is mentioned. But then Mr Prentice seems to sniff disapprovingly at most things.

On top of the twelve indoor staff (although Mr Prentice argues that Andrews the chauffeur should not be counted as indoor staff) there is Mr McIver, whom we all call Mac, and his assistant, Ned, who work in the grounds and have staff of their own. Ned is two years older than me and is one of the most handsome young men I've ever seen with his dark hair that falls in his face and his hazel eyes. When he'd said hello to me the first time, I'd felt my face burn and something inside me turn upside down. What a fool I am!

'It might seem a large staff to you, my girl,' Mrs Derbyshire says sadly. 'But back in the day when Her Ladyship was still alive, there were over thirty of us working indoors alone.'

I'm surprised by that, and it must show on my face because Mrs Derbyshire tells me to stop gawping and get on with my duties. I can't imagine there being over twice as many staff as there are now. They must have all been falling over one another in the servants' hall.

I walk down into the village towards my mother's house

and she is standing on the doorstep waiting for me. She waves when she sees me and I run down the cobbled street, straight into her arms. I hadn't realised just how much I'd missed her.

'Now now,' she says. 'Is that any way for a housemaid at Haverford House to behave?' Her voice is soft though and a smile plays on her lips as she looks at me. 'You look well, girl,' she goes on. 'The big house is suiting you I think.'

I don't know if the house is suiting me or not. I do know that my feet ache all the time and I've never been so tired. But I smile and tell her how much I'm enjoying working there because what choice do I have? I may as well try to enjoy it.

I follow my mother into our little house. It is as cosy as ever but to me it suddenly looks shabby and worn. I know that this is just in comparison to the elegance and splendour of Haverford House with its many rooms with their high ceilings, and the elaborately painted ballroom, so I say nothing to my mother and instead sit carefully in my favourite armchair while she brews the tea.

It has been just my mother and me for as long as I can remember. My father was killed on a field in France in 1915 when I was just three. I have no memory of him other than his name inscribed on the war memorial in the village. We have always managed on our own although we've never had much money. My mother takes in sewing and does other odd jobs around the village. Thanks to her I was able to stay at the village school until last year and I am so grateful for that. I wouldn't have wanted to be sent to Haverford at fourteen like Polly was, even if it does mean that I'm earning a wage that is really beneath me in terms of my age.

It doesn't matter. Whatever I earn is helping my mother out and that is the reason I'm doing this at all.

Like I say, we've always got by, but I feel as though I need to pay her back for everything she has done for me. She sees it as a great honour that I should be a housemaid at Haverford like she was, so the least I can do is bring my wages home to her. She won't be able to take in sewing forever.

'So tell me all about it,' my mother says as she sits down opposite me and starts to pour the tea. 'How are you settling in?'

I tell her everything. I describe my room and tell her about Polly, about how she has been teaching me my duties, about how she fluctuates between being my friend and bossing me about. I tell her about how Mrs Derbyshire has helped me settle in, and about Mr Prentice and his disapproving sniff.

'Oh Mr Prentice disapproves of everything and everybody.' My mother laughs, sitting back in her chair. 'It doesn't sound as though much has changed.'

My mother worked at Haverford House for five years until 1911 when she married my father. He was apprenticed to the local butcher and delivered the meat to Haverford House. That's how my parents met – at the kitchen door that I now pass through several times a day. I may not remember my father at all, but whenever I pass through that door I think of him, of what he might have been like, of how he must have made my mother smile. And I think of my mother when she was happy. I wish I'd known her then. I wish I'd known them both.

My mother has never really spoken about my father other than in terms of Haverford. She used to talk about

Haverford all the time when I was younger – about the sweeping driveway and the ornately carved staircase, the silver cutlery and the painted ceiling in the ballroom. She would tell me what a privilege it was to work there knowing, long before I did, that one day I too would have to move up to the house to clean and look after my betters. Not that I think of them that way – I don't think many of us younger staff do.

Things changed after the war and we know there is more out there for us, even for us girls. Factory work pays more than going into service, and many women had kept things running while the men were away fighting. We know what we are capable of. Not that I'd want Mr Prentice or Mrs Derbyshire to hear my thoughts, as Haverford is where my mother wants me to work and, if I'm honest, I want to stay near to her. For better-paying work I would have to travel to Harrogate or York. But they must realise, they must know by the diminished staff and the difficulty in getting a second footman, that things are different to how they were before the war. I've heard Mrs Derbyshire muttering about 'the Servant Problem'. Besides, Haverford itself is diminished since Her Ladyship's death. They do not need the servants they used to have.

'Have you met His Lordship yet?' my mother asks. 'Or the girls?'

I shake my head, swallowing the piece of sponge cake she has made especially for me. 'They're in London,' I say. 'Along with His Lordship's valet, the lady's maid and a new chauffeur that nobody has met yet.' I tell my mother about Mr Prentice's sniffing disapproval of poor mysterious Andrews.

'So you haven't met Carruthers yet?' my mother asks. 'She used to be lady's maid to Her Ladyship when she was alive and she looks after the girls now, I believe. You haven't seen disapproval until you've met Carruthers.' She chuckles to herself and I start to feel a little anxious about the staff I have yet to meet.

'What about Williams?' I ask. 'His Lordship's valet?'

'Oh they've been together a long time. Harry Williams is the son of His Lordship's father's valet as far as I remember. He's a nice chap. Quiet though, just like His Lordship.'

I put my plate back onto the table. I don't want to talk about my work anymore, or the house, or the staff and family I have yet to meet. 'Tell me all the village gossip,' I say.

The afternoon flies by and it isn't long before I find myself walking up the sweeping gravel driveway towards Haverford again. My mother has sent me back with a little packet of biscuits that she has made for me to share with the staff. I can still hear her voice in my ears and feel the touch of her lips on my cheek.

'I'll see you next week,' she'd said as I'd left and now I trudge back to the house with a heavy heart. It feels like leaving for the first time all over again.

Approaching the house, I see a car parked outside. Someone has arrived. I hurry towards the servants' entrance and bump into a young man with fair hair in a chauffeur's uniform. He tips his hat at me as I continue on my way. Is this Andrews and if so why is he back? His Lordship and the girls aren't due back for several weeks. Mrs Derbyshire has told me this many times.

As I walk through the kitchen door, the door where my parents first met all those years ago, the servants' hall is in chaos.

'What's going on?' I ask Lucy the scullery maid as she hurries past with a jar of flour.

'They're back,' she replies.

'Who's back?' I call after her retreating figure, as if I didn't already know.

'Annie, there you are.' Mrs Derbyshire hurries towards me, the keys at her belt jingling. 'How is your dear mother?'

'She's fine,' I reply, handing my packet of biscuits over. 'She made these for you.'

'Yes, well, never mind about that right now, girl. It's all hands on deck I'm afraid. I need you to go and change into your uniform.'

'What's happened?' I ask as I head towards the servants' staircase.

'His Lordship and Lady Prunella are back,' she replies. 'And there's been a terrible to-do by all accounts.'

# 4

Haverford House, Yorkshire – June 2003

Seraphina Montagu ran her hands through her short blonde hair and looked at Viola.

'The actors are arriving tomorrow,' she said. 'You must be excited to see Sebastian.'

From the rather worn Laura Ashley armchair opposite, Viola nodded. She was excited to see her brother again. It had been far too long since they'd last seen each other. But she wanted, desperately, to see her actual brother again – the person she could talk to about anything – rather than the famous actor he had become. She hoped they would be able to find some time alone together, just to talk.

'The beginning of summer,' she said quietly. And then she sighed and untucked her legs from under her, stretching them out and pointing and flexing her toes. 'I'm a bit worried that we should be busier than this.'

'You're still doing two tours every day that we're open aren't you?' Seraphina asked.

'Yes, but they aren't always as popular as I'd like and so far tomorrow afternoon's tour doesn't have enough people

on it to make it viable. I mean I'll still do it of course but…'
She paused. 'I worry that the Ghost of Annie Bishop isn't
enough to lure people in anymore.'

'There are other angles for the Annie Bishop story
though,' Seraphina said. 'The disappearance, the possible
murder…'

'Yes but the locals have all heard it before, and we simply
don't get enough passing traffic since the bypass was built.
But on the subject of Annie Bishop and tourists, I met an
American man yesterday…'

'Oh yes,' Seraphina interrupted, raising an eyebrow.

'Not like that,' Viola replied, trying not to think about
Chase Matthews' smile or the touch of his hand. 'Although
he was very good-looking. But anyway, he was talking
about ghosts and ghost stories and it got me to thinking
that in the autumn, once the actors have left for the summer,
maybe we could do evening ghost tours. It'd be something
different and…'

'Viola,' Seraphina said in the soothing voice she used
when she wanted Viola to calm down. 'Let's just concentrate
on the summer for now, shall we? The Shakespeare Festival
always brings in a good crowd who spend money on
refreshments and souvenirs as well. And this year we have
been sold out for weeks, even with more performances than
usual, thanks to your brother – the actual famous movie
star! Do we have the security to deal with it?'

Viola smiled indulgently. 'The theatre company are
dealing with that,' she said. 'They're used to it. We've got
Millie Springs this year too, fresh from playing Anne Elliot
in that new adaptation of *Persuasion*. Some people will be
coming to see her.'

'Yes, but she's not on your brother's level,' Seraphina replied. 'It's so exciting! Such a coup. I can't thank you enough for making it happen.'

Seraphina wasn't the only one buzzing with excitement for the arrival of Viola's brother. Everyone was talking about it, even though Sebastian had specifically asked for the entire thing to be kept as quiet as possible. How on earth could that be kept quiet? Viola felt as though she'd let him down somewhat with this level of excitement everywhere already.

'But we need to turn all these newcomers into repeat visitors!' Viola said. She saw this as a golden opportunity to get people interested in everything to do with Haverford House, not just the famous actor in their midst. 'Ghost tours might be just what we need as something new and different. Or I could think up something else…'

Seraphina stood up. 'Shall we have a cup of tea?' she asked. 'And then I think we probably need to talk.'

Viola nodded, a feeling of dread in her stomach. She wanted to keep this job more than anything. She needed to stay at Haverford House. She had no idea why, but she had felt so connected to it since she'd first read about it five years ago and took a risk that felt even bigger than the one that had brought her to England in the first place.

She'd been working with Seraphina Montagu ever since. Some days, like today, when they worked together organising each season of events at the house, it was easy to forget that Seraphina was the Dowager Countess of Haverford. Her son David, the seventh (and current) Earl of Haverford, lived in London and worked in finance and refused to have almost anything to do with the house. If he'd had his way the whole estate would have been sold to developers by now, but Seraphina had persuaded him otherwise. She was as attached to the estate as Viola – more so probably. They both wanted to keep the house as it was – open to the public as a piece of history funded by a few meagre grants and as many events as she and her team could put together.

Seraphina's husband Jeremy, the sixth earl, had died suddenly a decade before, leaving the entire estate and title to his son, who was only twenty-four at the time. That was when David first announced he had no intention of sitting about in the Yorkshire countryside desperately hoping that the house wasn't going to fall down around his ears like his father had done. Instead, he was going to actually earn some money and do something with his Oxford degree. Seraphina had moved out of the main house and into the dower house – a smaller separate house at the end of the sweeping gravel drive, built specifically for the widows of previous earls – and set about her plan to open Haverford House to the public.

David had thought she was mad, of course.

'You'll never make any money,' he'd said. 'The house is a dead duck, a money pit. We should knock it down.'

'It's my home David,' Seraphina had replied.

'And I'm the earl,' he'd argued, but he'd been smiling indulgently and Seraphina had known then that she'd win.

'You can do what you like with it,' David had capitulated in the end. 'But as soon as the last bits of money run out, I...'

She'd held up her hand. 'I know,' she'd said.

Seraphina had told Viola all of this over coffee on that

first morning over five years ago. She'd told her that her daughter, Belinda, was much more sympathetic and hadn't wanted the house to be sold either, but she lived in Canada now so was no help at all. Then Seraphina had done a hilarious impression of her son, which had turned out to be absolutely spot on when Viola finally met the seventh earl – who looked disappointingly unlike a member of the English aristocracy and just like all the other suits in the City.

'Miraculously the money has held out so far,' Seraphina had said to Viola on that morning. 'But, honestly, I'm desperate. I need help. Maybe David's right and I should sell it.'

'Oh, let's not be too hasty,' Viola had replied as she'd launched into the sales pitch that she had hoped would land her the job as the assistant that the dowager countess hadn't known she'd needed.

Viola had been in the middle of another silent Sunday brunch with Robin in the café across the road from their flat off Chiswick High Street when she'd first read about Haverford House. Their Sunday brunches, and their lives in general, had become increasingly more silent over the last year since Robin's promotion. All he had seemed to care about was work and even then, as they sat in the café, he had been engrossed in some paperwork or other for over half an hour while shovelling eggs and bacon into his mouth mindlessly.

Viola had known then that she was going to leave him; she'd known for weeks. His salary wasn't so important to her that she was going to sacrifice her own happiness. She just hadn't worked out the details – where she'd go or what she'd do. She'd finished her breakfast and, knowing that she wouldn't get a word out of Robin for a while yet, she'd picked up a nearby magazine. That was where she'd seen the interview with the dowager countess.

To this day she couldn't work out what it was that had sucked her into that article so much, or what it was that had made her feel as though she was right there with the dowager. Seraphina Montagu had talked about the history of the estate and about her decision to open the house and grounds to the public after her husband died. 'My children have no interest,' she'd told the interviewer. She'd relied almost entirely on volunteers up to that point, according to the interview, 'but now I'm desperate,' the dowager had gone on. 'I probably need someone who knows what they're doing – an events manager or something I suppose.'

And that was the moment Viola had known. This was the opportunity for the fresh start that she needed. She was the events manager the dowager was asking for. She'd folded the magazine in half and slipped it into her bag.

'I'm leaving,' she'd said to Robin, who'd nodded, not lifting his eyes from the pile of paper in front of him. At that point he'd probably just thought she was leaving the café.

The sales pitch to Seraphina that had taken place just a few weeks later had worked.

'When can you start?' she'd asked.

'Straight away if you like,' Viola had replied.

Five years later she was still here, still desperately trying to keep the house open and, each summer, wondering if it would be her last. She didn't know what she'd do when her last summer finally came.

She looked up as Seraphina brought the tea tray into the living room of the dower house. Even after all these years Viola couldn't believe that she regularly spent time drinking tea with a dowager countess. In her mind dowager countesses were terribly old and terribly bossy (not that she'd ever met one before) but Seraphina was neither of these things.

Now in her early sixties, all Seraphina wanted was for her children to be happy and for the house she used to live in to stay standing. It wasn't very much to ask was it?

'Here you go.' Seraphina handed Viola a mug of the chamomile tea that she liked to drink in the evenings. 'Biscuit?'

Viola took a jammy dodger and waited for Seraphina to sit down and say the sentence that she had been dreading for so long.

'I think this might have to be our last season.'

Haverford House and gardens were open to the public every day except Monday from March until October. Before Viola had taken over as events manager (which, if she was honest, was just a fancy title for general dogsbody) the house had only been open one day a week and the gardens just two. It was no wonder, she'd thought when she'd first arrived, that the whole enterprise was running at a loss.

Viola had used all the experience she'd gained in her various conference and events jobs in London to pull together an action plan. She'd done it in just a few weeks while in the process of leaving Robin and her job at Kew Gardens, and writing an introductory letter to Seraphina Montagu who, thankfully, still seemed as desperate as she had in the magazine and wanted to meet her as soon as possible. She packed everything she'd owned into just two suitcases (what a sad state of affairs that was) and boarded a train to Yorkshire without planning what she would do when she arrived.

Her action plan convinced Seraphina to hire her without really questioning her CV or asking any difficult questions about that gap between leaving Australia and Viola's first catering job in London. That meant Viola hadn't had to tell her about the place at St John's College, Oxford, which she had never settled into, or the unceremonious way in which she'd left (or was 'sent down' as the university preferred to say). That story could stay in London with Robin and her colleagues at Kew.

Her friends had thought she was mad to be leaving the civilisation of Chiswick for the wilds of the north. There were moments when she thought she was mad too. But most of the time, when she wasn't panicking or ticking off endless to-do lists, it felt right. Nothing had felt so right since she'd first left Australia. Maybe even before that if she was honest with herself.

It had been the tale of the disappearance of Annie Bishop that had first hooked her interest. Annie's story had been mentioned in the magazine interview and something about it had captured Viola's imagination. She'd spent most of the next day, a day off from work, in the archives at Kew looking for birth and death certificates, old newspaper articles, searching for Annie Bishop and what might have become of her. She'd found a birth certificate that informed her that Annie had been born in April 1912 in the village of Cranmere near the Earl of Haverford's estate, born on the very day that the *Titanic* hit the iceberg and the unsinkable ship sank.

She also found a few newspaper clippings, mainly local ones along with three lines in *The Times*. There was no death certificate because there had never been a body. From what Viola had been able to work out, a man who had been staying with Lord Haverford had been questioned but after that the matter seemed to have been dropped – Lord Haverford must have wanted the whole thing to disappear as quickly as possible, she suspected, and would have paid handsomely to make it do so.

It wasn't much, but it was enough to plant a seed of an idea in Viola's head. Annie Bishop, according to the article, had been planning a new life in America when she disappeared, which is exactly what Viola had been doing when she first came to England from Australia. It hadn't worked out for either of them, but Viola was still alive, she still had the chance to start again if she was brave enough. When she'd walked out on Robin at brunch the previous day she hadn't really known what she'd meant by 'I'm leaving', but after her day going through the archives she'd known exactly what she must do.

Five years after leaving London on what was essentially a punt, Viola had built a life for herself at Haverford House and in Cranmere itself. She had built a team of both paid and voluntary workers who ran the house and gardens like clockwork throughout the year. The gift shop, café and second-hand bookshop were all doing well under Viola's watch and she'd been particularly proud of the way she'd decorated these public areas in muted vintage colours that matched the rest of the house and conjured up a feeling of the period between the wars for the visitors. They even served afternoon teas on the lawn in the summer. The team both worked and played together – it was impossible not to in a village as small as Cranmere – enjoying quiz nights and slap-up dinners after work on Fridays in the local pub.

Winters were harder than summers up here on the edge of the North York Moors. The weather could be bitter and the days felt very long and dark when the house and gardens were shut to the public. Viola would spend the time working out what needed fixing around the estate and calling in the appropriate trade and craftspeople. She would also apply for any grant she thought they could get – anything to keep them going during the cold winter months. She'd managed to get funding to fix the roof the previous winter, which had been a huge relief. Without it, the servants' rooms in the attic upon which her tour so relied would have been out of bounds.

Viola's great mission, as she saw it at least, was to successfully apply to the Conservation Trust. The trust bought, repaired, restored and helped manage historic houses and land all over Britain but to be convinced to do so there had to be a reason, something special that was worth holding on to. A Georgian estate, similar to many others across the country, a few antique dollhouses and Viola's dubious stories about Annie Bishop did not seem to be worth conserving in their eyes. But she was determined to find a way; she had to.

The local council had made an offer to buy the house and grounds and run it as a going concern but the price had been pitiful. David Montagu had actually laughed when Viola had shown it to him and threatened, once again, to sell to developers. If he did that, Seraphina would lose her home and many local people would lose their jobs. She simply couldn't let it happen.

If Haverford House was sold, Viola too would lose her home – a small flat conversion on the first floor of the main house – and she had nowhere else to go. She couldn't turn to Sebastian. His life was too different to hers. Sometimes she thought about the flat she used to share with Robin in Chiswick. Sometimes she even thought about her home in the small town in New South Wales that she had left fifteen years before, full of excitement, ambition and a side serving of crippling grief – grief that got the better of her in the end.

But she didn't want to go backwards and saving the house had become the most important thing on her list of things she had to do.

'You mean this will be the last Shakespeare Festival?' Viola asked now in response to Seraphina's rather worrying statement. 'But why? It's been going really well for years now.' Her brother's involvement had been a huge draw of course.

The Shakespeare Festival took place every summer at Haverford. The entire enterprise had been Viola's baby right from the start. Watching Shakespeare outside on a balmy evening was one of Viola's favourite things to do. While English summers were not guaranteed to be balmy as they were in New South Wales, she'd been to enough outdoor Shakespeare productions to know that people in England would happily turn out even on a chilly summer's night and if it rained, they would just put up their umbrellas and carry on.

'Do we have the summers for it?' Seraphina had asked when Viola had first presented her with the idea. 'I mean we don't have Sydney summers up here. I'm not sure we even have London summers.' Viola, who by then had lived through one disappointingly damp Yorkshire summer, was sure that with enough rugs and umbrellas for people to borrow, and with the right plays, the right actors, everything would fall into place.

She'd been right and had seen the surprise in Seraphina's face when the first festival had sold out in just a few days. It had continued to be a success ever since.

The idea had come, not just from her own love of outdoor theatre, but also from something she had read about Thomas Everard. There was frustratingly little to be found about the American with the mysterious connection to the disappearance of Annie Bishop, other than he had been staying at Haverford House during the summer of 1933 and there had been talk of him marrying the then Lord Haverford's youngest daughter. The other snippet of information Viola had managed to find out was that Thomas had been an up-and-coming actor and, a few months before arriving in Yorkshire, had played Horatio in a London production of *Hamlet*. Haverford House wasn't old enough to try to claim any connection with Shakespeare himself, but as Chase Matthews had said, Thomas Everard had put on a production of *Twelfth Night* in the summer of 1933. From that connection Viola had launched the festival to much success.

She had worked so hard on the festival over the years, as well as on the house itself. While a part of her had been waiting for the conversation with Seraphina that she knew was about to happen, she also knew she would never be ready for it.

Seraphina put down her mug of tea and reached across

to take Viola's hand. 'Yes,' she said softly. 'But not just the Shakespeare Festival.'

This year's festival was bigger and better than anything they'd put on previously, mostly due to her brother and the publicity his name brought. Sebastian was playing a starring role in all three plays the festival was putting on that summer – Oberon, Banquo and Duke Orsino. But it still didn't seem to be enough to save Haverford.

'What then?' Viola asked, although she already knew. She could already feel the news sitting in her stomach like lead.

'It's time, Viola. It's time to put Haverford on the market. We've had a good run and tried our best, but David's right. It's just not financially viable anymore.'

'But there's so much we haven't tried yet.' Viola could feel the panic rising in her throat. 'There's still grants to apply for. We could try the ghost tours, maybe we could have overnight stays in the grounds – glamping or something and…'

'Viola, we've tried everything – you know that. And we need hundreds of thousands a year to keep this place viable. I can no longer see a way of guaranteeing that.'

She knew they'd tried a lot of things. But she remained convinced that there must be something they'd missed, something that could save Haverford House and its grounds from the developer.

'But what will you do? Where will you live?'

Seraphina leaned back in her chair and picked up her mug again. 'Well, in an ideal world I'd like to stay in the dower house but I think we both know that won't happen. A developer is hardly going to let me live here for free when they can sell the dower house for several million.'

She stopped for a moment and Viola watched her catch her breath. Seraphina wanted to stay here – she knew that. 'David wants me to take one of the London properties, probably the Kensington flat. It will certainly do temporarily. If I can't stand it, I'm sure I can persuade David to sell the flat and let me buy somewhere in Harrogate.'

'But what…'

'I know that you'll be losing your home too,' Seraphina interrupted gently with a sad smile. 'But it's not going to happen overnight. You'll have plenty of time to find an even better job somewhere else. You're an incredibly talented young lady, Viola. You'll be snapped up in no time.'

Viola put down her empty mug. She desperately wanted to get out of the dower house and back to her flat before she started crying. 'One last summer,' she said as she started to get ready to leave. 'Let's make it the best summer ever then, shall we?'

'That's the spirit!'

As Viola was leaving, heading off back to her own flat in the main house, Seraphina called her back.

'Viola, I can see this is incredibly hard for you,' she said. 'And I know how much Haverford has come to mean to you.'

Viola nodded in response, unable to find any suitable words.

'I am truly sorry.'

# 5

Haverford House, Yorkshire – August 1928

The 'to-do' that Mrs Derbyshire warned me about carried on for some days. Not that I heard anything mind – there was just a strange atmosphere in the house and Mr Prentice and Mrs Derbyshire fussed more than usual about clean aprons and best behaviour.

Despite my impeccable manners and immaculate apron, I don't see either His Lordship or Lady Prunella for nearly a week after their return from London. I am still too young to wait on table and my duties – bed making, fire lighting, dusting and the like – are done when the rooms are empty. I do, however, meet the infamous Andrews, Lord Haverford's new Scottish chauffeur. He seems nice and I don't really understand what the fuss is about. Cook says he has 'dangerous political views' but when I heard him talking during dinner in the servants' hall it seemed as though he was a supporter of the Labour Party, which doesn't seem dangerous to me as they are meant to be supporting working people like Cook herself.

'He isn't in any position to have views at all,' Cook had said.

Mr Prentice seems to object to Andrews eating in the servants' hall with the rest of us. I'm not really sure where he is meant to eat. In the garage with the cars?

I don't have much to do with Williams, His Lordship's valet, who has also returned from London as he is a long way above the likes of me in the pecking order of the staff at Haverford and Mrs Carruthers has remained in London with Lady Cecily. I'm not sure why Lady Cecily is still in London. Nobody seems to be talking about it in the servants' hall and if they mention it at all Mr Prentice silences them pretty quickly – but I do wonder if this is the root cause of the 'to-do'.

I find out what happened a few days later.

The staircase at Haverford House is breathtaking. When Mrs Derbyshire first showed it to me, I didn't hear what she was saying for a few minutes because I was staring at the curve of the steps and the shining mahogany banisters. I could imagine glamorous ladies coming down these stairs on their way to attend a dance in the ballroom.

'It will be one of your duties to keep this staircase looking spick and span,' Mrs Derbyshire had said when she'd finally got my attention again. 'Polly will show you what needs to be done, but I want to be able to see my face in these banisters.'

It is the banisters I am polishing – using a little beeswax and a lot of elbow grease as per Polly's instructions – when I finally meet Lady Prunella. She is running down the stairs in a manner that I'm sure both Cook and Mrs Derbyshire

would disapprove of, when she sees me and stops suddenly.
I remember what my mother has always drilled into me –
to carry on with my work as though I'm not really there.
Much as I want to look up, I keep my gaze on the banisters
and just catch glimpses of Lady Prunella from the corner of
my eye.

'You must be the new housemaid,' she says. I hadn't
expected her to talk to me and I almost forget to curtsy.

'Yes, my lady,' I say quietly.

'What's your name?' she asks.

'Annie Bishop, my lady.'

'Oh you can stop all that "my lady" nonsense with me,'
she says, although I know of course that I can't. Mr Prentice
would have my guts for garters. I'd probably be sacked on
the spot. 'It's nice to have another young person around the
place,' Lady Prunella goes on, although that doesn't seem
very fair on Polly. I suspect what she means is it's nice to
see a new face. I know already from Mr Prentice that His
Lordship's youngest daughter is the same age as me, give or
take a week or two.

'It's very boring being back here,' she continues. 'After
weeks in London where there is so much to do.'

I don't know how to reply to that, having never been
to London, having never even left Cranmere. I turn back to
the banisters.

'Such a fuss.' Lady Prunella seems to be talking to herself
now and when I look at her out of the corner of my eye she
is slumped a little, a deflated version of the girl who was
running down the stairs only a few moments ago. 'It's my
sister's fault of course that we had to come back. Such a row
with Papa. Nobody ever rows with Papa and Cec should

know better. Just because she wants to go to university. Is it really worth it do you think, Annie, tearing your family apart just to sit about reading books?'

'I couldn't say, my lady,' I mutter, although sitting reading all day does sound wonderful to me. To have such an opportunity. Imagine! I have a feeling that Lady Prunella is expecting more from me, an opinion on her sister's mysterious behaviour. But it is not my place to give an opinion. Surely Lady Prunella knows that.

I am saved by Polly.

'Have you finished those banisters?' she asks after bobbing a curtsy to Lady Prunella. 'Mrs Derbyshire says you're to come with me.'

I follow Polly down the stairs and across the hall.

'I'll see you again, Annie,' Lady Prunella calls after me.


'You've no business to be talking to the family,' Polly says as she bustles down the corridor. I follow with my duster in hand. I want to tell her that I hadn't said anything, that I'd just stood and listened. What choice did I have? But I don't say a word; I just trot after Polly, clutching my duster.

She opens a door and leads me into a room I've never been to before.

'Lord Haverford's library,' she says as we walk in. I look around me in awe. 'We have to clean in here at least once a week, His Lordship's instructions. It's a boring old job but somebody's got to do it.'

'And that somebody is me,' I say.

She nods with a smile. 'You and me.' I try not to let her see how much the idea of spending time in Lord Haverford's library pleases me in case she takes the job away. 'But just you for this morning as I have duties elsewhere. Mrs Derbyshire will be along in a minute.'

I can't remember a time when I didn't want to read. My mother taught me my letters before I started at the little village school and I would pull out one of the few books that we had at home and try to make sense of those letters on the page. I was a quick learner once I started at the school and I suspect my enthusiasm was quite unusual at a time when most mothers needed their children to help out at home while all the men were away at war. Miss Timmons, the schoolmistress, lent me whichever books I wanted to read and I consumed them with relish, eager to talk about them, eager to read whatever came next.

I was lucky that my mother allowed me to stay at school until I was fifteen and I was lucky that she encouraged me to read at home – we read from my father's *Complete Works* of Shakespeare together in the evenings.

My mother had told me about Lord Haverford's library but nothing could have prepared me for the sheer splendour of seeing all of those books before me for the first time. After Polly leaves, I stand in the middle of the room, my duster still clutched in my hand, and turn around slowly.

'Now, Annie, that doesn't look like dusting to me,' Mrs Derbyshire's voice echoes from the door. When I look at her though she is smiling. 'It's a beautiful room isn't it,' she says. 'All these books.' She pauses and frowns at me. 'Do you read, Annie?'

'Oh yes, Mrs Derbyshire. I love to read.' The words are out before I can stop them. I hadn't been planning on telling anyone how much I love to read, certainly not so soon.

'Me too,' the housekeeper replies, surprising me. 'I do so love Jane Austen. Have you read Austen?'

I nod and Mrs Derbyshire takes me aside and explains to me that Lord Haverford is generous with his library. We can take out books whenever we want as long as we record what we have in the ledger. And then, very particularly, she shows me where the Jane Austen books are shelved.

'But only after you've finished all your duties, or Mr Prentice will have your guts for garters,' she says, her voice stern again as she turns to go.


Nobody in the servants' hall mentions the row between Lady Cecily and her father that Lady Prunella hinted at. A few times I have opened my mouth to ask and then thought better of it, remembering the lecture Mr Prentice gave to me on my first day about respect and not gossiping. It feels as though the whole thing is blowing over, the atmosphere in the house settling again. I wonder if perhaps Lady Cecily will come home when Mr Prentice receives a letter from Carruthers. He shakes his head as he reads it before refolding it again along the creases and putting it in the inside pocket of his coat.

'Well?' Mrs Derbyshire asks.

'It seems Lady Cecily is set upon her endeavour to go to Cambridge,' he replies with one of his disapproving sniffs. 'Term begins in October.'

'And what about Carruthers? Will she be returning to Haverford then?'

'She will,' Mr Prentice replies. 'To look after Lady

Prunella. She writes that she hopes she does not fail Lady Prunella as she has done Lady Cecily.'

Mrs Derbyshire laughs harshly. 'There's a lot I could blame that woman for,' she says. 'But Lady Cecily having a brain isn't one of them.' I know that there is no love lost between Mrs Derbyshire and Mrs Carruthers – James the footman has told me that the two women bickered constantly about how the house should be run – and I wonder what it will be like when Carruthers returns to Haverford.

'It isn't right if you ask me,' Cook says. 'Women have no need of an education.'

'Well luckily nobody is asking you,' Mrs Derbyshire snaps at her, showing a rare glimpse into her inner thoughts. 'Women have as much right to an education as men.'

'Times are changing, Mrs Jones,' Mr Prentice says and it is clear from his tone that he is not happy about that.

I find out more the next day from Lady Prunella who wanders listlessly into the library while I am cleaning. Polly had said it was a job for both of us but I can't help noticing that she is rarely here to help. Not that I mind. I love being in the library by myself.

'Oh hello, Annie,' Lady Prunella says. I stop what I'm doing to curtsy. As I do I notice how sad she looks, how pale and tired. I suspect she is missing her sister. 'I suppose you've heard that Cecily is staying in London and then going up to Cambridge. Can you believe it? And Papa isn't stopping her. He says he's tired of the whole thing. She told Papa that if our brother would have been able to go to university then so should she and Papa says he can no longer argue with that.'

She sighs and slumps into one of the chairs, plucking a

book off the shelf without enthusiasm. 'She won't even be able to get a degree,' Lady Prunella goes on. 'Women can study at Cambridge but don't get a degree. What's the point in that? She should at least go to Oxford and get a degree at the end of it all. But no, she insists on taking Daniel's place at Cambridge, although of course she'll be at Girton rather than King's, and now I'm stuck here on my own forever.' She sighs and begins to leaf through her book and I turn back to my dusting.

I find myself thinking about the mysterious Lady Cecily who seems to have defied all conventions, upsetting everyone from her own family to Cook and Mr Prentice. Only Mrs Derbyshire had seemed to be on Lady Cecily's side. I wonder why Lady Cecily has done it and I think about Daniel Montagu, Prunella and Cecily's brother and His Lordship's only son. I've heard whispered conversations about Daniel – heir to his father's estate, who was only sixteen when he died of the Spanish flu just as the war ended. My mother had told me that Lady Haverford had followed her son to the grave two months later – both of them were dead before the war had been over a year.

Prunella begins talking again and I'm not sure whether she is talking to me or to herself. My mother has always said that the family ignore the staff most of the time. But Lady Prunella appears to be defying convention almost as much as her sister.

'I shall call her bluestocking from now on,' she says. 'Who would want to be a bluestocking rather than a beautiful lady? I don't understand it at all. She had her coming out this season, but she wasn't interested in that either. She says she doesn't want a husband. All she has talked about for months is Cambridge.' She throws the unread book down. 'Such a bore.'

There is something about Lady Prunella that draws you in. She is warm and funny and, while not conventionally beautiful, she has an aristocratic presence much like His Lordship. She has inherited his long nose and blonde hair. I realise that I have stopped my duties to look at her. I turn away just as her eyes flick up towards me. 'You know all about Daniel and Mama I suppose?' she asks and before I can answer she tells me the story I am already half aware of. Somehow it sounds all the more heart-breaking coming from her. I don't say anything though; I just nod and dust and bite my lip.

But later as I'm lying in bed, Polly snoring softly in the bed across from mine, I think about how Prunella must feel alone in this house with only her taciturn father for company – a house that echoes with the absences of the rest of her family.

# 6

Haverford House, Yorkshire – June 2003

Viola had been fourteen when she'd first seen *Twelfth Night*, the play she and her brother had been named after. Her mother had taken her and her brother in to Sydney on the train, a rare occurrence in Viola's childhood, and she could still remember feeling nervous in the city when she arrived, terrified of the noisy crowds of people and the tourist boats in the harbour, but also amazed – by the blue of the sky, the height of the trees in the Botanical Gardens, the shock of the Opera House. In the little New South Wales town of Kiama in which she'd lived her whole life, being a fourteen-year-old girl had felt like being almost grown up, but here she was astonished like a small child. Sydney had made Viola realise how young she still was.

She could still remember slipping her hand into her mother's rather childishly as they'd walked to the theatre (not the Opera House, much to Viola's disappointment) and her brother looking at her scornfully for doing so. He hadn't wanted to be there at all that day. He'd wanted to be back at home, helping his father run errands and complete chores around the property they lived on. He didn't think the theatre a manly enough pursuit for him. If Viola closed her eyes she could still feel her mother's hand, the dry calloused on her fingers. Sometimes Viola still dreamed of that afternoon in Sydney. It felt so real that the shock of waking up and remembering that she was on the other side of the world and her mother had been dead for fifteen years was almost too much.

The play had been spectacular. Viola hadn't understood all of it, but enough to know to laugh at Malvolio's yellow stockings and the constant mix-up of identities. Enough to feel her heartbeat when the Viola on the stage was reunited with the brother she'd longed for, the brother she'd thought was dead. She'd looked over at her own brother then, hoping to share a moment of sibling affection, but he too was engrossed in what was happening on the stage. Viola could barely believe it, that her surly brother, the boy who insisted he was going to be a farmer one day and had, therefore, no need of school or culture, was transfixed by a performance of Shakespeare.

Their mother was delighted at how much Sebastian had loved the play and, once again, he became the centre of attention as his obsessions turned from farming to acting. That afternoon had changed everything for him.

Viola had never minded being in her brother's shadow. She preferred to be out of the limelight. It was Shakespeare's words, rather than the actors, that had got under her skin that afternoon. It had been love at first play. She'd wanted to consume everything Shakespeare had written. She ploughed her way through her mother's *Complete Works*, following the adventures of these characters invented by a man who'd lived four hundred years before, feeling as though she knew them all personally.

'I knew you'd fall in love with the playwright too,' her mother had said to her. 'I knew you'd understand.'

Meanwhile Sebastian had finally found his forte. His sudden interest in acting had been a surprise to friends and family alike – until they saw him in his first play, a school production of *Annie* in which he played one of the nameless orphans. Despite his small role, his performance had, much to the chagrin of the girl playing Orphan Annie, stolen the show. Everyone talked about how one day Sebastian would be a star.

And everyone had been right.

That was why, when Chase Matthews had been talking to her after the tour the previous afternoon, Viola hadn't wanted to turn the conversation to her brother. Because quite often, as soon as people found out she had a twin called Sebastian, that he grew up in Kiama, that he acted for a living, everything changed. 'You're his sister?' they would ask, the excitement already pitching in their voices, along with a vague disbelief that someone like Viola could possibly be related to Sebastian. And when it came to Chase Matthews, he would already have seen the posters all over the estate with her brother's picture emblazoned upon them. When she talked to people about Haverford she wanted them to be interested in what she was saying, in the house, not in her movie-star brother. Although why she was still thinking about yesterday afternoon and Chase Matthews, she had no idea.

Sebastian and Viola had come into the world together just five minutes apart on a hot January day in 1970

– Sebastian first of course, a fact he'd never let Viola forget – and named after a play that meant so much to their mother. A play that, according to local newspapers of 1933, Thomas Everard had been rehearsing the members of Lord Haverford's household to perform in the grounds – a fact that Chase Matthews seemed to know about. Which was very interesting and…

*Stop it*, Viola said to herself. *Stop thinking about him.*

It had been fifteen years since Viola last set foot on Australian soil, or heard the kookaburra's call, or felt the difference in pressure that the other side of the world brought. Sometimes she felt homesick, but mostly she thought of Haverford as home. She missed Sebastian much more than she missed Australia these days.

They'd always been so close, especially after they'd seen *Twelfth Night*. The natural differences that had been becoming more obvious as they'd grown older had melted away over their mutual love of that play and, growing up, they had been each other's biggest cheerleaders. They had pressed each other to follow their dreams – Viola to Oxford and Sebastian to drama school. Sebastian's dream had been the more successful and it was his success that meant they saw each other so much less than they would like. He spent so much time in America now or travelling around the world filming. Viola knew she should make more effort to see him, but his life felt so alien to her, as though she barely recognised him.

The advent of Hotmail a few years ago had helped – they wrote long rambling emails to each other about the minutiae of their disparate lives. But it wasn't the same as having her brother there for more than a day or two at a time. He was her only relative. When she had to leave Haverford, he would be all she had.

The morning after Seraphina's gentle bombshell, Viola woke early. While she always tried to get up early – there was always so much to do after all – she wasn't a naturally early riser so, at first, she was surprised by how wide awake she felt. And then she remembered what Seraphina had told the night before, the heaviness she'd felt as she'd walked back from the dower house, the tears she'd shed before bed, and the strange dreams that had plagued her all night. Dreams of the beach she'd grown up on, dreams of a childhood almost forgotten, dreams of her twin.

Her twin who would be arriving at Haverford the next day. She would finally see him again, finally spend time with him. If there was ever a time that she needed him it was now.

Underneath everything, under the fame and the fortune, he was still her Sebastian and she still knew him, even though most of their communication was on the phone or by email. There had been a sadness in his voice when she'd first spoken to him about the Shakespeare Festival and she was worried about him. Was his lifestyle taking its toll? And if so, was it her business anyway?

Rather than just throw herself into the usual round of morning jobs and in an attempt to clear her mind of both the remnants of her dream and thoughts of Chase Matthews, Viola decided to take advantage of the beautiful June morning and go for a walk in the grounds. It was her favourite time of year at Haverford when the roses were in full bloom and everything was so green. She set out to walk towards the folly, to spend a few minutes sitting quietly and looking out over the lake in the hope that it would quieten her anxious mind and help her think more clearly.

The grass was still damp with dew as she walked across the lawn and she took long slow breaths of the morning air. A new day, a new page of the diary of her life. And perhaps, if her conversation with Seraphina last night was anything to go by, the beginning of the end. Could this really be the last summer she would spend here at this beautiful estate? What would she do next? Where else could she go?

The actors had already started to arrive and Viola could see the outline of the trailers through the early morning mist on the far side of the estate. While this might be her last summer here, she also knew these next moments might be her last chance for some solitary quiet for weeks. Once rehearsals began and the festival got under way she would barely have time to think. But perhaps that was what she needed right now. She was really looking forward to the Shakespeare Festival this year. The acting company were performing *A Midsummer Night's Dream, Macbeth* and, much to Viola's delight, *Twelfth Night.*

Her stomach rolled with excitement at the thought of Sebastian's arrival. When would he get here? she wondered. Would he call her when he arrived? Or in advance perhaps? She pulled her phone out of her pocket and flipped it open. No missed calls yet.

She sat in the folly for a few moments, enjoying the early morning light, and wondered what on earth life held in store for her next. Because if Haverford did close down at the end of the summer, she had no idea what to do.

*

Making sure that Haverford House was ready for opening time and looking its very best was one of Viola's favourite tasks. The quiet of the empty house before the visitors arrived, interrupted only by the arrival of the staff from the village, was usually a contemplative time for her, a time when she always felt grateful for what she had, grateful to her past self for getting on that train to Yorkshire to bombard the dowager countess with her grand plan to help.

But this morning was different. Viola stood in the old nursery and looked out of the window towards the folly and the lake beyond. The nursery always got the best of the early morning sun and this morning – a gloriously warm morning – the sunbeams caught the dust motes that danced through the air. Viola began to prepare the display of vintage dollhouses, dusting their roofs and opening their doors for the visitors to inspect. The dollhouses were part of a collection that had belonged to Lady Arabella and which had been kept almost perfectly intact after her death by her daughters, Cecily and Prunella, until the fifth earl had moved the family away and had the house locked up in the autumn of 1933. Viola always started the day in the nursery – as Cecily and Prunella would have done as children – and usually loved admiring the dollhouses in the early morning sun. But today she couldn't concentrate on anything.

The shadow of impermanence hovered over her. She'd known that Haverford House couldn't go on as it had been doing. She'd known that some months they could barely afford to pay the staff, but she'd hoped she could make a miracle happen, pull a rabbit out of a hat. She'd thought that was what she'd done when her brother had agreed to the Shakespeare Festival, but apparently even that hadn't been enough. It was only one summer after all and she needed a more long-term miracle than that.

She'd so wanted to get the Conservation Trust interested, but she hadn't been able to. but there had to be something she could do. Something she hadn't thought of. She had until September to think of it. Nothing would happen before the end of the Shakespeare Festival.

As Viola carefully opened the fronts of the dollhouses and checked everything was in order within, she thought about the day her brother had left for drama school in Melbourne – just a week before she had boarded a flight to London. Neither of them had any idea of what the future would hold but it was Sebastian on whom the light had shone so brightly. A recurring role in a soap opera after drama school – he played the long-lost son of one of the long-standing characters – and then after two years he'd left to find his fortune in LA with so many other Australian hopefuls. Except for Sebastian it had all worked out – several major film roles, a stint on Broadway and then a long-running role as a police detective on an HBO crime show.

But since the superhero film, the premiere of which had brought him to London three years ago to see Viola, he hadn't done as much – a few smaller films, a cameo on a television show – but she hadn't known why. She'd tried to ask him, tried to get him to open up about it all but he'd brushed off her concerns, and she still didn't know why he sounded so sad when they'd talked about his upcoming summer at Haverford.

Which was a strange place for an A-list actor to end up, even if his sister did run the show. She was still surprised she'd finally been able to convince him and wondered if his apparent sadness was something to do with his capitulation.

Viola went through the rest of her morning – opening up the house, the tearoom, the shop, and conducting the first tour – on a sort of autopilot. She'd been doing this job for nearly five years, essentially keeping most things the same. And yet this was the first day she could remember since she'd arrived in Cranmere that she'd done her job without really thinking about it.

She'd had many of these 'autopilot' days when she'd worked at Kew. Her brain was always elsewhere then – should she take a trip back home, should she make more of an effort with Sebastian, should she find another job, another boyfriend, another life? But since she began working at Haverford House she had really felt this was where she was meant to be and had been engaged in every aspect of her job. Yes, of course some days were better than others and, essentially, the tours she conducted six days a week through the summers were the same with many of the same questions asked day after day. But she had never once felt as though she wasn't present with the job.

Until today.

All of the questions that plagued her when she'd been in London were swarming around her head again now. If Seraphina was right and they would have to close at the end of the summer, was this the sign Viola had been waiting for to go back to Australia?

Later, after the morning visitors had either disappeared to the picnic grounds or the tearoom for lunch, Viola took a sandwich and a book down to the far side of the lake, away from the main estate – walking the long way around so she didn't bump into any of the actors who were starting to arrive – and sat in her favourite spot just by the old boathouse. The lake was a wonder of Victorian engineering and was built in a series of levels to stop the grounds of the Haverford estate from flooding. The boathouse had been closed not long after Daniel Montagu's death in 1919 and nobody went near it much anymore. The structure was very probably unsound and eventually something would have to be done about it – probably a complete dismantling. Neither Viola nor Seraphina had ever had anyone in to do anything about the boathouse. There had never been enough money.

It was a peaceful place to sit – visitors hardly ever came down this far, preferring the upper parts of the lake where the ducks and swans resided. But today Viola couldn't find any peace. Eventually, she closed her book after realising she had read the same paragraph at least six times.

She was sitting looking out across the lake, her back against a tree and her book abandoned next to her when Seraphina found her.

'I thought I might find you here,' the dowager countess said, squatting down next to Viola. 'You've got a visitor.'

A visitor? She never had visitors. Everybody she knew worked at Haverford. Unless Seraphina meant Sebastian of course. Had he arrived early?

'An American visitor. Very good-looking and asking for you specifically.' She paused. 'Very white teeth.'

'Oh.' Viola felt herself blush. 'He was on the tour yesterday. He seemed to know a lot about Thomas Everard. Usually people aren't interested in…'

'I think he might be more interested in you than Thomas Everard.'

'Don't be ridiculous.'

'Well, he's booked on to this afternoon's tour. Explain to me why else he would want to do the tour again so quickly?'

Viola felt herself blushing again and looked away, over the lake. She couldn't think of any other reason why Chase Matthews would be here. The thought of walking around the house with him, in a much smaller group than the day before, actually made her feel uncomfortable. Chase had seemed kind and was good-looking, but she wasn't looking for anything with anyone and particularly not something with an American who was passing through the village. Because he must be passing through surely? There was nothing in Cranmere to keep a man like Chase Matthews here for very long.

It had been five years since she'd left Robin in that café in Chiswick stuffing bacon into his mouth, dripping grease onto his paperwork. She'd never had a single regret about leaving and hadn't missed either London or her ex-fiancé. Since she'd left she hadn't felt attracted to anybody and wasn't interested in changing that. She wanted to learn to live with herself, to love herself, to be happy with her own company. What concerned her was that, after all these years, she was only happy with the version of herself that lived at Haverford. She had changed so much since she'd moved here, mostly for the better, and she had grown to love the Haverford version of herself. What would happen when she wasn't here anymore?

'So you'd better get ready,' Seraphina was saying.

'Ready for what?'

'For goodness' sake, Viola.' Seraphina laughed as she stood up. 'To see the mysterious Mr Matthews of course.'

'He's only here for the tour though, isn't he?'

Viola watched Seraphina roll her eyes. 'No harm in getting a bit spruced up is there? Just in case.'

Against her better judgement Viola did as Seraphina suggested. Going up to her apartment via the back stairs to avoid the tourists she was about to meet, including Chase Matthews, she changed quickly into a sundress, put her hair up and applied a little lip gloss and mascara. That was as far as she was prepared to go. She couldn't really believe she'd done that much. She was usually happy to take the tours around while wearing one of her burgundy 'Haverford House' polo shirts, but it was a very hot day. She'd be cooler this way at least. She pinned her name badge to the front of her dress to make herself look at least a little bit as though she worked here.

The tour went much the same as every other tour Viola had ever led. It was a small group this afternoon so Viola was able to answer a lot more of the questions and had time to listen to more of their many theories as to what happened to Annie Bishop – forcing herself to concentrate on the group rather than on Chase. When she eventually allowed herself to look over at him he caught her eye and smiled. It sent a tingle down her spine that she hadn't felt in years.

The group spent more time in the nursery than usual – one of the women on the tour collected vintage dollhouses and knew a lot of interesting facts about them so Viola let her take over for a few minutes for anyone who was equally interested.

'I have to say I've never seen one like this before,' the woman said, turning to Viola. 'Do you know anything about it?'

'That one was actually custom-made for Lady Haverford.' She paused. 'Lady Arabella Haverford who was married to the fifth earl. They married in 1901 and this dollhouse was a wedding present from her husband. It's one of a kind, I'm told, and is a replica of the couple's London home, which is where they spent the first year of their marriage.'

'It's truly magnificent,' the woman replied as other members of the tour group started to inspect Lady Arabella's dollhouse more closely. 'I've never seen anything like it.'

'So this Lady Arabella would have been the lady of the house when Annie Bishop went missing?' an older woman asked.

'Arabella died in 1919 of the Spanish flu,' Viola replied. 'Lord Haverford never remarried and, as you know, the house was closed up in 1933 for many years so there was no Lady Haverford living here when Annie Bishop went missing.'

There was some mumbling and exchanged whispers among the group at this but, much to Viola's relief, no further questions about either Lady Haverford's dollhouse collection or Annie Bishop. She was in no mood to answer a barrage of questions, which she usually loved to answer. She really wasn't herself today and her mind wasn't on the job at all.

'Shall we move on?' she asked the group and they all made murmurs of consent as they followed Viola towards the staircase. It was only then that she noticed Chase was missing. He probably wasn't very interested in dollhouses.

He didn't rejoin the tour until it was nearly at its conclusion in the grand entrance hall. Viola always finished her tours here as the visitors were then in close proximity to the café, the gift shop and the gardens should they want to take a look around any of them. She was telling the group about what the house had been like when the sixth earl, Jeremy Montagu – husband of Seraphina and father of David, the current earl – first decided to open it again in the 1970s, when Chase reappeared from the direction of the ballroom. She wondered for a moment where he had been but instead had to deal with the visitors asking where the toilets were, how far it was to the lake and when the Shakespeare Festival began.

The group dispersed, hopefully to spend lots of money, and only Chase was left.

'Not a fan of dollhouses then?' Viola asked him with a smile.

'Sorry for disappearing like that,' he replied. 'I'm more of a fan of real houses. The architecture of this place is amazing.' He paused for a moment. 'And Shakespeare too. I was disappointed that the festival was sold out but I'm not surprised with actors like that on board.'

Viola smiled, apologised. Should she try to get him a ticket? Or would he be back in America by then? Now would also be a good time to tell him exactly who the famous Seb McKay really was.

'I was wondering,' he went on before she had a chance to say anything, 'if perhaps you'd join me for dinner tonight.

I'd love to know more about the house and...' he caught her gaze with his own '...a little more about you.'

Viola hesitated. It had been a long time since she'd been out to dinner with a man. But really, what did she have to lose? He wasn't from around here after all. He would be back in America before she knew it, long before he had a chance to break her very carefully guarded heart.

'I'd love to,' she replied.

# 7

Haverford House, Yorkshire – April 1932

Much has changed at Haverford over the last four years and yet, at the same time, nothing has changed. I still share a room with Polly and get up at half past five to begin my duties. The indoor staff remain largely the same, and each day passes in a blur of exhaustion and abject boredom. Not that I would dare to say that to Mr Prentice or Mrs Derbyshire. I get one half-day off a week, which I spend in the village with my mother. I look forward to it more than I ever thought I would, and it has become the highlight of my week. I never mention my feelings to my mother either. I let her think I am happy, that my time at Haverford is the privilege that Mr Prentice tells me it is.

Despite what I told myself on my very first day here, I am still dreaming of something else and I spend all my free time reading the books from His Lordship's library, escaping into a world less mundane than this. I remind myself that I am lucky to work here, lucky to be able to be near my mother – but it doesn't always feel quite enough.

I've got to know Ned – the gardener's assistant – better

over the last few years. I am older now, and slightly less bowled over by his looks although I still get that tingling feeling inside whenever he smiles at me. He has shown me around the grounds and lake and taught me to identify different plants and flowers. He's also shown me all the different species of birds that live in the gardens of Haverford and now I can tell the difference between a thrush and a female blackbird, a coal tit and a great tit.

Outside of Haverford times are changing and of that I am hopeful. Andrews keeps us abreast of political issues – by us I mean me and James the footman. I feel as though, out of all of us, we are biding our time the most, hoping for something better, wishing that change would come more quickly. I know the days of this kind of servitude are coming to an end and there was hope when Ramsay MacDonald of the Labour Party became prime minister again in 1929 but the Conservative Party are back in power now. There are rumblings in Germany too, Andrews tells us, talk of an election and a new chancellor, and he wonders if there will be another war. James and I look at one another when he says that. James had been too young for the last war of course, but if war were declared again things would be very different.

'Sometimes it takes great suffering to bring about great change,' Andrews says in his soft Scottish accent before folding his newspaper and taking himself back to His Lordship's garage. He doesn't want Cook to catch him saying such terrible things after all.

It is fortunate that Cook doesn't hear some of the things that Lady Cecily says either, some of the rather angry discussions she has with her father. I serve at table occasionally now, helping out Mr Prentice and James when His Lordship has guests – another sign of how times are changing and how difficult it is to find young men willing to go into service. Lady Cecily is down from Cambridge where she spent three years at Girton College studying for, but not actually being awarded, a degree in English literature. She is determined, however, that women at Cambridge should be awarded full degrees and she talks about it all the time, especially when her friend – a lady called Hannah Rivington whom Lady Cecily met at Girton – comes to stay at Haverford.

'We can't go on like this forever,' Lady Cecily says at dinner one night when I am helping to serve. 'Living in the past, expecting people to wait on us.' I watch His Lordship's eyes slide from his guests to his daughter, hear the grumble in the back of his throat. 'You must know your servants are voting for the Labour Party, basically trying to overthrow you.'

I nearly drop the cutlery I'm carrying when I hear her say that, and Lord Haverford bangs his fist on the table.

'That is enough,' he says, and Lady Cecily shrugs and returns to her meal. She isn't wrong though. I am to turn twenty-one in just a few days and intend to vote for the Labour Party at the next election now that the voting laws have been changed. As long as I'm allowed the time off to do so of course.

Lady Prunella has already turned twenty-one. There was a big party in the ballroom to celebrate. I was assigned duties in the kitchen on that evening, helping Lucy and the women who come in from the village as Cook barked orders at us. Polly reported back that Prunella had danced with everybody, had been giddy with celebration and champagne, but that Lady Cecily had stood at the edge of the ballroom with Hannah Rivington, smoking constantly and looking scornfully at anyone who dared to try to ask them to dance.

Polly had giggled about it as she'd told me while we'd been getting ready for bed, dreading the morning duties after only three or four hours' sleep, but I hadn't found it as amusing. Both of the Montagu girls had been out in society for years now but there had been no offers of marriage. I had wondered that night if there ever would be. The next morning when I'd ventured to mention it to Mrs Derbyshire she'd turned to me in a moment of candour and had looked me straight in the eye.

'There are a few reasons,' she'd said. 'But mainly it's because there's no money. No man wants to marry the daughter of a penniless earl.'

She hadn't said anything else but she knew as well as I did that in other parts of the country, houses like Haverford have become too difficult to run and have been shut up and the staff dismissed. What do people like Mrs Derbyshire do then? She has worked at the house since she was fourteen.

It's not just Mrs Derbyshire either. Most of Cranmere are employed by or earn their living through the Haverford estate. If His Lordship were to shut up the house and move away what would become of everyone? What would become of Cranmere? It would have no reason to exist.

And yet even I, a lowly housemaid, can see how things are changing. Over the four years that I've worked here more rooms have been closed off, more furniture covered in dust sheets. I even know that one or two of the less important paintings have been sold at Christie's, an auction house in London. Sometimes the Montagu family forget that their staff have ears and hear every conversation – even if I did have to ask Andrews to explain what an auction house was. Despite that though we all carry on as normal, as though nothing has changed.

As well as the money problems, there is the whiff of scandal that surrounds Lady Prunella – the reason she no longer spends the season in London, why her twenty-first birthday was heavily supervised here at Haverford. None of us are completely clear about the details although Carruthers claims to know all about it but intends to take the secret to her grave. This is typical of her, though, so who knows if it is true or not. She probably knows no more than us.

All I know is that Lady Prunella became embroiled with a married man. I have no idea who he was or what exactly happened other than His Lordship knew the man in question and, when he found out about it, went down to London with his valet Williams to hunt them out. They were found in a jazz club in Soho, dancing the foxtrot and drinking cocktails. There must have been more to it than that but whatever it was I certainly don't know. What I do know is that a very strict eye has been kept on Lady Prunella ever since, and she feels as trapped up here at Haverford as I do. I wonder if she dreams of another life somewhere else, like I do?

There is more bad news coming for Mrs Derbyshire. A few weeks after Lady Prunella's twenty-first birthday party, Carruthers announces that she is leaving. She is the first person to leave since I arrived.

'I've done my duty to Her Ladyship, God knows,' Carruthers says dramatically as she enters the servants' hall. 'And what with Lady Prunella turning twenty-one I've kept my promises.'

'But where will you go?' Mrs Derbyshire asks.

'That's no concern of yours, Mrs Derbyshire,' Carruthers says, turning her back on the housekeeper.

I won't be sad to see her go. Edna Carruthers is one of the most sour-faced, unpleasant people I've ever met and her waspish remarks, particularly the ones about my mother, will not be missed by me. Or by anyone I should imagine.

When I tell my mother the news on my next afternoon off, she raises her eyebrows.

'I thought the only way Carruthers would leave Haverford would be in a six-foot box,' she says in a remark almost worthy of Carruthers herself. 'I have no idea what Lady Arabella saw in her but she brought her to Haverford with her when she married His Lordship. They'd known each other since they were teenagers apparently. When she didn't leave immediately after Lady Arabella's death I assumed she'd stay forever.'

'She says she made some promise to Her Ladyship on her deathbed,' I tell my mother. 'Do you know anything about it?'

My mother rolls her eyes. 'I've no idea,' she says. 'But she's probably made it up to sound self-important.'

I walk back to the house through the gardens that afternoon. It's a beautiful spring day and I want to see the bluebells that grow in the woodland around the lake. Polly had shown me this shortcut through the grounds of Haverford to the village when I'd been at the house about six months. I'd had no idea it existed. I'm hot by the time I've crossed the meadow and I stand for a few moments in the shade of the trees, listening to the thrushes and blackbirds and to the honking sound of swans and the ripple of water coming from the lake. The grass under the trees is carpeted in bluebells and I wish I could sit here until the sun sets and it becomes too cold to stay outside. But I know I have to head back to the house and after a few moments more I walk slowly over the bridge by the boathouse.

Mac and Ned are fixing the door of the boathouse that nobody uses anymore. Daniel Montagu had spent a lot of his time here when he was home from Harrow – rowing on the lake with his friends, fishing on the deck. Lady Prunella had told me once that when they were children the three of them would run away from Nanny and come up here to swim on hot afternoons. She had sighed and looked away when she'd told me. 'Nobody uses the boathouse anymore,' she'd said. 'It doesn't seem right somehow.' It feels like a sad place now, and I know that neither of the girls come here very often. But the grounds staff keep it in good repair in memory of His Lordship's only son.

The gardener waves at me as I pass and Ned comes over to say hello. He takes his hat off, running his hand over his hair, damp with sweat, and asks if he can walk me back to the house. Polly has been telling me for a while that Ned is sweet on me. 'Why would he spend so much time with you if he wasn't?' she asks, but I don't know how I feel about that. I let him walk with me to the house though, as he starts to tell me about his day.

We take a detour through the kitchen garden. Ned wants

to check on the early peas and beans, he says. I love the kitchen garden where all the fruit and vegetables that the house consumes are grown. It amazes me that all that produce can be grown from such tiny seeds.

'One day I'll have a garden of my own,' Ned says with his back to me as he turns towards the peas, which are beginning to flower. 'I'll be a head gardener like Mac, and I'll have a little house and a family…' He trails off. I know why. Ned has no family of his own; his parents died when he was still a child. He must long for one. I only have my mother but she is my whole world. I don't know how people manage without anyone, although Mr Prentice would say that the staff at Haverford are family.

Ned turns to me and smiles his handsome smile. He steps towards me and I feel his fingers brush against mine. 'I just need to find a nice girl who'll put up with me,' he says.

I suddenly realise what he is saying and why he is saying it to me. Polly is right. Ned is sweet on me, perhaps more than sweet. I don't know what to say or do. I certainly don't want to get married. I don't feel old enough and I want to experience something, anything, outside of Cranmere before I have to settle.

'I have to go,' I say eventually. 'I'm late getting back to the house and I don't want to annoy Mrs Derbyshire.'

Ned steps away and I start to walk very fast, as though I'm trying to outrun his words.

When I get back to the house, Mrs Derbyshire calls me into her parlour. She stands with her arms folded across her chest and I think I am in trouble for being late back, for lingering too long with Ned in the kitchen garden.

'You will be lady's maid for Lady Prunella and Lady Cecily when Carruthers is gone,' she says.

I'm astonished and stand staring at the housekeeper. I've not seen anyone promoted in all the time I've been at Haverford and I'm the one who had been here the least amount of time. Even little Lucy, the scullery maid, has been here longer than me.

'Don't stand there gawping, girl,' Mrs Derbyshire says. 'It's quite normal that eventually one of the housemaids becomes lady's maid.'

'But Polly…' I begin, my mouth dry.

'Polly will continue her duties as housemaid and you will help her, but your duties looking after the girls will take priority. Do you understand?'

'Yes, Mrs Derbyshire, but…'

'There are no buts to be had,' she replies. 'Lady Prunella asked specifically for you.' Had she? I wonder why? Since the day in the library when we were both only sixteen and she spoke about her brother and sister, I hadn't been aware of her noticing me in any particular way. Which is as it should be of course. That is the natural order of things, as Mr Prentice would say.

'Thank you, Mrs Derbyshire,' I manage.

'Well don't thank me, thank Lady Prunella. I'm not sure if you're ready for it at all. You'll have a lot to learn over the next couple of weeks and you'll have to listen carefully to everything Carruthers tells you between now and when she leaves if you want to do a good job, and I know you'll want to do a good job.'

I nod, not really knowing what I'm agreeing to.

★

The last month that Carruthers is at Haverford, I spend almost entirely with her as she teaches me everything that Lady Prunella and Lady Cecily would need me to do. I try to silence the voice in the back of my head that wonders why on earth grown women need so much help getting ready every day, as though they are dolls rather than human beings. I put up with Carruthers' endless nagging all day and then, in the evenings, I listen to Polly moan about all the work she has to do now I'm otherwise engaged.

Things improve after Carruthers is gone.

'We'll have so much fun together, Annie,' Lady Prunella says one evening as I help her get ready for dinner and again I wonder why she chose me over Polly, or even a new and experienced lady's maid. 'I'm glad that old goat Carruthers has gone. She was only here because she'd made some promise or other to Mama. Apparently when Mama was on her deathbed, she made Carruthers swear to look after Cecily and me until we were both twenty-one. It doesn't sound like the sort of thing Mama would have said if you ask me. It was just some ploy made up by that battleaxe so Papa wouldn't dismiss her I suppose.'

I try to hide my smile but Lady Prunella must have seen me because when she catches my eye in the mirror she winks at me.

As we get ready for bed that evening I tell Polly that now Carruthers has left and isn't insisting I shadow her every move, I'll have more time to help her again.

'I know the lady's maid job should really be yours,' I say. 'You've been here longer than me after all. I'm sorry.'

'Don't be sorry,' she replies snuggling down under the blanket. 'Brushing out their hair is the last thing I want to do. I've got bigger dreams than that.'

This is the first time I've ever heard Polly admit that she too dreams of a life outside of Haverford and I want to ask her what she wants, what she would do if she could. But I don't ask, because then she would ask me the same question and I'm not ready to admit that to anyone yet.

Not even myself.

# 8

Chase picked Viola up in a little sporty Audi outside the front of Haverford House. She wasn't really supposed to see guests on the premises, especially at the main entrance of the house, but Chase insisted on picking her up – he would have it no other way in fact – and after their conversation at the lake earlier that day, she didn't think Seraphina would disapprove that much. As Chase drove his car far too fast past the dower house, spraying gravel in his wake as he turned onto the main road, she did wonder what the dowager countess would think.

'I've booked us a table at a restaurant in Harrogate,' Chase said as they left Haverford House behind. 'I figured you might not want to eat in the village, seeing as everyone I've met so far seems to know you.' He turned and grinned at her for a moment. 'I hope that's OK.'

'That's great,' Viola replied. She was relieved that the first date she'd had in five years wouldn't be taking place in the pub where everybody knew her and everybody would feel free to comment loudly. 'I guess you must be staying at Cranmere's only dining establishment?'

'At the pub, yes!' he replied enthusiastically. 'It's so charming and I'm told it's about four hundred years old.'

Viola laughed. 'Well I think there's been a pub or an inn on that site for four hundred years. I'm not sure if any of the current bricks that hold it together are that old.'

'But still,' Chase went on, his excitement undeterred. 'Isn't it amazing? I must confess that I'm a bit of an Anglophile. I was at Oxford for a year on an exchange programme and that was it for me. I was in love.

'You must be used to old buildings if you were at Oxford though,' Viola said. If he'd stopped at every building to be amazed by how old it was he wouldn't have had much time to study.

'Yes, but your little village is something else. Everyone knows each other. I mean, everyone knew each other at Oxford, but this is like a proper community.' He had the enthusiasm for the English village of somebody who has never lived in one.

'We are only a tiny village,' she said. 'Things can be a bit…' She paused, trying to find the right word.

'Quaint?' he asked.

'I was going to say claustrophobic. Like you say, everyone knows me these days.'

'Does that bother you?'

'Not really, but I get to escape into Haverford whenever I want. I'm incredibly lucky.' She stopped herself thinking of what might happen if she could no longer escape to Haverford; she was on a date after all. Happy thoughts only.

'So,' she went on. 'You haven't told me what has brought you to our quaint little village of Cranmere.'

'I just needed a break and I felt like going to a part of England I'd never been before.'

'You've never been to Yorkshire before?'

'Yes, but only York and Leeds. Work has been really hard and I was thinking about taking a little time off and then I read about Haverford House in one of my mother's magazines. It was an article about the decline of the English country house.'

Viola groaned. 'How depressing,' she said. 'It's true though. It's becoming almost impossible to keep many of the smaller houses open. Families are selling up all the time.'

'That's what the article said,' Chase replied. 'There were various lords and ladies mentioned but Lady Seraphina's story stood out to me somehow.'

'Because of the disappearance of Annie Bishop, no doubt.' Viola smiled. 'And the American connection with Thomas Everard.'

'Right! I really wanted to see the house as soon as I read about it.'

'Funnily enough I felt the same the first time I read a magazine interview with Seraphina. That's how I ended up with this job in fact.'

'Tell me about it.'

And so she did. Or at least she told him as much of the story she was willing to tell, skipping the reason why she came to England in the first place, for now at least, and definitely passing over the image of Robin shovelling his breakfast into his mouth. Instead she concentrated on the magazine article that had sucked her in, much as a similar one had done with Chase, and stuck to the topics of the Shakespeare Festival and the disappearance of Annie Bishop.

'Don't read too much into it all though,' she said as Chase parked the car around the corner from the restaurant. 'I don't think her ghost is really wandering the estate you know.'

'But you do think something happened to her don't you? Or have you made that up for the tourists too?' Chase grinned.

'Most people in the village think she made it to America and started a new life but...' Viola paused. 'I just think something must have happened to her before she left the estate, otherwise wouldn't she have let somebody know she was safe?'

'But her body has never been found.'

'No, but the grounds are huge – if she'd had an accident that night as she went to meet Thomas Everard she could be anywhere.'

'So she was definitely meeting Thomas Everard that night?' Chase asked.

'She left a note with Prunella Montagu – she was one of the ladies Annie looked after. Apparently at the time it was assumed that Thomas would ask Lady Prunella to marry him – that was the reason he and his family had been invited to Haverford for the summer. Annie left on the night of a huge party that took place at Haverford – the last party Lord Haverford held before shutting the house up. Anyway in this note Annie said that she was leaving with Thomas, that they were going to America to start a new life.'

'But you don't think she ever got there?'

'No, and she never met up with Thomas either. Some people say Thomas let her down but I don't believe that. Why would he be out in the grounds looking for her like he told the police he was if he had intended to let her down? Wouldn't he have just stayed at the party and married Prunella?'

'It must have been a downer for this Prunella, to find out that the man she thought she was going to marry wanted to run off with a lady's maid.' Chase made the statement with laughter in his voice and, although she knew what he was saying must be right, Viola felt a desperate need to defend Annie, this woman from the past whom she felt so akin to. A woman who had just wanted so much better but never seemed to get it. She took a breath, not wanting Chase to see how passionately she felt about the whole story.

'Who knows,' she said diplomatically.

'So, Thomas is found in the grounds looking for her when the police arrive?'

'None of us are too sure of the details, but from what I understand by the time Thomas returned to the house, Annie's letter to her employer had been discovered. He had blood on his shirt apparently and Lady Prunella took one look at that and insisted the police were called.'

'Thomas went back to America with his family eventually.'

Viola nodded. 'Yes, once the police investigation was closed, but he died in 1944 during the war. Shot down over Dresden.'

'And Annie has never been found.'

Viola made a non-committal noise. Suddenly she didn't want to be talking about this anymore. What if Seraphina and David did sell to developers and they dug up the grounds and found Annie's body? What would happen then? They couldn't arrest Thomas Everard as he'd died during the Second World War.

Or worse. What would happen if the whole site was excavated and nothing was found? How would Viola feel then? She'd invested so many years in the story of Annie Bishop and the various theories as to what had happened to her. But why? Why did the story mean so much to her? If Viola was honest with herself it was just a story – something that happened a long time ago to people she had never known. But she remembered what it felt like to be planning an escape, a journey to another country for a fresh start that didn't work out.

'Perhaps she did leave the grounds,' Chase was saying, thinking out loud. 'Perhaps she saw a break for freedom and took it. It was 1933 and people didn't want a life in service anymore. Maybe she just ran away. Maybe your friends are right and she did get on a boat New York.' He paused. 'Hey, I could be living next door to her descendants for all I know.'

'Is that where you live?' Viola asked as they climbed out of the car. 'New York?'

'Yeah.'

'And what do you do there? What's the job that you needed a break from?'

'I work in finance,' he replied dismissively. 'Nothing as exciting as working in a haunted house.'

Viola laughed. 'How many times do I have to tell you that it's not haunted. Now I don't know about you but I'm starving. Where are we eating?'

*

Viola couldn't remember how long it had been since she was last in Harrogate. She rarely left the confines of Cranmere these days and she suddenly realised how small her life had become, how much she had shut herself away from everything. It was nice to be out for a meal with a handsome man. She couldn't live alone and closeted in her little flat at Haverford forever could she? Much as the thought of anything else made her positively anxious, she knew she had to start getting out and about again, away from Cranmere. Especially now it looked as though she wouldn't have a little flat for much longer.

Dinner was a tasting menu – small portions of ten different courses – and Viola hadn't eaten so much rich food since she'd left London. Mac and cheese at the pub was about the limit of her culinary experiences these days and, even though it was delicious, she struggled to finish.

Over dinner, as she and Chase talked, she realised how attracted to him she was feeling. Every now and then their legs would touch under the table and she would feel that same tingle she had felt when her eyes had met his that afternoon. For a man he talked surprisingly little about himself. Instead they talked about England, about life in rural Yorkshire, about Haverford.

'The house isn't that old,' she told him.

'Really? It seems old to me.'

'Well, not by British standards.' She smiled. 'Not when you consider we have castles that are nearly a thousand years old – including one in Oxford that pre-dates the Battle of

Hastings.' There was a lot she could tell him about Oxford, a lot they could talk about. But she wasn't willing to get into that conversation with him. He would only be around for a few days, a couple of weeks at most. He need never know she had set foot in Oxford, let alone been sent down. 'A house built in the 1760s is quite young by comparison.'

'It's a beautiful house,' Chase said. 'Has it always belonged to the Montagu family.'

'Yes, it was the Montagu family who had the house built when the position of Earl of Haverford was first given to Lewis Montagu in 1759. David Montagu, the current earl, is a direct descendent of Lewis.'

'That house must have seen a lot – war, illness, death, countless kings and queens.'

'Absolutely. Kings have even visited,' Viola went on. 'George V came just after the First World War and there's a rumour that Edward VIII visited too when he was still Prince of Wales but we've never found any evidence of that.' She paused. 'I told you all this on the tour.' She smiled. 'Weren't you listening?'

'Of course I was.' He grinned back. 'But English history is so much bigger than American. It takes a while for all the stories to sink in. Now correct me if I'm wrong but Edward VIII married the American woman and abdicated right?'

'Wallis Simpson, yes. But all that happened after Haverford was closed up.'

'So how come royalty visited Haverford so often?'

'Well, we don't know they came that often. Like I said, we don't have any records of Edward visiting, but he was a personal friend of the fifth earl, Albert Montagu. They knew each other at Dartmouth Naval College although the earl was a lot older of course.'

'And King George V?'

'That visit we do have records of,' Viola replied. 'It was an official visit after the First World War to thank the Montagus for opening up the house as a military hospital. You remember that bit from the tour surely?' she teased.

Chase smiled. 'Of course,' he said. 'I've been thinking about it actually. It must have been quite an intrusion for the family.'

'It's a huge house and lots of families did it. It was their way of doing their bit for the war effort. Unfortunately, they think it was one of the soldiers at the hospital who brought the Spanish flu into the house that killed Lady Arabella and her son Daniel, Lord Haverford's heir. They died within a couple of weeks of each other about six months before King George came to visit.'

'So was this all while Annie Bishop was working at the house?' Chase asked and Viola shook her head. She hoped that Chase Matthews was better at whatever it was he did in finance than he was at remembering dates.

'No.' She laughed. 'We've been through this. Annie wasn't born until 1912 and would only have been about seven when the king came to Haverford. She started working at the house in 1928 when she was sixteen.'

'How do you remember all this, Viola? I'm terrible with dates.'

'It's my job to remember,' she replied. 'And speaking of jobs, I think that's enough work talk for one evening.'

'OK,' Chase said. 'Then tell me about you.'

Viola took a breath then. *Here goes*, she thought. 'I'm

from a little town in New South Wales called Kiama,' she began. 'I grew up there with my mum and my twin brother Sebastian.'

'Really? You and Sebastian are twins exactly like *Twelfth Night*? That's amazing! Twins!'

'And we spent our lives finding it excruciating.'

'I can see that. Do you even like the play?'

'*Twelfth Night?*' Viola asked. 'I do. I love Shakespeare and that play in particular. It was the first play our mother ever took us to see. I fell in love at first play and it changed my brother's life.'

'How?' Chased asked, and then he stopped, his brow crinkling. 'Did you say you grew up in Kiama?'

Viola tried not to sigh. 'Yes.'

Chase said her brother's stage name in a sort of awed whisper. 'He's your brother?' he said.

'Is that so unbelievable?' Viola replied, trying to smile.

'Sorry,' Chase said. 'You must hear that all the time. I saw that he was performing at the Shakespeare Festival – I did wonder how you got such a big star.'

'To be honest that was a surprise to me too. I'd been asking him for years and I never thought he'd say yes. I can't believe he did.'

'I bet the tickets sold out really quickly.'

'Lightning fast.' Viola smiled. 'But I'm sure I could get you a ticket if you wanted one.'

'That would be amazing, Viola, but…' Chase hesitated. 'I hope you don't think that was the reason I asked you for dinner tonight.'

'I'm used to people picking my brains about my brother.'

'Because it's not the reason,' he went on, holding her gaze

84

until she felt herself blush and ducked her head. 'Although I am interested to know what it's like to have a famous brother like that.'

'It's strange,' she replied. 'Because to me he's just Sebastian, you know? The brother who was born a few minutes before me and embarrassed me at school but always had my back. But to everyone else he's Seb McKay. For me it's really hard to see the movie star.'

'Hmmm,' Chase replied. 'I guess I can understand that. I don't have any siblings so it's always interesting for me to hear other people talk about their brothers and sisters.'

'I've always thought it must be lonely for people who don't have siblings,' Viola mused before realising what she'd said. 'Oh I'm sorry I didn't mean...'

'Don't worry about it,' Chase said. 'Now shall we have dessert?'

He smiled at her but there was a sadness there and Viola wondered if he was lonely and if that was the reason he had asked her here tonight.

By the time they got back to Haverford, Viola was so full of food that she thought she may never eat again. Dessert had been some sort of Pudding Club where guests tried several desserts and voted for the best one, which was then crowned Pudding of the Night. She wondered if they should do something similar with the cakes in the tearoom at Haverford.

If there would even be a tearoom at Haverford in a few months.

'That was a lot of food.'

'You sure do love your sponge puddings in England don't you?'

'Are they too much for you?' she teased.

'Treacle sponge, sticky toffee pudding and the unbelievably named spotted dick may just have been a bit too much,' Chase patted his flat abdomen.

'I had a lovely evening,' she replied. 'Despite the sponge overindulgence.'

'Lovely enough to want to do it again while I'm here?' he asked.

'Yes,' she replied bravely. 'Lovely enough for that.'

'Tomorrow?'

'Sebastian is coming tomorrow,' she said. She looked at him and noticed his eyebrows shoot up. 'And no, I'm not introducing you to a movie star, not just yet anyway.'

'I wasn't even going to suggest it!'

'I'm not sure exactly when he arrives but why don't I meet you here tomorrow afternoon about four? I can show you some of the grounds of Haverford that you don't see on the garden tour.'

'It's a date.' Chase grinned, his teeth very white in the evening gloom.

She got out of the car and walked around the house to the side door, a door that would, years ago, have been the servants' entrance and was now the way in for staff, including herself. As she turned the corner she smelt cigarette smoke and stopped for a moment as she saw a shadowy figure hovering near the door.

'Who's there?' she called, wondering what she would do if it was an intruder lurking about. She wished that Chase was still here.

'Hello, Viola Hendricks,' a familiar voice said. 'It's been a long time.'

It had been three years since she'd last seen him, the brother she'd shared a womb with, since she'd spent two days with him in London after the premiere of his last movie. She missed him every day.

Seb McKay. A name known all over the world these days. He'd chosen to use their mother's maiden name as his stage name. There'd been another Seb Hendricks on the Australian acting scene when he'd first been picked to play a starring role in the soap opera *Sunset Bay*.

And then unable to help herself any longer, she threw herself into the arms of the only person who she felt really knew her, the only family she had in the whole world. He picked her up and spun her around, just as he'd always done since the day he'd shot up to be so much taller than her.

'Christ it's good to see you, Vi,' he said.

Part Two

# ARRIVAL

Central Park West, New York City – August 2003

*The writer has lived in this apartment since her second husband died – she didn't even move buildings, she merely moved two floors down to somewhere less ostentatious and more to her own taste.*

*Her second husband had passed away quietly in his own bed. She was there with him of course, as were his children from his first marriage. He died an hour before four gunshots killed a Beatle just a block or two further along Central Park West. The writer had heard the gunshots and wondered what they were. She had been writing murder mysteries for nearly thirty years by that time and had never heard a gun fired before. For some reason she had been more surprised by that in the days that followed than she had by her husband's death. He had been dying from blood cancer for years.*

*It wasn't that she had fallen out of love with him, it was more a case of having never been in love with him in the first place. How could she ever love anyone after what she'd felt for her first husband? How could anybody ever compare to the man who had saved her? Who had rescued her from everything?*

*Her second husband was called Sylvester Myers and she had been fascinated by him. He wasn't good-looking, or particularly charming. He was tremendously wealthy, but that hadn't been it either; her first husband had left her well enough off. She thinks it was the fact that when she told him she was a writer, he didn't laugh, or call it a 'little hobby'. Instead he wanted to know what she wrote, how she wrote, how she came up with her plot.*

*It had started, as she had told Sylvester, with a magazine column when she'd first arrived in New York. Her first husband had helped her get that. She'd written about being an Englishwoman in New York, the alienness of it, the differences, the similarities, the confusions. It had been funny and poignant and writing it for almost seven years – well into the Second World War – had taken her mind off everything that had gone before.*

*But now, she had written a detective novel.*

*'Can I read it?' Sylvester had asked.*

*'When it's published,' the writer had replied.*

*Five months after they met, in the spring of 1952, Sylvester Myers and the writer were married. A few months later the first Elizabeth Smithson novel was published by The Bodley Head. The writer had signed the contracts in the Flatiron Building on a wet Thursday afternoon in June. She had taken her pen name from Sylvester's mother – her maiden name had been Smithson. She had wanted a level of anonymity even then and was glad she had. If she'd known then, when she signed her first contract, what a long and illustrious career she was going to have she might have worked even harder at the anonymity from the start. These days she was seen as reclusive and difficult.*

*But she's never really minded what other people thought of her.*

*It is what she thinks of herself that matters.*

*And that is why she has to return to England one last time.*

*When Emily arrives that morning the writer is still sitting at her desk looking out over the Park with a copy of* The New York Times *in front of her.*

*'Have you ever been to England, Emily?' the writer asks. Despite working together for nearly eight years now, she knows remarkably little about her assistant.*

*'Once when I was eight,' Emily replies. 'I went to London for a few days with my family.' She pauses for a moment as though unsure whether to say more. The writer and her assistant rarely exchange anecdotes from their private lives. 'I've always wanted to go back though,' she says quietly.*

*'Well,' says the writer, pushing her chair away from her desk and turning to face Emily. 'Today is your lucky day.'*

# 9

Haverford House, Yorkshire – June 1933

Today is the fifth anniversary of my arrival at Haverford House. To say that the last five years have changed me is an understatement. I feel like a completely different person to the young girl who walked up the sweeping gravel drive on my first day as a housemaid. I was nervous then, and timid. I had no idea what I was in for and part of me was sure that I'd lose my job within weeks when they realised that I had no idea what I was doing. Now I feel stronger, more confident, and the world of Haverford doesn't scare me anymore. I may still spend too much time daydreaming, but I am a lady's maid now and, despite what I might secretly think about grown women being able to dress themselves, there is still a lot to be proud of there. Not too proud mind – I wouldn't want to upset Mr Prentice who is always warning us about the dangers of pride.

Every week, on my afternoon off when I go back to the village to see my mother for tea, I realise again how much I have changed. I am a different person to the one who left home five years before and that is partly to do with the other staff at Haverford. They have become friends. I hadn't realised I was lonely before when I lived at home. Perhaps it's not until things change that we notice what they were like before.

My mother and I don't talk about it – we while away the afternoons with small talk and village gossip – but I wonder if she notices too. I wonder if she recognises the daughter who left home for Haverford House anymore.

Meanwhile things continue to change around me as well, and the biggest change has been quite a shock to everyone, even to me who should perhaps have seen it coming.

Polly is leaving. It seems the 'bigger dreams' she spoke of when I was first promoted to lady's maid must have come to fruition, because she is to marry a Harrogate solicitor who moved, with his mother, to one of the large houses on the other side of Cranmere last autumn. I do wonder if marriage is the big dream she talked about or if this solicitor, Stephen Mather, is merely an escape route, a way out of domestic drudgery. Neither Polly nor I want to end up like Mrs Derbyshire. I keep my views about that to myself, but Polly has always been rather vocal about it, which has led to whispered conversations in the butler's pantry about 'getting ideas that are above her station'.

Her impending marriage has caused quite a stir in the servants' hall, I can tell you. There is much speculation about where Polly and Mr Mather met. They haven't known each other very long and the marriage seems sudden which has, of course, only added to the gossip. I've overheard some of the conversations about 'trouble' and 'the family way' that stop as soon as either Polly or I walk into the room.

She isn't expecting though – that much I do know. She is

far too sensible for that. She's waiting for her wedding night because, while Mr Mather may be infatuated with her red hair and her green eyes, this is Polly's escape and nobody ever escaped from anything by having a baby outside of marriage.

Speaking of marriage, Ned hasn't made any more comments about houses and families to me since that afternoon in the kitchen garden over a year ago. The next time I saw him everything seemed back to normal – gentle chatter as we walked in the grounds – and I wonder if I imagined the whole conversation, or at least read far too much into it. Either way I am glad of it. I cannot think about much else now that I am a lady's maid and with Polly gone I'll be busier than ever.

The rest of the servants may speculate about Polly's upcoming nuptials, but she and I do share things – it's impossible not to when you live in such close proximity with somebody for so long. I know that she met Stephen Mather at the Easter Fair in the village and has been sneaking out at night to see him ever since. She's very secretive about him though. She won't tell me how they went from secret meetings to being almost married and she never tells me what they talk about, what they have in common. In fact, when I think about it I realise that she hasn't told me much about Mr Mather at all other than he has the most beautiful blue eyes. Well, Ned has lovely eyes too but I'm not going to marry him on the strength of that alone.

We do speculate about what her life will be like after the wedding though – life as Mrs Mather won't be like life for Lady Prunella and Lady Cecily, but it won't be like life as a housemaid either. She'll have a maid of her own, just the one she tells me, and a cook.

'I won't know what to say to them,' she tells me. 'It'll be peculiar not having to do the dusting myself.'

I ask her what she will do all day but she doesn't really seem to know. They will be living with Mr Mather's mother after the wedding so she will probably have her work cut out there – or so my own mother tells me when she hears Polly's news. My mother never got on with my father's parents and they drifted apart after his death.

Today we have a new girl starting to replace Polly, not that Polly could ever be replaced in my view – where would we find someone with such pre-Raphaelite beauty and such a sharp tongue? The new girl's name is Katy and she'll be sharing with Mrs Derbyshire until next week when she'll move into Polly's side of my room. A change is as good as a rest, the housekeeper tells me, but I'm not so sure about that. As I wait in the kitchen for Katy to come down so I can go through her duties with her I feel restless. Things are changing all the time. I have read the headlines of Lord Haverford's newspapers every day since Andrews first started to introduce me to politics and world affairs. I know what's going on in America and Germany. I know the war that Andrews mentioned is gathering on the horizon like an encroaching storm, and I know that I am powerless to fend it off, if it heads this way.

With Polly leaving I feel this sense of restlessness even more. Everything is changing and I am being left behind.

I am in the library with Katy, the new housemaid, showing her how to dust Lord Haverford's vast collection of books. It is a delight to be back in my favourite room. I miss it now that I'm a lady's maid and have no real excuse to spend time here during the day. I still come to the library to borrow books as often as I can, along with Mr Prentice who loves detective novels and Mrs Derbyshire who continues to take out her beloved Austen novels again and again.

'I don't know where you all find the time for reading,' Polly says regularly. In my opinion you make time for the things you love but she has no interest in fiction, or books in general. She hated dusting the library, but lucky for her I was always willing to do it.

'You have to be careful,' I say to Katy now. 'Some of these books are worth a lot of money and can't be damaged.'

'How much money?' she asks, eyes wide.

'Never you mind how much money,' I say, taking a breath and trying not to be impatient. I remember how the house overwhelmed me when I was new. I wonder how often it overwhelmed my mother. I sometimes think that nothing could overwhelm her.

'What does His Lordship do with all these books?' Katy asks, staring along the shelves.

'He reads them of course,' I say with a laugh. 'He's generous with them too. He lets the staff read them as long as they log them here.' I start to show her the ledger but she turns away.

'I don't care for all that,' she says. Another Polly then. I sigh quietly to myself. I'd been hoping that I'd find a like-minded soul in Katy, but I suppose it was too much to ask. Girls who are interested in books don't become housemaids anymore these days unless they are very unlucky. I try not to wonder about whether my luck will ever change or if, despite my protestations, I will stay here for as long as Mrs Derbyshire.

If His Lordship's money lasts long enough to keep paying me, of course. I shake my head and look around the library again, trying to be grateful for what I do have.

It was in the library that I'd first met Lady Cecily. We were a week away from Christmas. The tree had been cut and erected in the hallway, waiting for the girls to decorate it as they had done when they were children. Lady Prunella had told me so much about her sister and I'd found myself full of anticipation on meeting this enigma of whom so much was spoken.

I was still rather in awe of Lady Cecily and her university studies then. It all sounded marvellously exotic to me, the idea of studying literature, and I saw no reason why women should not have the same advantages as men, no matter what Cook might think.

Since Lady Prunella had often referred to her sister as a bluestocking, I had been expecting Lady Cecily to be very plain. So I had been surprised when she drifted into the library on that bitingly cold December morning. She was plainly dressed, yes, and her hair was drawn back in an unelaborate, unflattering style, but she was beautiful in a way Prunella could never be. Prunella takes after her father – a square jaw and strong nose. But Cecily is beautiful to the point of being ethereal, despite her plain, almost dowdy clothing.

There is a photograph in the nursery of Lady Arabella – the girls' late mother. It is still part of my duties to clean the nursery each day even though it is barely used. Both girls still like to sit with the dollhouse collection from time to time and so I must keep the room tidy for them. In the photograph Lady Arabella is sitting with all three of her children. Judging by their ages I think it must have been taken during the war, perhaps to send to Lord Haverford in France. You can see that Lady Cecily looks exactly like her mother – dark hair and eyes in contrast to Prunella's fairness. It's uncanny in fact. Daniel took after his mother too from what I can see.

Cecily hadn't noticed me at first, that first time we'd met in the library. She had gone straight to the bookshelves clearly looking for something particular. I hadn't been able to keep my eyes off her. Eventually she'd looked up and I'd turned away, continuing with my dusting.

'You must be Annie,' she'd said. I'd turned around and curtsied.

'Yes, my lady,' I'd replied.

'Pru's told me all about you.'

I hadn't known what to say to that so I'd bobbed my head and turned back to my dusting.

'Pru's missed me I think,' she'd said after a while. I hadn't been sure whether or not she was talking to me or herself. 'She must be so bored rattling around here with only Papa for company.' She'd paused. 'It's such a sad house.'

Once again I hadn't replied, but I'd understood the sadness she meant. You could feel it everywhere – in the very walls of the house, in the rooms that were kept empty and locked. My mother had never told me how empty Haverford could be, but then I suppose it was a happier house when she was here. And I supposed that she was happier then too. Everybody was happier before the war.

I'd always been used to sad houses because I'd grown up in one too.

'Is that him do you think?' Katy asks now interrupting

me from my memories. I'm always surprised by how many memories I have of the last five years – Haverford seems so much more like my home these days than the house in Cranmere that I grew up in. I notice Katy peering out of the window, her dusting forgotten.

'Who?' I ask.

'Mr Everard of course!' Katy says turning towards me, her face filled with delight and excitement. 'I've never met an actor before.'

I hear the sound of an engine and realise that Katy is right. Our much-anticipated guest has arrived. Everyone has been on tenterhooks all day – we don't have very many guests at Haverford anymore.

'And you won't be meeting an actor today either,' I snap at her. 'You'll be in here dusting and then you'll be helping Cook with the dinner.' I may have been just a housemaid when I first met Lady Cecily but now I am a lady's maid to both the girls. And I serve at table when needed. It's not conventional but it's a product of the Servant Problem that Mr Prentice is always bemoaning.

Katy pulls a face at me and I suddenly feel sorry for her. She's only fifteen and probably has much bigger dreams than dusting books. 'When do I get to meet the important people?' she asks.

'Well,' I reply, trying to soften my voice. 'You'll meet them as you go about your duties around the house, no doubt, but you mustn't disturb them you know.'

'I know that,' Katie replies still peering out of the window.

'And,' I continue, 'if you work hard and prove yourself you may be allowed to serve at table.'

Katy nods vigorously and returns to the dusting with gusto.

Thomas Everard is indeed an actor, although I'm not sure he's as famous as Katy has built him up to be in her head. More importantly though, Thomas Everard's father is a very wealthy, very influential American financier 'whatever that is', to quote Cook. Haverford House doesn't just have a servant problem, it also has a money problem. As in there isn't any. Everyone knows it and nobody talks about it, but I've seen Mr Prentice sighing over the ledgers. I've overheard His Lordship talking to his bankers. I might be invisible but I'm not stupid. Things have only got worse since Mrs Derbyshire first confessed the matter to me last year.

Thomas Everard's parents will be joining us later in the summer but for now we just have the pleasure of Thomas himself, fresh off the stage in London, so far as I understand it. I wonder which of the girls he is here to be thrown at and then I chastise myself quietly. It isn't my business who Mr Everard marries. Or doesn't marry for that matter.

Lady Cecily comes into the library then.

'He's here,' she says. 'He has one of those little open-top cars.'

'Oh, how wonderful,' Katy says.

'Katy,' I warn quietly. 'You're forgetting yourself.' I don't like myself when I have to chastise her. Especially when she looks at me as though she doesn't understand what she has done wrong. Why shouldn't she express her delight after all. But it is not 'the done thing' as Mr Prentice would say and five years here has taken its toll. Those old-fashioned rules have been carved into me. Katy turns back to her dusting and Lady Cecily turns to me.

'Like Toad of Toad Hall,' she goes on and I hide my smile behind my hand.

'Or Bertie Wooster,' I say quietly and Lady Cecily nods. It was she who introduced me to the Wodehouse stories that even Polly had enjoyed when I'd read them out loud to her at night. Lady Cecily knows how much I love to read and is always recommending new books to me. She is the only person in the house other than Polly who knows how much I love stories. Unlike Polly who dismisses it with wild indifference, Cecily always asks me about what I am going to read next. Not today though, not in front of Katy when there is the excitement of Mr Everard to contend with.

Poor Mr Everard, I think to myself as Lady Cecily goes off to find her sister – who is as excited as Katy at the prospect of a resident actor. I wonder if he knows why he is here – I wonder if he realises how badly the estate needs his father's money? And I wonder what it must be like for Prunella and Cecily, being duty-bound to marry somebody they might not even like, let alone love.

# 10

Haverford House, Yorkshire – June 2003

Sebastian and Viola met at the folly the next morning. The sun was still low in the sky and the light was golden as Viola walked across the dewy grass. She smelled his cigarette before she saw him.

'You should give up,' she said as she climbed the steps towards him, sitting down next to him.

'I know. I keep telling myself I'll do it next month.'

'I used those patches,' Viola replied. 'They really work.'

He nodded.

'I'm sorry I cut your date short last night,' he said. 'I wanted to surprise you.'

'It wasn't a date. I told you that last night.' Viola was trying for that same teasing tone that came so easily to her brother, but it just sounded a little bit whiney. 'I'm sorry I wasn't there when you arrived but I'm really glad you're here.'

'Quite the coup for you getting me for the Shakespeare Festival.' He beamed. But Viola still wondered why he was here and why he had taken so little persuading this year.

'That's not the only reason I'm pleased to see you.' She sat down on the step next to him and he draped an arm around her.

'So tell me everything,' she said. 'Where you've been and what you've been doing.'

He could have told her everything the night before but unlike her brother Viola was not a night owl.

'You're tired, aren't you,' Sebastian had said, after he'd teased her about her date for a little while. 'We can do this again in the morning if you'd prefer?'

'And will you be awake in time?' she'd asked, remembering all the times when, as children, she'd had to drag him out of bed in time to get the school bus.

'I promise,' he'd said.

And for once he had been awake in time.

'I've been back to Kiama,' he said now as they sat together, turning to face her.

'Really?'

'Really.'

'When?'

'Last month, just for a couple of weeks.' He paused, looked away. 'I'm sorry I didn't tell you.'

'Was that the first time since…'

'Since I went to America? Yes.'

'What's it like?'

'Still exactly the same. The house is still standing and the blowhole is still there.'

Viola smiled in spite of herself. Kiama was a sleepy sort of seaside town, beautiful and popular with holidaymakers from Sydney and beyond who filled the caravan and campsites every summer, but there was never a huge amount going on if you lived there all year around. Except for the blowhole of course. Formed in the rocks on the sea's edge over two hundred million years ago, and named *Khanterinte*, the blowhole sprays gallons of water up to twenty-five metres into the air. It was pretty impressive, and pretty dangerous. The local council's warning signs were always being ignored, as people wanted to stand right on the edge to have their photographs taken.

Remembering the blowhole made Viola smile, but thinking about the house just made her sad. They'd grown up on a smallholding on the edge of Kiama, the smallholding that had made Sebastian want to be a farmer until he changed course to acting. But a year after Sebastian and Viola had seen *Twelfth Night*, their parents lost a lot of money – neither Sebastian nor Viola were quite sure how, other than it had something to do with pensions – and the house and land had had to be sold. That was when their father left, moving further north to start again. Their mother's idea of starting again was to live apart from their father, and the twins became children of a broken home, like so many of their peers.

They moved into a smaller house in the centre of Kiama, nearer to where their mother worked. They saw their father once a year if they were lucky. But the upside of that was Viola's relationship with her mother. They'd grown closer as Viola grew up – unlike many of her friends who seemed to find themselves arguing with their mothers more as they got older. By the time she was sixteen, Viola felt her mother was her best friend – clichéd as that sounded – and together they were Sebastian's biggest fans, always there at every play he was in, however small, supporting him from the sidelines in any way they could. The three of them became, after their father left, a little triangle that they thought could never be broken.

And then, just months before Viola and Sebastian turned eighteen, their mother died – her car hit by a drunk driver as she drove along the coast road. She was dead before the ambulance got to her.

The twins had been left alone, the house had become theirs and their father moved back to Kiama for a little while, just long enough to convince social services that his children were being looked after. Then he left again, leaving them to fend for themselves.

'You'll be eighteen soon enough,' he'd said as he'd gone.

Viola wouldn't have got through those months without her brother. He'd done everything for her back then. She was almost embarrassed about how badly she'd coped – both in Kiama and, later, in Oxford.

'What made you go back?' she asked. 'After all this time?'

'I...' He hesitated just long enough for Viola to realise that he was avoiding the truth. 'It just felt right,' he said.

She was about to question him further, find out what was really going on and whether it was connected to the sadness in his voice and the furrow in his brow, when she heard his name being called across the grounds from the direction of the house. Surely it was too early to start work just yet?

He stood up. 'Early morning read-through,' he said. 'I'm sorry. We can meet after lunch?'

'I've got a house tour after lunch and then...' She hesitated.

'What is it?'

'Well, I'm meeting someone at four. It shouldn't take too long. I should be free after a couple of hours and we can...'

'Meeting who?' Sebastian asked, the teasing glint back in his eyes.

Viola looked away. 'Chase Matthews,' she said quietly.

'The guy from last night.' Sebastian laughed. 'I thought you said it wasn't a date.'

'I... well... look I'm sorry. I can cancel. I'll call him...'

'That's OK.' Sebastian smiled as he started to walk away towards his read-through. 'I'm here all summer. I don't mind coming second place to the mysterious Chase Matthews just this once.'


'So tell me about you,' Viola said. 'I feel like all we did last night was talk about Haverford and me and Sebastian.'

Chase smiled. After her last tour of the day Viola had met up with him and taken him down to the old boathouse, away from the tourists, the actors and everybody else who was crowding out Haverford on this beautiful June afternoon. It was quiet here, and so beautiful by the lake. A gentle breeze rippled the surface of the water, cooling the heat of the sun.

'Sorry if I talked about your brother too much,' Chase replied sheepishly.

Viola shook her head. 'Don't worry, everyone does when they find out who he is.'

'My life is rather boring I'm afraid. No film-star relatives or anything.'

'But you live in New York,' Viola prompted. 'That must be exciting!'

'It can be,' Chase admitted. 'There's always so much going on – theatre, art, music and so on. But I've lived there my whole life and all I seem to do is work. This is the first real break I've had in years.'

Viola wondered how old he was. She'd assumed, when she'd first met him that he must be the same age as her but she wondered today, as she noticed the creases around his eyes, if he was older.

'So you grew up and went to school in New York?' she asked.

'I grew up there but I went to boarding school upstate. After school I studied at Brown on Rhode Island, which I loved, and majored in economics, which I didn't love so much. After graduation I had my Oxford year.'

'When was that?

'I started in the October of '91.'

'We were there at the same...' Viola began, the words escaping before she had a chance to stop them. She'd had no intention of telling him about her own time at Oxford.

'You were at Oxford too?' Chase seemed surprised and she didn't blame him. She didn't exactly have Oxbridge graduate written all over her.

'For a while,' she admitted. 'I won a scholarship at St John's to study English but... well... I was a long way from home and I missed my brother and my mum had passed away the year before.' She stopped, blinked. She'd told him too much already. 'Let's just say things didn't work out and I never graduated.'

Chase didn't say anything. He didn't ask the series of awkward questions that Robin had asked when she'd told him the longer, more complicated version of this story – such as where her father was or what she'd done after she was sent down – and she was grateful for that. He just placed his hand on her shoulder and squeezed gently. It felt comforting and she leaned into him a little.

'So what did you study at Oxford? Economics still?' she asked after a moment.

'PPE,' he replied. 'Politics, Philosophy and Economics although I have to admit that I felt very much out of my depth – British political systems are very different to ours in America.'

'That's the degree to study if you want to be prime minister in the UK,' Viola said and laughed. 'Is that what you had in mind?'

'No,' Chase said. 'And if it had been I would have been terrible at it!'

'And what did you do after Oxford?'

'I went back to New York and worked for my father and I've been there ever since.'

'And there's nobody special waiting for you back there?'

Chase turned his head to her and she looked up at him. 'I wouldn't have invited you for dinner if there were,' he said. He held her gaze for a moment, just as he had the night before. And just like the night before Viola looked away first.

'It is so beautiful up here,' Chase said, walking away from her a little towards the edge of the lake. 'And you say nobody comes up here?'

'It's not exactly closed to the public but we don't encourage it,' Viola replied, walking over to stand next to him. 'The boathouse is pretty dilapidated.' She explained its history to him.

'So it's been shut up since 1919?' he asked.

'It was always well maintained though – in memory of

Daniel Montagu. Or at least that's what my boss tells me. It's only in recent years that things have fallen into disrepair.'

'And why is that?'

'Simple,' Viola replied. 'Like so many minor estates across the country we're running out of money. In fact the Montagu family have been talking about selling up, which would mean I'd lose my job and…' She stopped. She was telling him too much again.

'And you'd hate that,' Chase finished for her. He was looking at her strangely, as though he was trying to figure something out.

'I love it here,' she replied simply.

The silence between them, which up to this point had been so comfortable, felt suddenly awkward and Viola wondered what had changed. Had she shared too much?

'We should get back,' she said. 'I'm supposed to be having dinner with my brother. If you're lucky we might even bump into him.'

The awkwardness lifted as they walked back towards the house and Chase's car.

'I really am sorry about your job and the house,' he said as they walked.

'I shouldn't have landed all that on you. It was supposed to be a nice summer stroll, not an afternoon of sad confessions.'

'That's OK. I've enjoyed getting to know you…'

Before either of them could say any more, Viola heard her name being called and a figure was running towards them.

'Viola, there you are!' It was Libby who ran the tearoom. She was out of breath and still had her cream apron on.

'His Lordship's here...' Libby stopped, hesitated. 'I mean Mr Montagu.' David hated his title and being called 'my lord' even more than he hated the Haverford estate.

'What's he doing here? He's not due this week. Does Lady Seraphina know?'

Libby nodded. 'Someone's gone to the dower house to fetch her. But the earl isn't alone either,' Libby went on. 'He's brought someone with him and...' She hesitated again. 'Well, you'd better just come and see.'

Viola turned to Chase. 'Listen, I should go. Shall I...'

When she looked at him, Chase had gone very pale. 'I think I'd better come inside with you. There's something you need to know.'

Before Viola could question this, Libby anxiously led the way around the front of the house where, unusually, the huge double doors had been thrown open – nobody, not even the guests, used this entrance. It was too difficult to lock and unlock those magnificent doors each day. Neither Libby nor Viola had ever walked up the steps and through these front doors before, and Viola found herself wondering what it would have been like to be one of the Montagu family before the First World War, before everything changed, when all the staff would be waiting on the steps to greet you.

*What a strange world it must have been*, she thought.

David Montagu stood in the hallway pointing up at the stairs. His voice was loud, as so many ex-public school boys' voices are, and it carried through the house, easily overheard. Ranting about the house was his favourite subject.

'Of course you might find that Montgomery Hotels want to keep a lot of the original features – the staircase for example, even if you would be installing a bank of lifts. And the ballroom ceiling is something to behold – you could turn it into a function room I suppose. Weddings, parties, stuff like that.' David hadn't noticed Viola arriving and he waved his hand vaguely as though he didn't give a jot what happened to Haverford House as long as it was money in his pocket. Viola knew that even Seraphina had given up on preserving the house but she hadn't expected David to jump in Haverford's grave quite so soon. He was clearly talking to a developer, but who was it? Whoever it was had their back to her.

'Good morning, Mr Montagu,' she said. 'Is there anything I can help with?'

'Ah, Viola,' he boomed at her. 'Just the person – you'll be much better at this than me. You can...' He stopped, spotting Chase standing next to her. 'Oh you've already met Mr Montgomery then. Well, that will make all of this less awkward.'

'Mr Montgomery?' she asked, looking at Chase, but David's attention had turned to someone else who had strolled in the front door like he owned the place.

'Seb,' Viola whispered loudly. 'What are you doing here?'

'Who are you?' David asked rudely.

'I'm Viola's brother...' Sebastian began.

'He's one of the actors in the festival,' Viola explained. 'Seb McKay.' She saw Chase turn his head, as though to catch a glimpse of the famous actor.

'I've never heard of you,' David said, losing interest in

Sebastian. Viola hid her smile. Her brother secretly hated it when people hadn't heard of him.

'Anyway, you say I've met a Mr Montgomery,' Viola said, stepping away from her brother. 'Is this him?' She pointed to the man standing next to David.

'Of course not.' David goggled at her. 'Have you run mad? This is Mr Montgomery's assistant.' He turned to the man standing next to him blankly, clearly having forgotten his name.

'Evan Jenkins,' the man said.

'Yes that's right,' David said. 'Jenkins. But, Viola, Mr Montgomery is standing right next to you. You just walked in with him.'

'What?' Viola turned to Chase who was deliberately not looking at her. Sebastian meanwhile had leaned against the wall and folded his arms in front of him, clearly settling in to watch the floor show. She felt her stomach drop and she pressed her lips together, willing herself not to cry, not here, not in front of everyone.

'Yes, his father owns Montgomery Hotels. You've heard of them I suppose? Well, they're considering buying Haverford now Mother's finally come to her senses.'

Viola swallowed. She knew exactly who Montgomery Hotels were. The group had wanted to redevelop an old Victorian building in Chiswick but the council had refused to give them the go-ahead. They were a huge American chain and were not known for keeping original features.

And Chase was Charles Montgomery, heir to the whole fortune.

What the hell?

He had been lying to her from the start, pretending to want to take her out so he could pick her brains about Haverford House and its suitability for one of his father's clinical hotels. And she had fallen for it, hook, line and sinker. She'd thought he was genuine, that he was really interested in her. He hadn't even been too overexcited when he'd found out who her brother was. He'd played his role very well – Viola would give him that.

But now the truth was out, unravelling here right in front of the Earl of Haverford and her brother. Viola wanted to run upstairs to her flat, get into bed and pull the duvet over her head. Alternatively if the ground would like to open up and swallow her that would be fine too.

'So will you do it?' she heard David say through the noise of the thoughts swirling in her head. 'Show Charles around.'

Viola took another breath. She would not cry.

She turned back to Chase and poked him hard in the arm with her index finger. 'You're Charles Montgomery of Montgomery Hotels?' she asked, poking him again.

'Well yes I...'

'And you didn't think at any point during dinner last night or our walk this afternoon to tell me that?'

'Well, this is awkward,' David said, to nobody in particular. 'But at least you know each other and that's all that matters.' He seemed oblivious to Viola's anger and quite used to situations like this where everybody had met everybody else at some sort of event or other – Henley or Cheltenham. It didn't seem to occur to him that the son of a billionaire hotelier and one of his own employees probably wouldn't have had many opportunities to meet. Which meant, of course, that David had no idea that Chase, or

Charles Montgomery, or whoever he was had been poking around Haverford for the last few days.

Chase Matthews then was the son of Reese Montgomery who'd inherited the famous hotel chain from his own father – Chase's grandfather – back in the 1950s and turned it into the famous institution it was today. It explained at least where Chase had disappeared to when Viola was showing everyone else the dollhouses the previous day.

'Of course, Charles,' David bellowed, stopping Viola from asking any questions, 'as Viola shows you around you'll see a lot of old junk. Mother has been trying to preserve the place as it was in the 1930s when that bloody servant girl went missing, but you have to ignore that nonsense. It's time we all forgot about it and moved on.'

Viola heard Libby gasp next to her and could sense her stare. Of course Libby would have questions – she had plenty of those herself – but neither of them ever got much of a chance to ask anything because at that moment Seraphina walked into the hallway.

'What on earth is going on?' she said, her voice carrying across the space almost as much as David's, her tone clipped.

'Ah, Mummy, there you are,' David replied. He smiled but he also went very pale. It became clear that David had not told his mother anything about Montgomery Hotels. 'I'm glad you're here. This is Charles Montgomery and he's come to...'

'We've met,' his mother said, her voice cold. 'He's been poking around here for the last couple of days calling himself Chase Matthews.' She stopped and looked over at Viola but mercifully didn't mention anything more.

A look of confusion swept briefly over David's face. 'He

has?' he said. His bravado was slipping now his mother had arrived. 'Well, I suppose he wanted to check the place out incognito as it were, eh Charles?'

Chase or Charles smiled his very white smile and held up his hands, looking sheepish. 'You got me,' he said. He still didn't look at Viola, clearly not wanting to have to explain himself in front of everyone.

'Anyway Charles is here to…'

'I know who he is, David,' Seraphina interrupted with such authority that everyone, even Sebastian and Chase, turned towards her like troublesome children. 'And I know exactly what he is here to do. And I am here to tell you that Haverford House will be turned into an American hotel over my dead body.'

# II

Haverford House, Yorkshire – June 1933

Thomas Everard has not brought a valet. This has caused a lot of unnecessary fuss in the servants' hall and Mr Prentice is practically apoplectic.

'I asked him if his man was following behind, on the train perhaps. I asked if we should arrange for him to be collected from the station and Mr Everard looked at me as though I'd asked him if he'd brought the moon,' the butler tells us incredulously, as Polly and I hide in the corner and try unsuccessfully not to laugh. 'He had no idea what I meant but in the end it transpired that he hasn't brought a valet with him.'

'What is the world coming to?' Mrs Derbyshire replies, and I can't quite work out if she's being serious or not.

'Well, it's no good,' Mr Prentice goes on. 'No good at all.'

'Where is his valet?' James asks.

'He doesn't have one, can you believe? What is the world coming to?' he repeats and shakes his head sadly. 'James, there's nothing else we can do. You'll have to step up and help Mr Everard dress...'

'But I've never done anything like that before,' James protests. 'How will I know what to do?'

Mr Prentice holds up his hand. 'Williams will have to give you a crash course,' he says, looking at His Lordship's valet. 'We don't have long – there's less than half an hour until the dinner gong now.'

'But what about serving dinner?' James asks. 'I can't be in two places at once.'

Mr Prentice is so red now he looks like he might burst and luckily Mrs Derbyshire takes control of things.

'You two girls,' she says to Polly and me. 'You stop giggling in the corner. Polly, you can help Mr Prentice for now and you can serve at dinner. Once Annie has dressed the girls she can come down and help me and Cook. And as for James, as soon as he's done with Mr Everard he can come back down here and change into livery and be back in the dining room before anyone has noticed he's missing. It'll be a rush but it will have to do.'

'It's positively uncouth,' Mr Prentice says in a choked voice.

'Well, it's the best we can do for now,' Mrs Derbyshire replies. 'And perhaps tomorrow you can speak to His Lordship about another footman.'

'I'd rather we had another valet,' James says, but Mr Prentice gives him a look so severe that he turns away and goes to Williams for his crash course.

'We can't go on like this, Mrs Derbyshire,' Mr Prentice mutters as he and the housekeeper start to walk away.

Polly nudges me and giggles again. 'I'd best go,' she says. 'Or he'll…'

'Have your guts for garters,' I finish.

'Exactly.'

I watch her follow Mr Prentice to the staircase, as I wait for the dinner gong. Polly and I are like chalk and cheese in many ways, but we always have fun. Polly is one of those people who finds the funny side in everything and I realise that Haverford House will feel empty without her when she leaves to be married.

I go upstairs to help dress the girls. Prunella is in a state of excitement at the prospect of finally meeting Thomas Everard.

'When Papa first mentioned him I didn't allow myself to believe he would really come,' she says. 'It's not as though anything interesting ever happens in this house, is it?'

I don't say anything in reply and I certainly don't remind her that it isn't that long since her twenty-first birthday party. I continue to curl the front of her hair with the hot tongs, that I'm sure I will never get used to using. Mrs Derbyshire is always having to put cold tea on the little burns on my fingers.

'Have you seen him yet?' Lady Prunella goes on. 'Is he very good-looking?'

'I've only seen the back of his head, my lady,' I reply. 'From the library window when he first arrived. It was a very neat head though.'

'An actor,' she exclaims loudly, making me jump and almost burn her head. 'Can you imagine? What will Papa say when I marry an actor?'

She catches my eye in the mirror as she often does and I smile benignly, as I often do. 'I couldn't possibly say my lady,' I reply although even she must know that Mr Everard has not been invited to Haverford because of his acting skills – however brilliant they may be according to the review of *Hamlet* that Mr Prentice read out to us from *The Times*. He is here because his father is as rich as Croesus – or at least that was what Mr Prentice told us after reading the review to us, and the butler is not known for outbursts of hyperbole. Even Lady Prunella knows full well that if she were to marry Mr Everard, His Lordship would be delighted that some money was finally coming into the house.

'Oh, for goodness' sake,' Lady Cecily sighs from the corner of the room. I had dressed her first. She rarely needs much help, and she is waiting now, leaning louchely against the doorframe. 'Who says he's here to marry you?'

'Well, he's hardly here to marry you, is he?' Lady Prunella bites back, her eyes narrowing. 'How is dear Hannah? When will she be visiting again?'

The insult barely registers with Lady Cecily, even though both she and I know what her sister is insinuating. She turns away.

'I'm going down,' she says. 'Don't be too long. You don't want to keep Mr Everard waiting.'

After Lady Prunella has left, I tidy the girls' rooms and stoke the fires. Even though it is the middle of summer the family like to have fires in the evenings. I gather up some mending that needs to be done and go back down to the servants' hall where James is in a fury over our visiting actor.

'He didn't even want anyone to help him dress,' James is saying. 'Says he has never had a valet and has no need for one now that he travels about with his acting. I didn't know what to do.'

'As you're told, James,' Mrs Derbyshire says. 'You do as you are told and you were told to dress Mr Everard.'

'Which is what I did do but he just snapped at me and kept pushing me away. It was awful. I'm not doing it again and that's that.'

'Don't let Mr Prentice hear you talking like that,' Mrs Derbyshire replies. 'He won't like it.'

'And I don't like dressing people who don't want to be dressed.'

'Between you and me,' the housekeeper goes on. 'I think Mr Prentice would prefer you in the dining room tomorrow so I wouldn't worry too much. I'm sure Williams can help Mr Everard if need be.'

James scowls at me as he pushes past me, as though any of this is my fault. I brush it off. I know he gets as frustrated with his work as I do, and I ask Mrs Derbyshire what she needs me to do.


Lady Prunella is not as enamoured with Mr Everard after dinner as she was before.

'He just kept talking about Shakespeare for positively ages,' she says. 'It was tremendously dull.'

'Well, you were the one who wanted to marry an actor,' Lady Cecily replies. She often comes into her sister's room after dinner as though she is afraid to be alone. I think when she is alone she feels the sadness of the house a little more than usual.

'It's all right for you. You know all these plays and books that he's talking about, but ordinary people like me and Annie…' here she catches my eye in the mirror again and I smile again '…well, we don't know what he's talking about.'

'Oh come on, Pru, there's a whole library downstairs you could have learnt from but you chose not to. Annie is better read than you.'

I keep my head down and don't look up at either of them. Because it's true: I am better read than Lady Prunella, and it is Lady Cecily who has helped me become that way.

Lord Haverford's library has opened my eyes to more books than I ever thought possible, as Lady Cecily well knows. I am bowled over by it every time I go in there to dust – there are so many books and so much to learn. It would take several lifetimes to read everything in there. It is Lady Cecily who has helped me decide what to read, what to focus on, so that I am not overwhelmed. She tells me sometimes about the libraries at Cambridge that hold every book ever printed and she introduces me to modernism, which I have loved, even when it has felt very hard to get a grasp of. I particularly enjoyed the Virginia Woolf novel that she recommended: *Mrs Dalloway*. It took me a while to get into, to understand what was going on I don't have a Cambridge education after all – but I got there in the end. I was quite proud of myself about that. And it made me realise what women are capable of when they allow themselves, when they break free from what society tells them they need to be.

But my main love, as Lady Cecily knows, the writer whose words I turn back to again and again, is the bard himself. I take after my father in that, even though my mother has no idea where he got his big grey book of the *Complete Works* from. 'It must have cost him a fortune,' she'd told me when

I was fifteen and had recently left school. 'It's yours now. He would have wanted you to have it.'

Later, when it is finally time for us servants to go to bed, I take the blanket-wrapped parcel from my bottom drawer and carefully remove the book that used to belong to my father. I turn the pages carefully to the first scene of *Hamlet*.

'"*Who's there?*"' I whisper to myself, following the words on the page with my finger. '"*Nay, answer me. Stand and unfold yourself.*"'

'Oh no, please,' Polly moans. 'Not Shakespeare, we've heard enough of that for one night from Mr Everard at dinner.'

I'm rather pleased that she recognises the opening line of *Hamlet* but I don't push it. I ask her instead what our house guest is like.

'Extremely good-looking,' she says dreamily. 'Very tall and his American accent is rather lovely. Even Shakespeare didn't sound too bad with that accent.'

'Polly,' I chastise jokingly. 'You're supposed to be getting married on Saturday.'

Her face freezes for a moment and she nods slowly. 'Saturday,' she repeats.

'Last-minute nerves?' I ask.

'Don't be silly,' she says. She's smiling but it seems forced. 'Now get back to your boring Shakespeare.'

'You'll miss me when you're gone,' I reply.

'I know,' she says quietly and I wonder if I hear a hint of regret.

## 12

'Why didn't you tell me who you really were?' Viola asked Chase as they sat alone in the tearoom at Haverford, which had thankfully now closed to the public. She had told the increasingly curious Sebastian to go back to his trailer, that she would find him later, explain everything then.

'It's a bit complicated,' she'd said. She had been embarrassed and flustered and hadn't wanted to embarrass herself further in front of Lady Seraphina and the Earl of Haverford.

'It doesn't seem complicated,' Sebastian had said. 'It seems as though that bastard has lied to you. Do you want me to...'

'Please, Seb, go back to your trailer.' Obviously it wasn't complicated but that had been neither the time nor the place.

Chase shrugged now as he sat opposite her. His face was pale and he looked furious.

'I thought it was a done deal,' he muttered. 'He told me his mother was on side.'

'You haven't answered my question,' Viola said.

He turned to her and ran a hand across his forehead. 'Everyone calls me Chase,' he said. 'And I often use my mother's surname. It's easier than people making a guess at who my father is. I've done it since college and...'

'And it's stops people realising that you're only there to turn their place of work into another unit in an American hotel chain,' Viola interrupted.

'It's really not like that.'

'It looks a lot like that from where I'm sitting.'

What a fool Viola had been – wearing a pretty dress, accepting his dinner invitation, taking him up to the old boathouse, thinking he was interested in her – when all he'd wanted was the house, or at least enough anecdotes about it that he could turn into USPs when it came to opening his luxury hotel. Even though she'd known he probably wasn't going to be in Cranmere for very long, it had been nice to believe that someone had found her attractive. It had been nice to have an evening away from Haverford, even if it hadn't quite been a night off from talking about it. She'd even been looking forward to seeing him again. She should have known.

'I didn't mean you to find out like this,' Chase said.

'No, I suppose you wanted to wait until the ink was dry on the sale contract.'

He sighed. 'It doesn't look like there's going to be a sale contract now does it?'

'Oh, I don't know. David is the earl; he has the final say in what happens to the house so you might be in luck.'

Chase reached across the table towards Viola's hand but she pulled it away.

'Let me explain,' he said.

Viola folded her arms across her chest and leaned back in her chair. In the distance she could hear Seraphina and David who were still standing in the grand hallway of Haverford House shouting at one another. Whenever one of their voices got particularly loud the sound drifted towards the tearoom but Viola couldn't make out the words. She looked at her watch, glad that most of the visitors were on their way home now.

'What are you doing here anyway?' David had asked his mother sheepishly.

'I could ask the same of you,' she'd replied. 'But luckily my staff are very loyal and came to get me to tell me that you're about to sell the house to an American hotel chain so I'm here to tell you that you're not.'

'It's my house,' David had begun but Viola hadn't heard much more as she'd gently sent the staff who were still watching the floor show back to their respective jobs and steered Chase towards the tearoom. 'Let's just leave them to it,' she'd said. Chase had reluctantly allowed himself to be led. He'd been able to see that his prospective deal wouldn't be going anywhere under the current circumstances.

'Go on then,' Viola said now, her tea going cold in the cup in front of her. 'Explain.' She was furious too for so many reasons, not least that she had been planning to spend this evening with her brother whom she hadn't seen properly for three years. They had so much to catch up on and now there was the added mystery of why Sebastian had gone back to Kiama.

'I'm not angry because it looks like the deal might fall

through,' he said. 'The deal was a long way off being agreed anyway.'

'You just said you thought it was a done deal,' Viola snapped. Why were men so contradictory?

'From David Montagu's perspective it was a done deal. He wants the whole estate off his hands and he wants a lot of money for it. My father was willing to give him what he wanted and he said he could talk his mother around. But I wasn't so sure anymore. I was thinking about telling my father that it wasn't a suitable place for a hotel. I just wanted to be the one who pulled out rather than be sent on my way by David's mother.'

'Why don't you think it's suitable?' Viola asked.

'Well, that's partly thanks to you.'

'Thanks to me?'

'I've always had a soft spot for England,' he began. 'Ever since I was at Oxford, so when my father showed an interest in Haverford House I asked if I could take this one. The house seemed interesting and the area around it beautiful. I'll confess that when I booked on to the first tour I knew I'd be interested in the history but I didn't think I'd find myself so invested in it so quickly. I thought the whole thing – the myth of the missing servant girl and the American actor who got off with her murder – well...' He paused for a moment, smiled. 'I thought it was something and nothing. People go missing all the time and it just felt like Haverford was milking a non-story...' He paused for a moment, as Viola stared at him.

'You thought all that or your father did?' Viola asked.

'Well, my father mostly.'

'That's how you knew so much about Annie and Thomas

Everard then,' Viola said. 'You and your father researched it to belittle it.'

He held up his hands. 'Initially that had been my father's intention.'

'And what about your intention, Chase?'

'To do my job,' he replied.

'You know,' Viola said after a while, her voice resigned, 'there's a lot of people who would agree with your father. The story of Annie Bishop is not as popular as it used to be. I think everyone who wants to hear it has heard it.'

'But that's the thing!' Chase exclaimed. 'I thought I'd heard all I needed to hear, but when you told the story, when you showed us where the servants slept and what Annie's life would have been like it humanised everyone. I believed the story. I wanted to know what had happened to Annie and it made me wonder if Haverford would be a suitable place for a hotel after all.'

'Is that why you came back? To find out more?'

'I wanted to do the tour again and, yes, when I disappeared when you were showing everyone the dollhouses I'll admit that I was scoping the place out a bit but I was having second thoughts.' He paused again for a moment. 'And I did genuinely want to spend more time with you.'

'To pick my brains about royal visitors and other key moments in the history of Haverford so you could put it on a plaque on the wall of your hotel. You used me, Chase, to find out more about the house. That's all you wanted.'

'Not just that,' Chase said quietly.

Viola felt herself blush and turned her head away.

'Perhaps we could try again?' Chase went on.

'What, so you can pick my brain for more exciting

things that happened at Haverford so you can charge huge amounts for the hotel rooms?' Viola snapped back.

Chase sighed, holding up his hands again. 'Fair enough, I deserved that. I should have told you who I was but, honestly, I'm really not sure this place is right for a hotel. This history, these stories, they need to be preserved.'

'Well, that's something we can agree on. If only there was the money to keep it going. Even Lady Seraphina knows it's time to call it a day.'

'But she's not behind the hotel idea, I take it.'

'If she's going to lose her home I suppose she'd like a say in it.'

Chase didn't say anything to that, he just fiddled with his empty cup.

'When are you going back to America?' Viola asked.

'I'm not sure,' he replied quietly. 'I'll need to break this news to my father so I should probably leave as soon as possible. He'll be expecting me after what's happened.' For a brief moment Viola almost felt sorry for him. Having a father as famous and powerful as Reese Montgomery was never going to be an easy ride.

'So I suppose this is goodbye then,' she said.

'I suppose it is.'

Viola stood up. 'At least if you don't think it suitable for a hotel,' she said, 'that buys me some more time to find another source of funds to keep this place running.'

'I'm certainly going to recommend that Montgomery do not buy Haverford,' Chase replied. 'And for what it's worth, I wish I'd been honest with you from the start.'

★

Despite the events of the day, Viola's mind kept returning to her brother, and his recent trip to Kiama. She was desperate to talk to him about it more, to find out why he went.

And to ask him if it was time she did the same.

Deep down, no matter how hard she worked and how much she loved her job, Viola knew that she was still running – she'd run from Kiama, run from Oxford, run from London, run from Robin – the difference was that this time, after Haverford, she had nowhere to run to.

Except perhaps back home, to put the ghosts to rest. To deal with the grief that she had run away from in the first place, the grief that had followed her halfway across the world anyway. Was that what Sebastian had been doing? Had he never truly dealt with what had happened to their mother either?

She needed to talk to him. She had so many questions bubbling beneath the surface now she'd had time to think about what he'd told her.

As she passed through the hall of the house, leaving Libby to close down the tearoom properly and Chase to do whatever it was he had to do before he went home, David had got to the pleading stage of his argument.

'Come on, Mummy,' he wheedled. 'You must see why we have to do this.'

'If you want to use the word "we", David,' his mother replied coldly, 'then you should do me the decency of telling me what's going on.' She paused, looking in Viola's direction before glancing at her watch. 'Here's Viola now,' she went on. 'She needs to get the house ready for tomorrow and lock everything up so I suggest you and I go to the dower house.' And with a nod from the dowager countess and not even a glance in Viola's direction from the earl, they were gone.

It was almost eight o'clock before Viola had time to seek out her brother again to see if he was free to finish their conversation from this morning. As she walked over toward the area where the Shakespeare Festival took place, she realised that the actors were in the middle of an impromptu rehearsal so she leaned against a nearby tree to watch them. Her brother was in his element on the stage. His body moved fluidly, his voice loud and clear as he rehearsed his part.

Viola could still remember the day Sebastian auditioned for his first lead role in the local amateur dramatics society's production of *Oliver!* a few months after his debut in the school play.

'Come with me, Vi,' he'd said. 'I need all the moral support I can get.'

It hadn't sounded much like something Viola wanted to do but Sebastian had always helped her out when she was nervous or when she just needed someone to talk to, so now it was her turn. The auditions were in the same building as her Guides meeting and so she'd just had to run down the stairs ('No running, Miss Hendricks,' her Guide leader had shouted down after her) and poke her head around the door to watch him audition.

He'd got the part and he had been wonderful – the whole town had talked about it for weeks, and Viola had been there every night of the show. Sebastian had smiled at her, as everyone else congratulated him, because they always had to be there for each other. No matter what.

Until drama school and Oxford University had taken them to opposite sides of the world and a distance had formed between them, exacerbated by the grief they were both consumed by but never really talked about.

It wasn't the sort of dramatic breaking apart that happened to so many siblings – one that started with an argument and escalated into years of not speaking to one another. It was more an acknowledgement that some things were too insurmountable to overcome, and that sometimes even twins couldn't be there for each other.

Viola wondered if Sebastian was happy, or if he felt like she did: cut adrift. Even here at Haverford, a place where she felt so at home, there was still that sense of something missing. She had felt like that since her mother died and wondered if she always would. She remembered the sadness in Sebastian's voice when he'd told her about the summer he was spending at Haverford. Did he feel the same?

After a while the rehearsal seemed to stop and the director brought the cast together to tell them something. It was then that Sebastian looked up and caught Viola's eye. He waved and started to walk towards her.

'Hey,' he said. 'Is everything OK?'

She nodded. 'I'm finally done for the day. Are you?'

Sebastian nodded, looking over his shoulder at the other actors.

'I can come back later if now isn't…'

'Now is perfect.'

'I want you to tell me about Kiama,' she said. The only

way to get him to talk was to be honest with him. 'About why you went back and why you seem so sad.'

He nodded. 'And I want you to tell me what on earth was going on in the hallway of the house this afternoon,' he replied.

# 13

Today is the day! Polly is getting married. His Lordship said that she could marry from the house because she has nowhere else, no family of her own. She has never said it but I wonder if that is why she is in such a rush to leave service, to get married – so she can have the family that she had always wanted, much like Ned. Maybe I'm being fanciful though. Polly is far more pragmatic than me and doesn't have the romantic notions about life that I get from always reading books. She probably saw an opportunity when she first met Mr Mather and grabbed it with both hands.

Good for her.

Polly was abandoned as a baby on the steps of a church in Harrogate. She's never known who her parents were and was brought up in a convent until she was old enough to go into service. She'll tell you how much she hated the nuns, how much their education and religion was wasted on her, but the truth is Polly is smart as a tack and much cleverer than me in many ways. She knows exactly what she wants and today she gets to have it all. Her experiences have made her so much stronger and more resilient than me. She isn't tied to her mother's apron strings like I am. She doesn't hide from the world in the pages of a book.

Mrs Derbyshire has gone all out to give Polly a good send-off. We had a little party downstairs, late last night after His Lordship and the girls had turned in, just some tea and sherry and sandwiches. We're all exhausted this morning of course but it was worth it to see Polly so happy and excited and to see Mr Prentice wipe a tear from his eye as he gave a toast to Polly's seven years of service. In public he has always disapproved of Polly and her general desperation to get out of service, something Mr Prentice has dedicated his life to, but privately I think he's very fond of her. We all are. We'll miss her terribly.

Especially me. Who will I read my Shakespeare to now? I don't think Katy will be quite so tolerant when she moves into my room this evening.

Mrs Derbyshire and Cook have worked together late into the night all week to make Polly the most beautiful wedding dress.

'I'm not having any maid of mine going out on their wedding morning looking like anything less than a princess,' the housekeeper said. Cook has just complained a lot about eye strain and headaches while smiling indulgently at Polly. Everyone is happy to see Polly fall on her feet like this.

When Polly steps out of Mrs Derbyshire's parlour, where she and Cook have been dressing the bride-to-be, we all gasp. She looks so beautiful – almost unrecognisable from the housemaid whose hair was always falling out of her cap and who often had a smut of soot on her nose.

'I've had to use every spare hairpin in the house to keep your hair up,' Mrs Derbyshire says, fussing with a stray strand. 'So try not to move your head too much.'

'And keep away from any soot or dirt,' I tell her with a wink. She grins back at me.

'In an hour's time I shall be a solicitor's wife,' she says, trying and failing to put on a posh voice. 'I need to learn quick smart how to keep clean and tidy.'

His Lordship has let us all have the morning off to go to the church with Polly. Just the morning though. We have to be back to serve luncheon.

'Look here, Prentice,' Katy had overheard His Lordship saying. 'It's one thing letting the staff go to this wedding, but it's quite another to expect us to help ourselves to food in one of those buffets.'

'Indeed, my lord,' Prentice had replied. Prentice hates the idea of the buffet as much as His Lordship and I wonder if either of them will ever move with the times. We are well into the 1930s now after all.

Not that it really matters as none of the staff have been invited to the reception, which is to take place at Mrs Mather's house – or Polly's new mother-in-law, I should say. It seems so grown up to have a mother-in-law, but we are all grown-ups now. Lady Prunella told me that Mrs Mather did invite His Lordship to the reception, an invitation that he was swift to turn down. We will all return to the house as soon as the marriage service is over, and in time to prepare luncheon. We've done as much as we can this morning and Ned is coming in to help with the fires. I'm in the scullery when he arrives and he puts his head around the corner of the door and smiles his perfect smile.

'Skip the wedding and spend the morning with me,' he says. 'We can play house while everyone's gone.'

'I can't skip Polly's wedding,' I reply, trying to ignore the implication about 'playing house' – the first hint since the kitchen gardens that he may still think about a future for us. I wonder at him, at what he is thinking. We still spend a fair bit of time together when we're both free – we take walks around the estate and talk about our work and, occasionally, I let him kiss me. But sometimes, like today he seems overly familiar, as though our future together is already decided. Have I led him on? Have I let him think I am more interested in a future together than I really am?

I should say something, spend less time with him, not lead him to think things that aren't true, but whenever I consider broaching the subject I feel so sorry for him and how lonely he must be. He steals one of those kisses now before he disappears to deal with the fires. One day Mr Prentice will catch us and Mr Prentice is in such a state of perpetual anxiety about how much things have changed since the war that I cannot imagine how he'll react.

Things have changed since the war and for the best. There is so much more opportunity for girls like me if only we are brave enough to take it. Only the other day I heard that a girl from the village, a girl who had been at my school, has moved to York to train as a nurse. Some days I despair at myself and wonder if I will be a lady's maid forever, and I worry about what will become of me when Cecily and Prunella marry – which they will of course eventually – even Lady Cecily. I cannot stay near my mother for the rest of my life. There is a future out there for me somewhere. I know it, but I don't know how to begin to find it.

But today isn't a day for sadness. Today is a day for celebration.

We walk into the village together, Polly leading the way, holding on to Mr Prentice's arm. He will be giving her away in the absence of a father and when she asked him I saw him turn around and wipe another tear. Mr Prentice has shown more emotion in the last few weeks than I've seen from him since I began my duties at Haverford.

We are all wearing our finest clothes – although they are not very fine in the grand scheme of things and have needed a lot of help from Mrs Derbyshire's sewing needles – and there is a sense of excitement and possibility in the air. We are all in high spirits, mostly about our morning off, I think, rather than the wedding itself, and it is a beautiful morning as we walk through the trees and past the lake to the village. In the winter, when I walk back from my mother's this way, it can be a little dark and creepy, but on a day like this when the skies are cloudless and the sun is warm, when there is joy and birdsong in the air, it feels like the most beautiful place on earth.

But how would I know? I've never even left Cranmere. I don't have anything to compare it to. Sometimes it feels as though I will be here forever. Perhaps that is the real reason I never say anything to Ned; he might be my only hope.

The ceremony is very moving and all of us shed a tear – even if Mr Prentice, James and Andrews pretend they have something in their eyes ('It's a very dusty church, Annie,' Andrews says with a smile) and afterwards we throw rice at the happy couple as they head towards the open-top car that will take them to the reception about five hundred yards away. Mr Browne, the church sexton, glares at us all from the churchyard. It is he who will have to clean up the rice after all. But you have to throw rice at a wedding. It's bad luck not to.

Polly catches my arm as she passes.

'I'll come visit,' she says, her smile not quite as sure as it was this morning. 'I promise.'

I squeeze her hand, knowing that this is a temporary homesickness and that I'll probably never see her again. My stomach drops at the thought. We haven't been the best of friends, we have very little in common, but she has been a certainty in my life. A certainty that wouldn't be there anymore.

We arrive back at Haverford just in time to change and go about our duties. It is a cold luncheon, but not a buffet of course, and Mr Prentice asks me to help with service.

I haven't served at mealtimes very often recently. I think the butler is trying to pretend we still have enough staff to keep the house in the traditional manner, especially while Mr Everard is here, but James is run off his feet and Mr Prentice has a permanent worry line etched between his eyebrows. With Polly gone and Katy still so green, I'm not sure how we're going to manage. But I suppose we will. We always do. There is talk of agency staff when Mr Everard's parents arrive.

Today James and Mr Prentice need an extra pair of hands as the farm steward and some local landowners are joining

His Lordship for lunch. I suppose that's why he didn't want a buffet and why he gives Mr Prentice a hard stare when he sees that it's a cold lunch.

'Apologies, gentlemen,' he says, as though his two daughters weren't there. 'The staff were at a wedding or some such this morning.'

Nobody except him seems to mind, although everyone eats in a rather uncomfortable silence after that, speaking only about land-related matters and asking Mr Everard how things are done in America.

It is Mr Everard who tries to jolly things up a little.

'I was thinking,' he says placing his cutlery down on his plate in the American way that I've now learnt means he has finished. 'We should put on a play.'

'A play?' Lady Cecily drawls. 'How quaint. But are you so bored of English country life already, Mr Everard?'

'I do wish you'd call me Thomas,' he replies. 'And no I'm not bored of your country ways yet, Lady Cecily.' He smiles slowly at her and she holds his gaze. 'I just thought it might be fun.'

His Lordship makes a grunting sound and signals to Mr Prentice to start clearing the table.

Mr Everard has been at Haverford for three weeks now and I expect he is desperately bored. According to Lady Prunella he grew up in New York City. His father is known as one of America's most successful financiers who even managed to not lose too much money in the crash, and for the last few years he's been acting in plays in New York and, more recently, London. He is also, now I have seen more than just the back of his head, extremely handsome – just as everyone keeps saying.

'Well, I think it would be fun,' Prunella says now eagerly, smiling widely at Mr Everard. She always seems eager whenever she talks to him. Lady Cecily tells her that she is too eager.

'Well, it's not you who he'll marry is it?' Prunella snaps back whenever Cecily brings it up. 'Someone's got to appear eager to marry him after all.' In private Prunella has told me that she would marry him tomorrow if she could, so I wonder if Cecily is right, if she is too eager. And then I remember Polly's face as she took my arm after the wedding and I wonder if she has been too eager as well, if she has married her solicitor in haste to get away from Haverford, just as Lady Prunella seems to want to do with Mr Everard. Perhaps we women are not that different after all. We all piss into a chamber pot, as Andrews so eloquently puts it.

'What play were you thinking?' Lady Cecily asks, as we begin to clear the table under Mr Prentice's orders.

'*Twelfth Night* is my favourite,' Lady Prunella says. 'All that nonsense with the yellow stockings!'

'Then *Twelfth Night* it will be,' Mr Everard replies. As I take his plate, he catches my eye and smiles. It's the sort of smile that would give a girl goosebumps if I was the sort of girl who got goosebumps. Polly would be bursting with laughter if she were here. 'Perhaps,' he says, without taking his eyes off me, 'the staff would like to be involved.' I know I should move on and clear Lady Cecily's plate but I feel as though I'm frozen by Mr Everard's gaze. The way Ned looks at me pales into insignificance compared to the way Thomas Everard is looking at me now. My mouth feels dry and I try to swallow.

I hear Mr Prentice clear his throat and I spring back to life and back to plate clearing as His Lordship stands up from the table.

'Are we done here?' he says. 'Done with this nonsense?' He signals to the estate manager and the other gentlemen to go with him and Mr Prentice holds the door, following after them, no doubt to serve their coffee in the library. After all these years His Lordship still surprises me with his moods. Mr Prentice says he saw more in the war than I'll ever understand, but even I can understand that you could never be the same person again if you came home from the hell of war to find your wife and son dead.

'I can invite Hannah to help make up numbers,' Lady Cecily says as I turn away from the table. 'She was in the amateur dramatics group up at Cambridge.'

'Oh, must you,' Lady Prunella complains. 'She is such a bore.'

James nudges me gently and nods towards the table where I notice not only has Mr Everard not followed the other gentlemen to the library, but he is still looking at me.

'We'd definitely need some staff on board with the play if we want to make it work,' he says. 'What do you say, James, are you up for it?'

James nods. 'Yes, sir,' he says.

'And you, miss?' He doesn't know my name and I feel sudden disappointment. But why should he know? I realise he is waiting for an answer but my mouth feels dry and my cheeks are on fire.

'Of course Annie will be in the play won't you, Annie?' Lady Cecily says, smiling at me. 'My maid is quite the fan of Shakespeare you know, Mr Everard.'

'Is that right?' he says as James nudges me and the dirty plates out of the room.

'Annie knows more about *Twelfth Night* than any of us, I should think,' I hear Lady Cecily say as I leave.


'What was that all about in the dining room?' James teases once we are back in the kitchen.

'I don't know what you mean,' I reply, unable to look up at him.

'Mr Everard's play,' he says, 'the way he looked at you and all that about you loving Shakespeare.'

'It's nothing,' I say. I feel as though Lady Cecily has betrayed me with her comment. My love of Shakespeare, of books in general, had felt like a secret between us. Obviously everyone knows I love to read but this makes it seem like something more. James certainly wasn't supposed to know I loved Shakespeare, as this will just give him yet another thing to tease me about.

Cook comes to my rescue, which is something of a surprise. 'You know how much Annie loves to read, James,' she says. 'It's no surprise she likes the greatest writer of all time.'

James looks sceptical, glancing between me and Cook as though neither of us should know who Shakespeare is at all. 'That doesn't explain the way Mr Everard was looking at you,' he says, as though he's never seen anyone leer at a servant girl before.

'I was just clearing his plate,' I reply turning away from him, trying not to remember the way Mr Everard's gaze had made me feel.

I hear Mr Prentice clear his throat behind me. He has glided into the kitchen on noiseless feet as usual. 'Go about your duties, James,' he says.

When James has gone and Cook has turned back to the stove, Mr Prentice places his hand on my shoulder and leans towards me. 'Be careful with Mr Everard,' he says, a fatherly warning in his eye.

# 14

'I'm surprised you're still here,' Sebastian said as they walked away from the house towards the lake. 'I know things didn't work out in Oxford or with Robin, but I'm surprised you've stayed up here in this old house for so long.'

'It's more than just an old house,' Viola replied, reluctant to talk about Oxford and defensive about Haverford as usual. 'But why do I get a feeling you're deflecting? What are you doing up here at this old house rather than on some glamorous film set?'

'You know why I'm here.' He smiled. 'Making this the best Shakespeare Festival you've ever had!'

'While that may be true, isn't it all a bit... well... beneath you? A rural Shakespeare Festival in an old house?'

Sebastian shrugged and Viola looked at him. He seemed careworn somehow, as though life wasn't as kind to him as he always claimed.

'I just fancied a change,' he said.

'Don't get me wrong,' Viola went on, 'it's wonderful

to have you here and I hope we get to spend some time together with fewer interruptions but...'

'Yes, tell me what all that was about this afternoon,' Sebastian prompted.

'Don't change the subject.'

'But...'

'Please just tell me why you're here.'

Sebastian stopped and turned towards his sister. 'I wanted to see you, talk to you, talk about Kiama and if you'd ever thought about going back.'

'I... I've never thought about it,' Viola lied. She'd thought about it a lot, but always talked herself out of it. She wasn't sure she could face those ghosts.

'Really? But it's your home.'

'It's your home too and until this morning I never thought you'd go back either.'

'If we both really didn't want to go back then why have neither of us ever even mentioned selling the house, cutting ties with the place forever?'

'Well, the house brings in money I suppose and...' Viola trailed off. It sounded feeble even to her ears. Sebastian didn't need the money and if she was going to lose her job she might be better off selling the house rather than relying on the intermittent rent it brought in now.

They walked on in silence and Viola thought about Kiama for a moment, their house, their old school, the blowhole. She tried to imagine her brother as he was now back in that town, but she couldn't, and she wondered again what had taken him back. She knew that they had drifted from each other for so long that they didn't really talk about the things that mattered anymore. She knew that Sebastian didn't tell her almost as much as she didn't tell him, and she knew it shouldn't be like this. They were twins; they'd shared a womb. They should be able to talk about the hard stuff together. But perhaps they had both ignored the hard stuff for too long.

'Are you happy here, Vi?' Sebastian asked eventually. 'Because sometimes I wonder if you've been happy since you left Kiama. Even Oxford didn't make you happy in the end.'

Viola had become obsessed with Oxford as a teenager after reading *Gaudy Night* by Dorothy L. Sayers – it was always a book or a magazine article that led her forward. She'd felt somehow at home in the Oxford college of Sayers' imagination and had begun to read obsessively about the city and collect pictures that she'd cut from magazines. She began to feel as though she knew the medieval passageways of the university and wondered if she could ever go there – not as a tourist, of course she could do that, but as a scholar.

She had begun to research every possible scholarship going. With the help of her English teacher at school she'd worked for years to try to study there. She'd almost worked herself to death and, when she'd got an interview, had spent all the money her grandmother had left her on the flight to England where she'd finally seen the city she'd been dreaming about for years. It hadn't let her down, and she hadn't let herself down either, gaining the scholarship she'd never believed would be hers. It had been everything she'd ever wanted.

Until it wasn't.

'After Mum died,' she said, 'nothing was the same. Everything felt empty, even the things I'd been dreaming about for years. You know that. You must feel that.' She rubbed her forehead with the palm of her hand.

'I know that,' Sebastian replied quietly.

'I guess that sometimes what we think we want isn't good for us in the end.'

Oxford hadn't been the soothing balm she had hoped it would be. After the initial gloss wore off Viola had found it hard, impossible even to fit in. It had begun to feel like a 1990s version of the worst parts of *Brideshead Revisited*. She was still amazed she had managed to stick it out for nearly two years. She hadn't been able to find her way at all, hadn't been able to find her niche. And then there were all the men in tailcoats storming about shouting and breaking glass, men who would go on to run the country.

'I know you thought everyone there was a dickhead,' Sebastian said with a smile, his Australian accent suddenly stronger. 'But the idiotic Bullingdon Club can't be the only reason you left.' She'd told Sebastian about the strange clubs and societies of Oxford that other people took for granted because she'd thought he would find it funny and it was easier than talking about how lost she had felt, how the ancient university had not lived up to her hopes and dreams.

'I didn't leave,' she corrected him. 'I got sent down. It's very specific and it happened because I simply couldn't keep up with the workload. I guess there were a lot of reasons for that.'

They walked on in silence again, around the kitchen garden and towards the lake. They both knew that there were many reasons why things hadn't worked out for Viola after she left Kiama, but they also both knew that she'd been running away from her grief when she left and that she shouldn't have gone anywhere until she'd understood that grief more. She knew now that she'd been running ever since.

After Oxford she'd found a job, waitressing at a big hotel in London. It was a live-in position so she'd had just about enough money to survive. She had worked her way up into the conference and events team and then, later, had applied for a job at Kew Gardens, which she'd miraculously been offered. Kew had been the stepping stone that she'd needed. She'd gained a lot of experience and insight that she'd been able to take with her when she'd risked the move to Haverford House.

It sounded simple, but of course it hadn't been. She'd had a lot of fun, met a lot of amazing people, visited European cities she'd only ever dreamed of back in Kiama. But among the laughter there had been a lot of tears and loneliness, and a lot of forgetting – pushing down feelings of homesickness, of Sebastian, of Kiama, of her mother. And then she'd met Robin and life had felt as though it had come to a grinding halt until she read about Annie Bishop in a magazine one Sunday morning.

Viola and Sebastian sat down in the dappled shade under the trees.

'You said you were surprised I was still here,' Viola said quietly, looking out across the lake. 'And I know it's a bit strange, disappearing to the North on a whim and a magazine article like I did, but Haverford is the first place that has felt like home since I left Kiama. You're right when you say I hadn't been happy for a long time, but I'm happy here. It's the first place I've ever felt happy since Mum died. But now I could lose it.'

Sebastian's brow creased and she told him about the conversation she'd had with Seraphina, about how this was the last summer and about the earl wanting to sell.

'Is that what all that fuss was about?' Sebastian asked. 'I'll admit I lost all track of what was going on after the earl's mother started shouting at him.' He laughed softly. 'Posh people can fight as hard as us commoners, can't they?'

'It's all a bit embarrassing really,' Viola said. That was a huge understatement of course – she felt excruciatingly humiliated by the whole experience still as she explained to her brother that Charles Montgomery also went by the name of Chase Matthews, the man who she had gone out to dinner with the night before, the man she had put before her brother only this afternoon.

Sebastian blew air out of his cheeks. 'And you had no idea who he was or why he was here?'

'None.'

'I should find this Chase Matthews and hit him really, shouldn't I?' But they both knew that he wouldn't. Hitting people really wasn't Sebastian's kind of thing.

'He claims after meeting me he'd decided that Haverford shouldn't be a hotel after all,' Viola went on.

'That's good isn't it?'

'Even if Montgomery Hotels don't want it, somebody will. And then I'll lose everything.'

Sebastian sighed and looked away from her again. 'You know when you said that sometimes the things we think we want aren't good for us?'

'Yes.'

'Well, that sums up where I am too.'

'I knew there was something. I knew you didn't do this Shakespeare Festival out of the goodness of your heart.' She stopped, looking at him with concern. 'What is it?'

'The reason I was back in Australia…' He paused, cleared his throat. 'It wasn't just about a trip down Kiama's memory lane. I've been offered a job.'

'In Kiama?'

He shook his head. 'No, in Sydney. *Sunset Bay* want me to go back and I'm thinking about saying yes.'

'What?' Viola was surprised. *Sunset Bay* was an Australian soap opera set on the Queensland coast, but filmed just north of Sydney, in which Sebastian had played the part of Christian Stokes for three years straight after drama school. Viola had been in England by then where the soap ran almost a year behind but she had watched it religiously for the whole three-year period that her brother had been in it, until they sent his character off to an unspecified city for bigger and better things and Sebastian himself went to America. She wasn't going to admit it now but she still watched the occasional episode of *Sunset Bay* whenever she felt homesick.

'I know, it was a surprise to me too. They called my agent, paid for me to fly over to the studios and said they wanted to bring Christian Stokes back from wherever he's been as a teacher at the high school. It felt weird to be back there – it brought back a lot of memories.'

'I'll bet,' Viola said quietly. 'Are you going to do it?'

'I honestly don't know. I said I'd think about it. I have to let them know by the end of September.'

He told her then about how he'd decided to hire a car and drive up the coast and that stopping off in Kiama had been a whim. He certainly hadn't planned to do it.

'It was then that I realised that I can't do this anymore, Vi. I can't do all the travelling and the instability and the publicity and interviews. I just want to be in one place for a while. I just want to feel like I've got a home again and...' He stopped.

'And?' Viola prompted.

'Well, I wondered if you wanted to come back with me?'

'Oh, Seb,' Viola replied, surprised by how emotional she suddenly felt. 'If you go back I'll come visit, of course, but Haverford is my home now; I've told you that.'

'But you just said that you're about to lose it, that...'

'I can't lose it.' She felt defiant suddenly. She couldn't let this happen. There had to be something else she hadn't tried. Something else that would save Haverford.

Because she couldn't go back to Australia on the coat tails of her famous brother. It would be admitting, once and for all, that she'd failed at everything she'd tried so hard to do. And she wasn't sure she could go back to Kiama on a whim like Sebastian had either. How could she when all she could think about when she thought of her hometown were the blue lights of the police car that had come to tell them about their mother, and of the father who had abandoned them not once, but twice.

'But you said you'd tried everything,' Sebastian said. 'You said that the earl was ready to sell.'

'I have to keep trying until it's too late. He hasn't sold up yet so it's not too late.'

Sebastian smiled. 'Still the same old Vi. When you want something you really don't let it go do you? You really do love it here. What is it about this place?'

'You know what brought me here.'

'The missing lady's maid.'

Viola nodded. 'I know you think it's silly but the story, her legend, the house, this lake...' She paused, looking around her. 'It all means so much to me and I'm absolutely not ready to let it go.'

'And you still believe that your lady's maid is here somewhere, that she never left the estate?' Sebastian had heard Viola's theories plenty of times.

'Where else could she be? She must have had an accident or something. Surely if she'd run away she'd have turned up again somewhere?'

'Not necessarily. She could have changed her name, gone overseas. She was meant to be going to America wasn't she?'

Viola nodded.

'It was much easier for people to disappear back then. Perhaps she did leave. Perhaps she has had a happy life. Perhaps she is even still alive.'

Viola thought about all the conversations she'd had in the pub when the locals had laughed at her kindly and told her Annie had just left for a better life, and she thought about Chase Matthews laughing about the possibility of living next door to Annie's descendants. She'd never really considered that Annie had got away – it was almost as though she'd wanted to keep Annie to herself, for her to become part of Haverford so Viola could continue to compare their stories.

But what if she'd been wrong all this time?

What if she'd left that August night?

She stared at her brother for a moment as dusk began to settle around them.

'Perhaps it's time you left too,' Sebastian said.

# Part Three

# APPEARANCE

*A*ugust *has just slipped into September and the airport
is heaving with people travelling here, there and
everywhere. It has been a long time since the writer has
been anywhere so busy, but Emily soon finds someone to
help and a wheelchair.*

'We'll soon have you safely in the first-class lounge,
ma'am,' the man with the wheelchair says in that patronising
way she finds that so many young people speak to her these
days. She may be old and useless but money still speaks in
New York City – the same as it ever did – and the man is
right: they are soon in the first-class lounge.*

'I feel about a hundred years old in this contraption,' she
complains, and Emily raises an eyebrow. She isn't that far
off her century after all. She wonders, not for the first time,
if she will live to be a hundred and how many friends she
will outlive if she does. She has so few friends now; she sees
so few people. This is the first time she's been further than
the park in years. She knows this will probably be her last
trip anywhere, and she remembers the feeling she had as she*

*left that she may never see it again. Things are coming full circle, she thinks. It's about time.*

'Let's have a drink of something,' *she says to Emily to stop these maudlin thoughts.*

'Sure, what would you like. Coffee? Iced tea?'

'Let's push the boat out.' *She smiles.* 'Let's have a glass of champagne.'

*When Emily returns to the table with the drinks she asks the question that the writer had been expecting her to ask days ago.*

'So, this trip to England. Why after all this time?'

'I wanted to go home, that's all.'

*Emily looks sceptical.* 'Really? But you never talk about England; in fact I'm not even sure I knew you were English until you told me the other day.' *She pauses, chewing her lip.* 'We've worked together a long time now,' *she says eventually.* 'Why don't you tell me the truth?'

*The writer takes a large drink of her champagne and returns the glass half full to the table. She watches the bubbles float to the surface of the liquid for a moment before opening her handbag and taking out a copy of* The New York Times. *It is already open at the correct page and she places the newspaper on the table between them, smoothing out the pages. She has smoothed the pages of this article so many times over the last two weeks that she is surprised she hasn't worn them away.*

'I know I promised you some time in London,' *the writer says,* 'and I'm not going back on that promise. But after London we are going here.'

*She watches Emily begin to read the article.*

'Haverford House,' she says as she reads. She pronounces it with the emphasis on the last syllable, as so many Americans do. The writer does not correct her.

'I used to live there,' the writer says. 'A very long time ago.'

# 15

Haverford House, Yorkshire – July 1933

W e are to have a house party in August when Mr Everard's parents arrive, although how we will cope with so few staff nobody knows. Mr Prentice is in paroxysms about it all. His behaviour is easy to mock and Andrews does a wonderful impression of the butler in full flow.

'We haven't got time for this messing about,' Mrs Derbyshire says when she catches us laughing. 'And Mr Prentice is right. I've no idea how we'll cope with a houseful again. You'd all better hope that we find some agency staff who know what they're doing.' She sighs. 'And you'd better get back out to the garage, Andrews, before Mr Prentice catches you. You know how he hates you being in here in the daytime. What if His Lordship needs driving somewhere?'

Andrews nods, pressing his lips together to stifle his laughter, and leaves us.

'You should know better, Annie,' Mrs Derbyshire says to me. 'Mr Prentice has been nothing but good to you and your mother before you. He's devoted his life to Haverford since he first came here as a footman. He's been here even longer than me.'

There is a sadness in her face when she speaks of this and I realise for perhaps the first time the loneliness of a life spent in service. No husband or wife, no family, no children, just the people that you share the servants' hall with, random strangers thrown together. I suddenly feel desperately sad for both Mr Prentice and Mrs Derbyshire and the lives they could have had. I remember the butler's tears on Polly's wedding day as another member of his makeshift family left him.

I'm alone in the servants' hall after Mrs Derbyshire goes. I know I have duties about the house but I relish these tiny moments of solitude that happen so very rarely. I press my hand against the dresser and close my eyes, wondering what it would be like to not be below stairs, but instead one of the ladies upstairs. Wondering what it would be like if somebody dressed me every day.

My mother would tell me that these daydreams are a slippery slope. That if I wasn't careful I would be 'getting ideas above my station'. And it's only a few detrimental steps from that to 'forgetting my place'. My mother is very strict about this sort of thing. There is barely an afternoon when I go to see her that she doesn't mention it. But I've never been convinced about this idea of hierarchy, that some of us are better than others simply by way of our birth. Surely only fate decides that, and we are all the same really. We all deserve the same opportunities. I know my mother is proud of the fact that I work at the house as she once did, but I don't want to stay here forever, getting to Mrs Derbyshire's age and looking sad because I've missed out on so much in my life.

My mother would also say I was forgetting my place if she saw the way that Mr Everard looks at me, or if she knew how much pleasure those looks give me.

Don't misunderstand me, I may never have left Cranmere but I'm not completely naïve. I know what happens when men like Thomas Everard wink at the maid and I'm not intending to ruin myself for him, but oh, when he smiles it's as though the whole world lights up.

Oh, listen to me. I sound like Katy.

Mr Everard has a lot of opinions on British hierarchy, opinions that are more in line with those of Andrews than of His Lordship.

'In America,' he says one luncheon (he starts many sentences with the words 'in America' to which His Lordship responds with a sniff), 'everyone has the same opportunities to rise up through the ranks, no matter their lowly beginnings. My father himself came from very little.' I want to find out more about Mr Everard's father and his lowly beginnings but Mr Prentice chooses that moment to usher me down the stairs and back to the servants' hall.

'I've read about it,' Andrews tells me later when I relate what Mr Everard had said. 'Some of these wealthy American financiers that the British aristocracy now rely on came from bugger all like us. Of course half of them lost everything in the crash but...'

'Not the Everards,' I interrupt.

'No, not them. Imagine, Annie,' he goes on, his eyes lighting up, 'in America even you or I could be wealthy.'

'What about me?' James pipes up.

'Even you, James.' And it is then that Andrews tells us he is saving up his money for his passage to America. 'I don't just want to drive these cars,' he says. 'I want to own them and that's never going to happen if I stay here.'

'Enough,' Mr Prentice's voice echoes through the servants' hall. 'All of you back to your duties. I don't want to hear any more of this nonsense.'

Rehearsals for the play are underway and His Lordship disapproves wholeheartedly of it all. He absolutely refuses to let the servants join in, although we are secretly helping downstairs with the sewing of costumes and the making of scenery.

The performance will be held when Mr Everard's parents arrive and it will be a way for the Everards to meet some of the local families. Rehearsals are taking place in the grounds and I watch surreptitiously from the sidelines, wishing I could be part of it. Everyone looks as though they are having so much fun and I think again about another life, where I was born under different circumstances. And I think about what Mr Everard and Andrews said about America. Can it be true? Can anyone make it over there?

But if anyone can make it, then anyone can fall too. There are no guarantees in life, not for even the wealthiest people. Even His Lordship grieves every day for his wife and son.

I have been reading *Twelfth Night* again from my father's *Complete Works* of Shakespeare – just a few lines every night before I sleep. I tried to interest Katy in it but she has said it is the most boring thing she has ever heard. But I know almost every line off by heart and this afternoon as I watch the rehearsal I mouth the words along with the actors.

I use 'actors' in the loosest possible way. They are terrible. Local friends of Prunella's have been summoned to play the smaller parts and Cecily's friend, Hannah Rivington, is here, staying indefinitely in the blue room, to play Malvolio – an odd choice for a woman, perhaps, but she apparently feels more comfortable in men's clothes and appears to have almost perfect comic timing. She is also the only one who has learned their lines. Everyone else is still reading from the script that Mr Everard has provided.

'You should be our prompt,' Lady Cecily says, suddenly appearing at my elbow.

'Beg pardon, my lady,' I reply. 'I was just…'

Cecily laughs. 'It's all right, Annie. I know you wanted to be in the play. I wish Papa were less stubborn and stuck in his ways. It's 1933 for goodness' sake. The servants should be able to have some fun.'

'I don't think Mr Prentice would agree, my lady.'

'No, I'm sure he wouldn't.' She looks up at Mr Everard who is walking towards us across the lawn, leaving his actors in chaos behind him.

'I told you Annie knew more Shakespeare than any of us,' Lady Cecily says. 'She knows the whole play by heart. I was saying she should be our prompt.'

'God alone knows we need some help,' he says, speaking to Lady Cecily but looking at me. 'Will you be our prompt, Annie?' he asks. 'Please.'

'I'm sure His Lordship would never…' I begin. I realise I'm staring at Mr Everard again, at his dark blonde hair and blue eyes. And I realise that he is looking at me in the same way he looked at me in the dining room.

'You leave Papa to me,' Lady Cecily says, leading me

towards the actors, such as they are. 'As Mr Everard says, we need all the help we can get.'

July continues much as normal. The weather is warm and sunny, the days are long but as I go about my duties, I have a little light inside me that wasn't there before – I am the official prompt for the Haverford House production of *Twelfth Night*.

I know it doesn't sound like much, it isn't much really, but it's something to me. Something glamorous and exciting. Something that is just mine. Lady Cecily must have spoken to her father, as she promised, as there have been no more grumblings from him and I know that she spoke to Mr Prentice, who reluctantly agreed. He always has had a soft spot for Lady Cecily. I have kept the secret from my mother, however, even though I am so tempted to tell her. She didn't approve of the play in the first place when I mentioned it and if I tell her that I am now the prompt that will definitely be an idea above my station.

Every afternoon I join the cast on the lawn for rehearsals and as I prepare to leave the servants' hall Mr Prentice tells me to be careful in that fatherly way of his, although what trouble I can possibly get in, sitting on a bench in plain view calling out lines I do not know. And there are so many lines to call out as the cast, with the exception of Mr Everard and Hannah Rivington, still barely know a word.

'Lady Prunella,' Mr Everard calls loudly one afternoon. 'How do you still not know your lines?' There is a moment of silence then as though nobody can quite believe that an American with no title has spoken to the daughter of an earl in such a way. But he is unperturbed. 'Even your sister knows her lines now.'

'Thanks very much,' I hear Lady Cecily mutter to herself. 'Even dull old Cecily.'

Prunella has insisted that she take the part of Viola, and there are a lot of lines to learn. 'Perhaps I can help,' I say quietly, not wanting to draw too much attention to myself.

'Yes of course,' Prunella gushes enthusiastically as she always does when she is in the vicinity of Mr Everard. 'You can help me learn my lines, can't you, Annie? We'll start tonight and…'

But I don't hear any more of what she says because I see Mrs Derbyshire beckoning me from the side of the house. I close my copy of *Twelfth Night* and hurry towards her, as I'd promised the play would not get in the way of any of my duties.

'We have a surprise visitor,' she says.

# 16

Haverford House, Yorkshire – July 2003

One of the few things that Albert, Lord Haverford, had updated in Haverford House were the bathrooms. In the late 1920s he'd had enough bathrooms fitted to accommodate all the guests that would stay in the house. There was almost a bathroom for every two bedrooms. At the time this must have seemed utterly outrageous and over the top – a complete waste of money in fact, at a time when everyone knew the country house was on its last legs, even if perhaps they weren't admitting it out loud.

Viola had often wondered why he'd done it, especially as everybody knew that the Montagus, like so many minor aristocratic families at the time, had been running out of money. Still, she had always been glad he had because it meant that she had her very own bathroom, complete with art deco, claw-footed bathtub, a bathtub in which she was lounging now. Admittedly the hot water wasn't as efficient at Haverford as it might have been but it was turning out to be, according to the newspapers, the hottest summer for twenty-seven years, so a lukewarm bath was no hardship.

As she lay in the tepid water, she kept thinking over what Sebastian had said.

*Perhaps she did leave. Perhaps she has had a happy life. Perhaps she is even still alive.*

What if Annie had left of her own accord to live a life elsewhere? What if, as her letter to Prunella had indicated, she had gone to America? What if she had left without Thomas Everard? What if she had met up with him later when he too had returned to America?

Why had Viola never thought about these things before? Why had she always had a feeling that Annie Bishop had never left Haverford House on that fateful night in August 1933, despite her friends teasing her about it? Why had she allowed that legend to become such a huge part of her work, her life, her identity when she knew, deep down, that it was nothing more than a legend?

And then she thought about the other thing Sebastian had said to her.

*Perhaps it's time that you left too.*

Perhaps, by the end of the summer she wouldn't have any choice but to leave. But where would she go?

She couldn't believe that Sebastian was thinking of going back to *Sunset Bay*, and she couldn't believe he'd gone back to Kiama without her. When he'd talked about it, she'd felt homesick for the first time since she'd left. She'd thought about Kiama, of course, memories of her childhood, of her mother. But she'd never seriously considered going back. She didn't know anyone there anymore. Her father had barely been able to stay when she and Sebastian were there. God only knew where he was now. Viola and Sebastian had long since lost touch with him. Why waste energy on someone who clearly didn't care about them?

Could she go back if she had to? Not to Kiama necessarily but back to Australia with Sebastian as he'd suggested? She didn't know. She wouldn't be able to make that decision until she was sure she couldn't save the house, until David Montagu had sold it and turfed her out of her flat. And if she did go back it had to be on her own terms, not holding on to her brother's coat tails. She hadn't come this far to start relying on somebody else now.

But why was she thinking so negatively? Sebastian might think she should leave but he didn't understand how much she loved this job. There must be a way of saving Haverford House from developers, hoteliers, or whoever else might want to buy it. Yes, Seraphina had been pretty adamant that this would be the last summer, the last Shakespeare Festival. But when Chase Matthews had turned out to be Charles Montgomery and in cahoots with David to turn Haverford into a hotel, Seraphina had been equally adamant that was not going to happen.

If she could just think of something that could make the Conservation Trust listen and understand how important this house was, not just to her and the family (although perhaps not to David), but to the village and the local community as well.

There must be something on the estate that she had missed. If she could just stop thinking about Annie Bishop for one minute.

Viola took a deep breath and submerged herself into the bathwater.

'So what happened to the girls?' Sebastian asked as he blew smoke rings into the air.

'I do wish you'd give up smoking,' Viola replied as she always did. She worried about him. She couldn't help it.

'One day, I promise.' He'd been saying that for years.

It was still hot and Viola could feel a trickle of sweat slide down her spine underneath her polo shirt. They were sitting by the lake near the old boathouse, a place where they knew they wouldn't be disturbed.

'What happened to the girls?' Sebastian repeated.

'After Annie disappeared you mean?' Viola asked not taking her eyes off the golden light. 'After Lord Haverford shut up the house?'

'Yeah.'

'Well, the whole family moved to London and then, in 1934 Lady Prunella died in a car accident.'

'Really?' Sebastian turned to her, the sunlight catching the side of his face, his eyes wide in surprise.

'From what I understand she was very unhappy in London. Just before Annie Bishop disappeared and Thomas Everard was questioned, she'd thought Thomas was going to propose to her. She was drunk on the night that she died.'

'How do you know all this?' Sebastian queried.

'The dowager countess told me but she didn't seem to know much detail. Or at the very least she didn't seem to want me to know any detail. It's a big family secret apparently but it's not really her family, not by blood, and I think she still tries to protect her children from everything if she can.'

'From what?'

'She once told me, years ago when I first started working here, that she too had always been fascinated by the story of Annie Bishop but her husband, Jeremy…'

'David's father?'

Viola nodded. 'Yes, apparently he always thought about the family and the effects that Annie's disappearance had on them – the scandal and police investigation of 1933, closing up the house and then Prunella's death. They were his family and Lady Seraphina always tried to remember that, although they weren't her family by blood, they were her children's family. She tries to play down a lot of the aftermath of Annie's disappearance for that reason.'

'And what about Lady Cecily?' Sebastian asked. 'What happened to her?'

'She married,' Viola went on. 'The son of a banker – incredibly rich according to Seraphina. Old families like the Montagus needed money and the rich middle classes wanted titles. It happened a lot as far as I understand. Anyway, Lady Cecily and her banker husband were Jeremy's parents and Jeremy became the sixth earl.'

'And what about the actor, Thomas whatever his name was?'

'Thomas Everard. Well after the police dropped the case he went back to America. He was killed in the war.'

'Why did the police just drop the case like that?' Sebastian asked. 'Don't you think that's a bit odd?'

'Why all the questions all of a sudden?'

Sebastian lay back on his elbows allowing the evening

sun to warm his face. 'I don't know. There's just something about that story you told me, the story of the disappearance of Annie Bishop that doesn't ring true somehow.'

'It is mostly just a local story you know,' Viola said. 'One that we milk a little bit to get the punters in.'

'But it really happened,' Sebastian went on. 'That young woman did actually disappear one night and was never seen again and it's that story that made you want to work here. I guess I'm just surprised that you haven't dug into it all a bit more.'

'Annie's story captured my imagination. I was at a place in my life where I was really unhappy and I didn't know what to do about it. When I read the interview in that magazine I wondered if perhaps I could disappear too. I think that's what brought me up here in the first place. But...' She paused.

'But what?'

'There was more to it than that. Annie was leaving Haverford for America for a new life, a better life. There were so many opportunities in America back then, certainly far more than there were for a lady's maid in sleepy old Cranmere. And that's what I was doing when I left Australia for Oxford. I was trying for a new life, to leave my old self, my grieving self behind. Of course that was never going to work out and...' She stopped again, biting back tears. She was so much happier in Haverford than she'd been for years but it still hurt when she thought back on her life.

Sebastian turned to his sister then. 'Why didn't you tell me at the time how unhappy you were?'

'What could you have done? You have your own life to lead.'

'But we've always looked out for each other. We've always had each other's backs. I know I was on the other side of the world at the time but I'd have helped somehow if you'd just talked to me.'

'I wanted to work things out on my own.'

Sebastian smiled. 'You've always wanted to do that,' he said. 'Are you happier now?'

Viola nodded. 'Yes, I really am. I'm worried about what I'll do when David finally sells the house, but I'll work it out. I feel much stronger and more capable than I did five years ago.'

Sebastian nodded and turned his face towards the setting sun again. 'I have to go to London tomorrow,' he said. 'A quick trip before dress rehearsals start and the festival opens. I need to talk to my agent.'

'About going back to *Sunset Bay*?' Viola asked.

He nodded. 'I'm probably going to do it, you know. I miss home. Don't you?'

'Sometimes.'

'You could come back too,' he said again.

But Viola didn't want to talk about that. She was determined still, even though the odds were against her, to find a reason for the Conservation Trust to take an interest in Haverford. There had to be something.

When she didn't reply her brother stood up and stretched. 'I'll see you when I get back then,' he said. Their partings had always been like this, neither of them making a fuss, both of them already missing the other.

'Hey look,' Sebastian said suddenly. 'Isn't that guy Chase or Charles or whoever over there? You know, the guy you dated.' He pointed towards the other side of the boathouse.

'Where?' Viola asked, standing too, craning her neck to see.

'Why are you blushing at the mention of his name?' Sebastian teased.

'I'm not blushing,' Viola insisted even though she knew she was. She had been trying very hard to not think about Chase Matthews.

'Look there.' Sebastian pointed again. 'I'm pretty sure that's him, isn't it?' Sebastian started to wave at the shape in the distance.

'Be quiet will you,' Viola hissed, knocking his hand back down by his side. 'Don't draw attention to yourself.'

'Why?' Sebastian asked. 'Don't you want to see him?'

She ignored her brother. 'It is him, isn't it. What's he doing here?' She started to walk towards the boathouse. 'Hey,' she shouted. 'You're not supposed to be up here.'

'I thought we weren't drawing attention to ourselves,' Sebastian muttered as he followed her.

'Oh hello, Viola,' Chase said as she got closer. She saw his eyes widen as he noticed her brother behind her but he didn't say anything.

'What are you doing here?' Viola asked crossly.

'I've paid my entrance fee...' Chase began.

'You know members of the public aren't supposed to come up here to the boathouse and...'

'But I thought...'

'Well you thought wrong.'

'I was just looking at the lake here and...'

'Well go and look at the lake somewhere else please. I think we've made it quite clear that we don't want anything to do with Montgomery Hotels so just leave and tell your father that we said no.'

'This isn't to do with the Montgomery Hotels,' Chase began. 'If you'd just let me explain…'

'Just leave please,' Viola said, crossing her arms in front of her. How was she supposed to work out how to save Haverford if this guy kept hanging around, finding ways to persuade the Montagus to sell up?

'I think you'd better go,' Sebastian said quietly, placing a hand on Chase's shoulder. Chase seemed so shocked by this touch from a movie star that he nodded blankly and started to walk away.

'What is he doing here do you think?' Sebastian asked as Chase left.

'I'm not sure, but Lady Seraphina won't be impressed if she finds out he's still sniffing around.'

# 17

Haverford House, Yorkshire – July 1933

Polly is sitting at the large table in the servants' hall when I walk in. She has her back to me but I know it's her straight away. I am delighted to see her and rush to the table.

'Polly,' I exclaim. It's been a month since her wedding and I've missed her so much more than I thought I would. 'You should have said that you were coming. We could have had Cook make a cake and everyone could have...' I trail off as I look at her face. 'Where is everyone?' I ask.

'Polly just wanted to see you,' Mrs Derbyshire says. 'I shall fetch some tea.'

I sit next to my old friend and she reaches over to take my hand. 'I've missed you, Annie,' she says. 'I can't stay long but I have missed you.'

As she turns her head I can see her face more clearly and I know then that what I thought I saw wasn't a shadow. She is sporting a black eye fit for a boxer.

'I missed everyone,' she goes on, barely letting me get a

word in. 'I even missed the house and my duties.' She smiles sadly and looks away but that surprises me.

'You missed Haverford?' I ask. 'But you hated it here.'

'It's funny how things turn out, isn't it?'

We sit in silence for a moment and I wonder how to bring up her bruises. How did that happen? A dark thought comes into my head that I hope is not true and my mouth feels dry.

Mrs Derbyshire saves me by returning with the tea.

'What happened to your eye, Polly?' she asks, just like that. I wonder if that confidence comes with age. If I will ever be able to be as forthright as Mrs Derbyshire.

Polly laughs, but the sound is hollow, echoing off the walls. Nothing like her old laugh that rang through the house at inappropriate moments.

'Oh, I walked into a door,' she says, ducking her head so we can't see her eye anymore. 'Imagine that, me who has worked in the big house for so many years, having accidents in her own house!'

'Accidents?' Mrs Derbyshire repeats the plural that I had noticed as well. 'You've had more than one?'

'Oh, I burnt myself in the kitchen too, but it was nothing,' she goes on, still not looking at either of us, but I notice her hiding her hands inside her sleeves.

I decide to change the subject. 'Come on then, Polly,' I say, my voice unnaturally cheerful. 'Take your hat off and relax and tell me all about married life and I'll tell you all about the play that Mr Everard is putting on. Lady Prunella is…'

'Oh, I can't stay,' she interrupts, snatching up her teacup

and gulping down what must still be scalding-hot liquid. 'I have to be home before my husband gets back from work.' She glances at me then and I'm sure, just for a moment I see fear in her eyes. 'I just wanted to see how you were.'

Mrs Derbyshire stands up. 'I'll leave you to it,' she says.

'I've missed you, Polly,' I reply. 'Can't you stay a little while longer?'

She shakes her head, her lips pressed together, almost bloodless.

'Not today,' she says. 'Maybe another time.' She stands suddenly, the legs of her chair scraping on the stone floor.

'Polly, please.' I stand too and face her. 'Is something the matter?'

She takes my hands then and finally looks at me properly. I can see that the bruise on her face is beginning to yellow, which means it is a few days old.

'I just wanted to be sure you were all right, Annie,' she says. 'I wanted to be sure of you, that you were still here.'

I smile. 'Oh, Polly, I'll always be here – you know that. Where am I going to go?' I want to tell her about Thomas Everard and about how in America everybody has the same opportunities. I want to tell her about how handsome he is and how, if she was still here, we would giggle about him. I want to tell her all about the play and about my role as prompt but she is already pulling away from me.

'I must go,' she says, glancing towards the door.

'You'll come again?' I ask. 'Or I could come and see you on my afternoon off. My mother can be without me for one week.'

'No,' she says, that slightly panicked look coming back

into her face again. 'Don't do that. I'll come here again soon. I promise.'

'Do,' I say as I walk her out toward the courtyard. 'I've so much to tell you.'

When she smiles then it seems genuine. 'I can't wait,' she says. And then she's gone, hurrying away, her heels clicking on the cobbles.

When I return to the servants' hall Mrs Derbyshire is clearing the tea things.

'Go on now,' she says. 'Get back to your play before Mr Prentice finds you something more useful to do. He was mumbling this morning about the silver needing cleaning.'

I hesitate, fingertips touching the table. 'Did that seem strange to you?' I ask.

Mrs Derbyshire pauses and brushes imaginary dust from the table. 'Yes, Annie, it was strange. You will keep in touch with her if you can, won't you?'

I nod.

'And I'll tell you something for nothing,' she goes on as she takes the tea things out. 'It wasn't a door that caused that bruise.'

It isn't until I am lying in bed that night that I realise what she meant.


The next morning as we are finishing our breakfast the bells start ringing, each one summoning one of us from downstairs to assist in various locations upstairs.

'Chop chop, everybody,' Mr Prentice calls. For one reason or another none of us seem very interested in things this morning.

Neither of the bells from the girls' bedrooms have rung yet and I'm wondering if they have both overslept when a bell rings that I have never seen ring before. I watch Mr Prentice and Mrs Derbyshire exchange a glance.

'Her Ladyship's old room,' Mrs Derbyshire says quietly.

Mr Prentice clears his throat. 'That'll be the girls, Annie. They must be in their mother's old room for some reason. Why don't you take their tea up there and see what's what? You know where it is?'

I do know where Lady Haverford's room is, but I have never been in there. Polly used to tell me that it had been kept exactly as it was on the day she died. Nothing had been moved or changed on His Lordship's instruction. She would try to make me believe that it was haunted. Nonsense of course. I'm not easily fooled but I try not to think, as I carefully carry the tea tray along the corridor, that this was also the room in which she had died.

'Oh, there you are, Annie,' Lady Prunella says as I push the door open and place the tea tray down on a nearby table. 'You've found us. I hoped you would.'

Lady Cecily is sitting in her dressing gown on a chair in the window, smoking a cigarette and looking out across the grounds. She doesn't say anything as I enter.

'How can I help, my lady?' I ask.

'Oh, for goodness' sake,' Lady Cecily says, snapping out of whatever trance she was in and stubbing out her cigarette. 'Let's not stand on formality here. You have, after all, just entered Cloud Cuckoo Land.'

'Help me with these buttons will you, Annie?' Prunella asks, ignoring her sister.

'You will notice that my sister, having gone completely mad, is trying on a wedding dress,' Cecily says, her tone dry. She lights another cigarette.

'Is there to be a wedding?' I ask tentatively. I have seen very little sign of Mr Everard showing any interest in Lady Prunella. He shows more interest in me than he does in her. Only yesterday he had sat next to me during rehearsals and told me that my knowledge of Shakespeare was second to none. I had felt myself blushing and had to look away. I try to push that thought out of my mind. Now is not the time or the place. Perhaps one of Lady Prunella's friends who has been spending so much time at Haverford because of the play has proposed.

'According to Pru,' Cecily goes on, 'wedding bells are imminent any day now.'

'Are they?' I say, forgetting myself. It is not my place to ask such questions but it seems so unlikely.

'Nobody has proposed yet,' Lady Prunella says, her voice joyful and on the verge of laughter. 'But it is only a matter of time.' I set about helping with the rows of tiny buttons up the back of her dress, simply to give me something to do and to stop me asking any more questions.

'This is Mama's wedding dress you know,' Lady Prunella goes on.

'And Mama was a damn sight slimmer than you judging by the struggle Annie is having with those buttons,' Cecily snaps waspishly from the corner and unfolds herself from the chair. Even in just her dressing gown she is more beautiful than her sister will ever be. 'Leave it, Annie, for heaven's sake,' she goes on.

I step away from Prunella as Cecily starts to unbutton the wedding dress again.

'It is a little tight,' Prunella admits, her voice sounding flatter than it did. Does she really think that Thomas Everard is going to propose to her? I wonder, for a moment if I have the courage to ask him next time he talks to me at the play rehearsals. As I'm thinking about this I hear my name and I look up.

'Do you think you could do something with it so that it would fit?' Prunella asks, her face hopeful.

I have no idea at all, but Mrs Derbyshire might. 'I'll try,' I say.

'Let's have some music,' Prunella suggests as Cecily helps her into her dressing gown again. I notice a dusty gramophone in the corner of the room. The girls walk towards it and put one of the shiny black discs on the turntable. Music begins to fill the room, music I recognise as 'Alexander's Ragtime Band'. Gramophones astonish me. Where does the music come from? There is so much I don't know about the world and I seriously think, in my daydreams at least, that I could make it to America. I am as much in Cloud Cuckoo Land as Lady Prunella.

'This was one of Mama's favourites,' Cecily says. 'She used to sing it when we were little and twirl us around.'

'Let's dance now,' Prunella says. Her cheeks are flushed and her voice sounds as though it might break.

'Are you all right, my lady?' I ask.

Cecily looks up at me. 'Can you wait for me in my room?' she asks. 'I'll come to get dressed shortly.'

As I leave I hear her trying to get Prunella to drink some

of the tea I brought up. It is not my place to wonder what is wrong of course, but I can't help being curious.

By the time we begin the rehearsal that afternoon, Prunella seems her normal self again, or as normal as she ever gets at the moment. When I first started working at Haverford, when I first met her on the stairs and we were both sixteen, she seemed like any other sixteen-year-old girl. But recently she has become what my mother would call 'highly strung' and what Mrs Derbyshire has called on more than one occasion 'worrying'. I think I can see what is wrong though, as I feel some of those feelings myself. She is lonely, desperate for companionship and, I suspect, would marry anyone to get away from this life at Haverford.

I can't know this for sure of course – I am just an observer – but I've been thinking a lot about leaving myself recently, about a life outside of the Haverford estate, outside of Cranmere. Polly thought a lot about leaving too. She married her solicitor to do just that and now she has a bruise on her face and has lost her laughter.

Lady Cecily on the other hand always seems much more content to be at Haverford, especially now Hannah is here. Despite her beauty, despite her lofty monologues about women's rights, despite her time at Cambridge, she doesn't seem to want to go anywhere or do anything else. Perhaps she knows there are worse places to be trapped than the Haverford estate. I wonder if she will marry, if she will be forced to do so in the end, because of course there is the question of an heir, the next earl. Even us servants know that. Without an earl, who knows what will happen to the house and the title when His Lordship passes away. Mr Prentice says the house will go to Lady Cecily but he doesn't know who would inherit the title.

After the rehearsal is finished, Lady Prunella invites the whole cast to stay for dinner. 'We'll have a party,' she announces in a voice that is becoming, once again, worryingly like the overexuberant voice of this morning, before the tears began. I see Cecily and Hannah exchange a look.

Cook is not best pleased about the impromptu party of course. She fusses about and shouts at Lucy the scullery maid. But Cook tends to perform her best work under pressure and creates a feast fit for a king.

'I don't know,' she says. 'These young people and their impromptu dinner parties. It never used to be like this...'

'Times are changing,' Mrs Derbyshire interrupts, 'and I for one am glad about it.' The housekeeper is a huge embracer of the new, unlike Mr Prentice, and it is a bone of contention between them. Mrs Derbyshire has always been a quiet supporter of women's rights and she has seen so much in her lifetime. But then I remember the sadness in her face the other day when she spoke about how long she had been in service, how long she had worked at Haverford and how, for her at least, not much has changed.

I'm very aware of how easy it is to stay somewhere for too long, to not realise that the best years of your life have passed until it's too late. The times might be changing but, with the exception of the hot running water, the electricity and the telephone system, much has stayed the same at Haverford since Queen Victoria was on the throne. Will I be stuck here for decades like Mrs Derbyshire? Or can I escape? I think about America again, of things Mr Everard and Andrews have spoken about. I wonder if Andrews will get there in the end.

But as for me, I won't be going anywhere other than in my dreams. How could I go anywhere? How could I leave my mother all alone?

There is no formality to dinner that night. His Lordship disappears from the dining table as quickly as he can, shutting himself in his study with Mr Prentice, as James and I clear. There is no port and cigars, the ladies do not leave the dining table early, and Lady Prunella announces that they shall have dancing. James is sent to bring the gramophone down from Lady Arabella's old bedroom, and I send Katy to open up the windows in the ballroom as it is a stifling night and everyone is in need of some air. Lady Prunella insists on the ballroom being used as though this is a huge party when in reality there are so few people they will be rattling around in there like peas in a colander. But I can tell that Prunella is in the sort of mood where not even her sister will argue with her.

Knowing that everyone is busy and looked after, I let myself into the library after everything is cleared away. Lady Cecily has been encouraging me to read Dickens – his books have always rather intimidated me before due to most of them being so very long.

'Annie, you've read and enjoyed Woolf and Hardy,' Cecily had said. 'And you know Shakespeare better even than our resident Shakespearean actor, so I think you'll manage Dickens.'

I started with *Great Expectations* and then *Oliver Twist*, my copy of which I am bringing back to the library tonight, careful to use His Lordship's meticulous checking in and out process. I've come to collect a copy of *David Copperfield*. As I slide it off the shelf I see how thick the book is, his longest novel so Lady Cecily tells me. I try not to balk at the length of it and instead remember how Cecily's eyes lit up when she talked about it.

I go back to the servants' hall and ask Mrs Derbyshire if I can take my book into the yard for a little while. It's quieter there and nobody interrupts me to ask questions about what my book is about, and at this time of year it's still light enough for a while longer.

'Of course, but be ready for when the girls need you,' she says. 'And don't strain your eyes out there. Come in as it gets dark.'

I settle onto the bench by the wall, and begin to read.

*Whether I shall turn out to be the hero of my own life, or whether that station will be held by anybody else, these pages must show.*

I have barely got past the first sentence when I hear the strike of a match and smell the smoke of a cigarette. I look up, expecting it to be Ned. We meet here in the evenings sometimes, although I haven't seen as much of him since Polly's wedding. Perhaps he is tiring of me and my excuses about always being busy. Perhaps I should never have encouraged him in the first place.

I watch somebody step out of the shadows and I stand up.

'Hello, Ned,' I say.

'It's me,' a soft voice replies. 'Thomas.'

# 18

Viola found herself thinking about Chase Matthews again after her brother had left for London. Why was he still hanging around the estate? And why did it bother her so much that he was?

She hadn't seen either Seraphina or David for a few days and she wondered what was happening about the house, or if another buyer had been found. Since the argument with Chase, Viola had tried to go about her days pretending everything was as it should be, trying to believe that this was a normal summer, not the last one she might ever spend here.

Was there any way that Haverford could be saved? The only way she could think of was if there was some reason for the Conservation Trust to get involved, and even if she could find a reason to interest them, the trust would want to make substantial changes. The stories of Annie Bishop would certainly have to stop. The trust was a serious historical and conservational body – it was unlikely to want to keep peddling local legends. Annie Bishop would be confined to pub gossip.

*But at least I'd still have a job*, Viola thought to herself.

And keeping her job was important to her. She knew that her brother often thought her indecisive and she knew that indecisiveness frustrated him. But this time she knew exactly what she wanted – she wanted to keep Haverford open to the public. She just needed to work out how before David Montagu sold the whole estate.

She decided to call Seraphina and see how she was. She should probably tell her that she'd seen Chase wandering the grounds. He had been a paying visitor and was entitled to be on the estate during opening hours but she'd told him that they tried to avoid the public going near the old boathouse, so why had he chosen that specific place? It was a bit odd. She flipped open her phone and checked for reception. It was usually quite good on the estate since a new mobile phone mast had been built on the other side of Cranmere. Surprisingly, the villagers hadn't objected to it, instead embracing modern communication methods. Cranmere was remote enough, especially in the winter.

'Viola darling,' Seraphina said when she answered the phone. 'I've been meaning to call you. We must catch up.'

'I just wondered if there were any further developments on the sale of the estate,' Viola said. 'Sorry, I've been so busy with the festival since we last spoke.' She didn't mention that she'd been avoiding thinking about what might happen at the end of the summer and especially avoiding thinking about the house being turned into a hotel.

'We must catch up though,' Seraphina went on. 'I haven't

had a chance to apologise for all that fuss the other day over the hotel business. I'm so sorry. What must your brother think of us?'

'Oh, don't worry, he knows what families can be like.'

'I just can't believe that David didn't tell me he was trying to sell to Montgomery Hotels and that man you went out with was Reese Montgomery's son. Did you know?'

'Of course I didn't know! I would have said something if I'd so much as had a feeling about it.'

'Well, I'm terribly sorry about it all anyway. Come to dinner tonight and let me make it up to you. David is in America on business so he won't interrupt us with a new scheme. Bring your brother too.'

'Sebastian's had to go to London for a couple of days,' Viola replied, thinking that if David was in America there was definitely no need for Chase to still be here. What was he up to?

'Just the two of us then,' Seraphina replied. 'Shall we say about seven?'

After she'd finished work for the day, and before it was time to go down to the dower house for dinner, Viola walked out to the far side of the lake to where she and Sebastian had last seen Chase. She didn't expect to bump into anyone. The grounds had closed for the day and the Shakespeare Festival was yet to open, but she felt compelled to have a look, to check that he hadn't secreted himself somewhere after closing time, still in cahoots with David Montagu. Or even to go ghost hunting as he'd joked about the first time they'd met. He had seemed so genuine, so interested in the house and grounds and everything that had happened there. Viola had well and truly been taken for a fool.

There was definitely nobody about – just her and a few birds – but that didn't stop her wondering why Chase had been lurking around. What was his purpose? What had he seen when she'd brought him here that had compelled him to come back, despite claiming that Haverford shouldn't be sold as a hotel?

Viola decided to leave the birds to it and walked back across the grounds to the dower house. Perhaps she wouldn't tell Seraphina about seeing Chase again. It was just another thing to worry her with and until Viola knew more, perhaps she should keep it to herself.

They talked about the Shakespeare Festival over plates of spaghetti Bolognese.

'What's it like to see Sebastian again?' Seraphina asked. 'Has he forgiven us for our silliness? I must introduce myself properly when he comes back from London. I can't believe he saw me shouting my head off like that.' She looked embarrassed. 'A film star at Haverford and I'm screaming like a Banshee.'

'It's so lovely to have him here, to see him every day. I think this is the most we've seen of each other in one go since I left Australia. And don't worry about the other day. Seb thought it was funny to be honest.'

'I'm still so angry with David about it. I just don't think I can bear to see the house become a hotel.'

'Ultimately it will be up to David, though, won't it?' Viola said despondently.

'Well yes, but I think I've managed to buy us some breathing space for now at least. Although what good it will do I don't know. The estate will have to be sold eventually.'

They fell into silence for a moment so Viola changed the subject.

'You know, Seb really loves it here. He's been wondering what I've been doing out here in the middle of nowhere but now he's seen Haverford he understands. He's taken to wandering the grounds in between rehearsals.'

'That's lovely to hear.' Viola is sure she hears a note of sadness in Seraphina's voice.

'I took him up to the other side of the lake where the disused boathouse is the other day.'

'That was always one of my husband's favourite parts of the estate – it's one of the reasons why I don't advertise it to the public. If they come across it by accident that's OK, but it keeps it peaceful, doesn't it, if people aren't walking around there all day.'

'I can stop taking people up there if you prefer,' Viola said thinking rather guiltily that her brother hadn't been the only person she'd taken to the boathouse that week.

'No, no,' Seraphina interrupts. 'It's beautiful up there and I don't mind staff and so on going up. Jeremy and I used to walk up there a lot when he was alive but, well... I've told you about how Jeremy's mother and aunt closed up the boathouse after their brother died.'

Viola watched as the dowager countess sat back in her chair and looked away slightly as though remembering.

'This was before the First World War of course,' Seraphina went on. 'They kept a small boat in the boathouse and as soon as Daniel Montagu came home from boarding school each summer he and Cecily and Prunella spent their days there. I imagine in many ways they barely knew there was a war going on for half of their childhoods. Daniel and his mother died after the war and that was when they shut it all up. When we moved back here and Jeremy opened up the house, he tried to keep that area as private as possible in memory of the uncle he never knew.'

'He never knew his aunt either did he?' Viola asked, even though she knew the answer.

Seraphina shook her head. 'No, Prunella died before he was born as well. There was so much tragedy in that family.' She paused and looked at Viola. 'That was why it was so important to my husband to move back here, open the house up and breathe new life into it. Before the First World War Haverford was the hub of everything around here, but afterwards things were never the same I suppose.'

'That must have been true for so many similar families and estates,' Viola said quietly.

'Of course. The world changed a lot after that war. But locking up the house and moving to London didn't help. I do understand why Lord Albert did it but so many people lost their livelihoods because of it, and Jeremy used to think about that a lot. Then after Albert finally died – he lived to be ninety-two you know – and Jeremy became earl, he always wanted to do something about that. We'd only been married a year when Lord Albert died and it was a while before we had the money to put into reopening the house. It cost us a lot, both financially and emotionally, but it's not something I ever regretted.'

'When did you open it to the public?' Viola asked.

'After Jeremy's death. There were a lot of taxes and so forth to pay and it wiped the coffers out somewhat. I moved to the dower house and we began opening the house to the public. David and I have been arguing about it ever since, but it was something I wanted to do, something I had to try. And then you arrived out of nowhere and saved the day.'

'Only temporarily saved the day,' Viola said.

'Yes… well…'

'And how do you feel now?'

'The world has changed again, many times.' Seraphina sniffed and shook herself as though pulling herself together. 'And it's time for us all to move on.'

'No second thoughts?'

'We don't have the money for second thoughts anymore, my love,' Seraphina said leaning across the table and squeezing Viola's hand briefly. 'Besides, ultimately it's not my decision to make as you said. It's David's.'

Viola decided that tonight was definitely not the time to say anything at all about whether or not Chase Matthews was hanging about the disused boathouse.


'Have you made a decision?' Viola asked Sebastian when he had returned from London. 'Are you going back to *Sunset Bay*?'

They were sitting in the folly, which had become their favourite place to meet in the early evening. Today when they'd met, Sebastian had reached for his customary cigarette but had changed his mind, putting the packet back in his pocket. 'I'm trying to give up,' he'd said. 'You're right – it's a disgusting habit.' It wasn't often he listened to his sister.

Now he nodded slowly in response to his sister's

question. 'I'm going back,' he said. 'The studio want me to start filming in November so I'll probably fly out at the end of the summer.'

Viola felt her stomach drop and she wasn't really sure why. She knew now that he was unhappy, that he wanted more stability, and it was clear he wanted to go back to Australia even if she was still in two minds. And it wasn't as if she wasn't used to living on a different continent to him.

'Going back to Australia and giving up smoking,' Viola said with a smile she didn't feel. 'That's a lot of decisions for one day.'

'And what about you, Vi? Have you made any decisions? Do you fancy coming back with me?'

Viola sighed. By the autumn when Sebastian flew back to Australia it was looking increasingly likely that she would be without a job. There were jobs she could apply for all over the country – she'd been looking at the advertisements if not actually filling in any application forms – but none of them lit her up in the way Haverford House had when she'd first read about it. Besides, did she want to spend another cold, dreary winter in England in staff accommodation that would undoubtedly be badly heated? She didn't mind it at Haverford so much, not least because she got to spend so many evenings with Seraphina in front of the fire at the dower house but what would it be like somewhere new? Did she want to spend another Christmas alone, when her brother would be on the beach surfing?

'I don't know what to do,' she admitted, knowing how much those words and her indecision would frustrate Sebastian. 'I guess I'm still hoping that we can save the house somehow, and that I can save my job.'

'You love it here that much?'

'I really do. I can't imagine not living here.' She paused then, trying to imagine what would almost definitely happen in a few weeks' time. 'But the chances are I'll have to leave before the winter,' she went on turning to her twin. 'Can I let you know then?'

'Of course,' Sebastian replied, putting an arm around her and giving her a squeeze. 'It's an open offer. You can come out and join me anytime.'

'I've been up to the boathouse again,' Viola said changing the subject. 'But it doesn't look like Chase has been back.'

'Oh, you've been looking for him have you?' Sebastian teased, a glint in his eye. 'I knew you liked him. Waiting for another date are you?'

'It's not like that,' Viola said, but she could feel herself blush and knew that it was a little bit like that. If he hadn't lied to her about who he was she would have jumped at the chance of another date. 'I can't date him anyway after what he did.'

'Seems to me he was just reluctantly following his father's orders. That doesn't make him a bad person.'

Viola hadn't thought about it quite like that but she didn't want to start now.

'Anyway,' Sebastian went on. 'I'll leave that mystery in your hands while I solve another one for you.'

'What mystery have you solved?' Viola asked.

'Well, none really,' Sebastian admitted. 'In fact, I might have made things more complicated actually.'

'What are you talking about?'

'The mystery of Annie Bishop.'

'What have you found out?' Viola asked. 'And how?'

'I have this friend,' Sebastian replied. 'He works in historical research, and he helps me when I'm working on a role set in the past – like that detective show on HBO. I asked him to see what he could dig up on your lady's maid.'

'Really?' Viola felt her stomach fizz, and not about Chase for once. 'Does he know what happened to Annie?' Did she want to know if he did?

'Well no. Annie Bishop disappeared without a trace that night and nobody can find any records of her afterwards but two other people disappeared on the same evening.'

'The gardener's assistant,' Viola said suddenly, remembering something somebody had told her in the pub one night years ago when she first came to Haverford. 'Didn't the police eventually blame it on him or say he ran off with Annie or something?'

Sebastian nodded. 'Edward Callow, or Ned as everyone called him. He was never seen again after that night and, like you say, he was probably used as a bit of a scapegoat after they stopped questioning the American actor.'

'But who was the other person?'

'A young woman called Polly Mather. She was married to a solicitor who lived in Cranmere, but before she married him guess where she worked?'

'Here at Haverford?' Viola asked, the fizzing in her stomach getting stronger.

'Yup, she was a housemaid.'

'Which means she must have known Annie Bishop.'

'Probably knew her quite well, if you think about it. All those servants living on top of one another in those attic rooms.'

Viola was silent for a moment wondering how it all fitted

together. 'If you're right,' she said slowly. 'If Annie left and lived a life somewhere else, she probably did it with this Polly woman.'

'Maybe. Or with Ned. Maybe the three of them ran off together.' He stopped, shrugged. 'You never know.'

'You're right – you have made this more complicated than it was!'

'Sorry but that's all my research guy could find in the time he had. Records for the lower classes weren't exactly meticulously kept in the 1930s, especially for women. Like I said, it was a lot easier to disappear back then.'

'I wonder what they were disappearing from,' Viola mused.

'So you think they did disappear now do you?'

'I have no idea what to think anymore!'

If what Sebastian was saying were true then it was definitely an argument for Annie Bishop getting away from Haverford that night. But what was she getting away from? Something, or someone specific? Or just running from the drudgery of domestic service? And what about this Polly? What did she have to do with it all, if anything? 'You found all this out in two days?' she asked.

'Jonathan's pretty fast and has access to records that the rest of us would have to apply for special permission to see.'

Viola nodded slowly. 'What about police records?' she asked.

'Such as they were in rural Yorkshire in 1933,' Sebastian replied. 'He's going to do a bit more digging but it doesn't look like much was recorded. The case seems to have just fizzled out, like you said.'

'Seraphina seems to think that Lord Haverford paid the

police off to drop it.' The dowager countess had told this to Viola in confidence when she'd first started working at Haverford. She'd made it very clear that, while she didn't mind the legend of a disappearing lady's maid being used during the tours of the house, she didn't want her husband's family to be dragged into it. It had felt like double standards to Viola at the time. Why should Annie's life be worth less than the Montagu family's reputation? But that was the way it was seventy years ago. In truth it was the way it was now, whether Viola liked it or not.

# 19

## Haverford House, Yorkshire – July 1933

'You're not supposed to be here,' I say to Thomas as he steps towards me, but I hear the smile in my own voice. I'm secretly delighted that he's here in the servants' yard. Delighted and somewhat apprehensive. I'm relieved when he stops a little distance from me, not coming too close.

'I wanted to see you,' he says. 'Alone.'

I feel a wave of apprehension at that and step away from him.

'I'm sorry,' he says holding up his hands, palms towards me, the cigarette burning between the fingers of his right hand. 'I didn't mean to frighten you. I just wanted to talk, but I can leave if you'd prefer.'

I hesitate. I know I should ask him to leave. I know I should close my book and step back inside the kitchen to the safety of Mrs Derbyshire and the others, but I realise that I don't want to. My heart is beating harder and my breath is coming a little faster than it should do. I'm not nervous that Thomas is here though. I'm excited to see him, delighted that he has sought me out.

'Stay,' I hear myself saying.

He steps closer and I turn to sit on the bench again, gesturing that he should sit down too. He does, as far away from me as he can and us both be on the same bench.

'What are you doing here?' I ask. 'I thought you were all having dancing in the ballroom this evening.' I think of Prunella with her mother's wedding dress and gramophone. I shouldn't be sitting here and encouraging Thomas. I should be sending him back to the ballroom to be with her.

He shrugs. 'Not really my thing,' he says. 'They won't notice I'm gone.'

I find that highly unlikely considering how relatively few people will be in the ballroom tonight, compared to the old days, or even Prunella's twenty-first birthday. I don't say anything though, just as I don't encourage him to return to Prunella who is convinced he will propose any day.

'What are you reading?' he asks. His American accent is soft, softer than it sounds during the day somehow. I could listen to him speak forever. He sounds so exotic.

I show him my copy of *David Copperfield*. 'We're free to use His Lordship's library,' I tell him.

'That's good of him.'

'He's got the most wonderful selection of books and Lady Cecily is helping me widen my reading.'

'Have you always liked to read?' he asks and I tell him about the school in the village and the teacher who encouraged me, the books I'd read as a child and my father's copy of the *Complete Works* of Shakespeare.

'Ah so that's why you know *Twelfth Night* so well.'

He smiles at me, his white teeth gleaming in the twilight (I make him sound like the wolf in Little Red Riding Hood, but it isn't like that at all) and I feel myself blush. I hope he can't see. 'It's my second favourite Shakespeare play,' I tell him. 'After *Hamlet*.'

'I can see how much you love Shakespeare when we're in rehearsals,' he says. 'I feel as though you and I are the only people there who care about Shakespeare. Everyone else seems to be there to just pass the time, to waste the summer away. I guess that's…' He falters, suddenly less sure of himself. 'I guess that's why I'm here,' he goes on. 'I feel as though we have a connection.'

'But I'm just a maid,' I respond. 'That's why you shouldn't be here. You're to be with…'

'Don't you see that doesn't matter to me?' he replies. 'I didn't grow up believing in these ridiculous societal constructs. In my world it's money that talks, not class distinction.'

I almost laugh at that. 'I don't have any money either.'

'That came out wrong.' He smiles and looks away. 'I meant that you English have created a society that isn't fair, that doesn't give people equal opportunities.'

I know exactly what he means, but despite all our talk in the servants' hall it feels like make-believe to me. All my life I've been preparing myself in some way for this – to be a maid at the big house. It's hard to believe that there is anything more, even though a part of me knows there must be.

He tells me then about when he played Fortinbras in a production of *Hamlet* in New York. 'The smallest possible part,' he says with a grin. 'But it was still *Hamlet* in New York, you know?'

I nod even though I don't know. How could I possibly know?

And then he tells me about the production of *Hamlet* in London in which he'd played Horatio right up until he'd arrived at Haverford last month.

'How's *David Copperfield*?' he asks then, pointing at my book.

'I've only just started it.'

'*David Copperfield* was the first Dickens I ever read,' he says. He tells me that *Little Dorrit* is his favourite although he is still to read *Barnaby Rudge* and *Our Mutual Friend*. And then he asks me if I've ever read Wilkie Collins and he tells me that he's always preferred *The Woman in White* to *The Moonstone*. I've seen both of those on His Lordship's library shelves and I make a mental note to take a closer look at them.

As he talks he seems more relaxed and content than I've ever seen him. He never looks completely comfortable in Haverford House, as though the formalities and rituals of the English country house are too much for him. He is perhaps too American, too independent, for life here. Even when we are rehearsing the play he seems a little overwound and holds himself too tightly, as though just being near Cecily and Prunella makes him nervous and he doesn't really know how to speak to them. I wonder if he knows that he is here in the hope that he will marry one of them and that his father's money will save the Haverford estate before it's too late.

That makes me think about Lady Prunella in her mother's

wedding dress again and I stand up, stepping away from him and towards the kitchen, my book pressed to my chest as though I'm defending myself against something.

'I should get back,' I say, 'before I'm missed.'

'Of course,' he replies, standing too and looking, just for a moment, as disappointed as I feel, which in turn takes the edge off my disappointment a little. Would he really rather be here in the yard with me than inside with the others?

'Could I come to see you again?' he asks.

'Not here,' I reply. We can't meet here again – I know that. We're lucky nobody came out and spotted us tonight. 'I'll think of somewhere we can meet and let you know.' I don't look at him as I say it because I think, if I saw him in his hand-tailored clothes with his expensive smile and perfect skin, that I would lose my nerve. And I don't want to lose my nerve because there is so much I want to know about him.

'Until then,' he says with a small bow as he turns on his heel.

I decide on the kitchen garden as a good place to meet and talk with Thomas. There is a place, between the shed and the water butt, where Ned and Mac eat their lunch each day in the summer, with a bench and a makeshift table. The gardeners will be long gone by the time I can sneak away to see Thomas for a while and nobody comes down into the kitchen garden after supper. Nobody will see us, or even suspect us, and the evenings are warm and dry enough for us to not have to worry about rain or being cold. It is, in my head, the perfect place and I marvel at my own inventiveness, and at how sneaky I can be. Who am I all of a sudden?

I manage to get the message to Thomas at our next play rehearsal and he nods once to show he has understood.

That evening I take my book, a cover really just in case anyone does see me – I've barely read a word of it since Thomas came to see me in the yard – and I tiptoe down to the kitchen garden. The sun has set and the sky is a mix of pinks and greys, but there is still enough light to see by. It is coming back that will be the problem. I'll have to be very careful not to break an ankle walking through the grounds as I have no light. I have no way of telling the time either and hope I can rely on the sky to tell me when I must head back. Either that or Thomas's pocket watch.

As I wait for him on the bench between the shed and the water butt – a bench I last sat on with Ned back in May, before we had even heard of Thomas Everard, as he told me about the different vegetables that were being grown in the kitchen garden and when they would be ready – the tendrils of guilt begin to contract around my stomach. Guilt about Ned of course and the way I have led him on, with no intention of a future on my part, but mostly guilt about Prunella. When I close my eyes I see her again in her mother's wedding dress, like a modern-day Miss Havisham, waiting for Thomas to propose. Perhaps he still will, perhaps I am merely a dalliance. I remind myself of Mr Prentice's words.

*Be careful with Mr Everard.*

I know I will be. I have no intention of getting myself in trouble for a handsome face and a beautiful smile. I tell myself I'm just curious, about him, about the theatre, about America. That's all. I try not to think about the fact that I will be alone with him, that nobody knows where I am. And when he finally arrives and says my name in that accent of his, I ignore the way my stomach feels as though it has just turned over.

'I've been thinking about you,' he says as he sits next to me. 'I can't stop thinking about you.'

I haven't stopped thinking about him either, but I can't admit it. I shift away from him just a little bit because I know what he is saying is just words. He must notice because he apologises then for being so forward.

'I know what you must be thinking,' he says. 'I know how it looks when the rich house guest shows an interest in the maid and I know there's nothing I can say that will convince you that I'm not here to take advantage of my position. I just want to know a little more about you.'

I swallow and look up at him. 'I want to know more about you too,' I say. 'I want to know more about Shakespeare and about why you love him, why you want to be an actor.'

'There is just something special about Shakespeare,' he begins. 'He's like Mozart, only with words – one of a kind, you know?'

I nod because, for once, I think I do know.

'Whatever is going on in my life there is some wisdom to help me in Shakespeare – his plays or his sonnets – there's always something that makes me feel better, makes me feel alive.'

Alive. I understand that too. My life is mundane. It was always going to be, but when I read Shakespeare I don't feel mundane anymore.

'Although,' Thomas continues, 'his plays are meant to be heard, not read alone like a book.'

'Oh yes,' I say, finally finding my voice. 'The words are so much more powerful when they are read aloud.' That was why I always tried to read to Polly, whether she liked it or not.

We meet in the kitchen garden most nights after that. We have to be careful to make sure nobody spots us making our way there. Some nights I can only stay for a moment and some nights I cannot get away at all and have no way of getting a message to him. I imagine him sitting on the bench, smoking, waiting until it is almost too dark to see, but when we do spend time together it feels as though we have a connection that I've never had with anyone, the connection that Thomas spoke about himself. Later, after he has gone and I have returned to the servants' hall, I chastise myself for being so stupid. Of course there isn't a connection. Some men just have a thing for the servant girls. There's hundreds of housemaids who will tell you that, hundreds who would rather lose their virtue than their job. Not that anything like that has happened to me. Not yet anyway.

But when we're together again, when we talk about Shakespeare and books and he tells me what it's like at the theatre, what it's like to act on the stage, all of my misgivings disappear. This is something else, something different.

Something I can't tell anyone else about. I don't think I'd even talk about it to Polly if she were still here.

He tells me about the first play he was ever in – a production of *A Midsummer Night's Dream* when he was at school.

'I played Titania,' he says with a wink. 'It was an all-boys school.'

'But only boys and men could act during Shakespeare's

time so it would have been quite apt,' I say, trying to imagine Thomas as the fairy queen.

'You're wasted here, Annie Bishop,' he says softly to me. He is sitting so close to me on the bench that I can feel his breath against my cheek. 'You could be anything you wanted in America.'

'You make America sound like a fantasy,' I say, looking down at my lap so my face doesn't give away how much I've thought about America and what it would be like to go there. 'I can't believe anywhere allows absolutely anyone to be exactly what they want.'

'What do you want?' he asks. 'If you could have or do anything?'

'I'd like to be a writer,' I reply in a heartbeat and then I clamp my hand over my mouth, unable to believe I'd said it out loud. I've never shared that with anyone. I barely even admit it to myself. It is the secret I have held inside me since I was a child, almost since I first learned to read. I've made up stories in my head my whole life. It's how I pass the time during the long boring days of duties here at Haverford, but I have never written one down. How could I? What presumption. People like me don't get to write books, no matter how much we might want to.

I expect Thomas to laugh at me. To tell me how that couldn't happen even in America. But he doesn't. He merely carries on the conversation because to Thomas Everard, nothing is impossible.

'What sort of writer?' he asks.

'A mystery writer,' I continue. 'Like Agatha Christie.'

He doesn't say anything for a moment and I wonder

if this time he will laugh at me. Who could possibly be anything like Agatha after all?

'Then you must write,' he says simply. 'You must write as much as you can.'

And I know he's right. It really is that simple. It doesn't matter who I am or where I come from. I have been blessed with an education that many girls in my position haven't. I shouldn't waste that.

I marvel at how obvious it is and how it took a man from the other side of the globe to point it out to me.

As he leaves the kitchen garden that night he kisses me for the first time. It is soft and gentle and he asks permission first, unlike Ned who has always taken me by surprise. I find myself kissing Thomas back, with a little too much enthusiasm. *No*, the voice of restraint says in the back of my head. *Not yet, not now.*

I pull away.

'I'm sorry,' he begins. 'I…'

'No,' I interrupt. 'Don't be. It was lovely.'

He smiles then. 'Until tomorrow?' he asks.

'Until tomorrow.'


It is the day after Thomas kisses me that I see Polly again. It is my afternoon off and I am rushing through Cranmere village to my mother's house. I'm late because, as I'd walked through the wood and past the lake towards the village, Ned had stopped me.

'I haven't seen you for a while, Annie,' he'd said, and for some reason I'd become nervous. I'm never usually nervous in Ned's company. I've always felt before that I have the upper hand when it comes to him. But today I had cursed myself for that confidence – Ned is still a man and could still easily overpower me if he wanted. And today when he'd appeared on the path out of nowhere there had been a look in his eye I had never seen before. A look that frightened me.

'I'm sorry,' I'd said. 'We're so busy at that the house preparing for this party when Mr Everard's parents arrive. As soon as that's over...' I'd trailed off then, not wanting to promise anything, but it seemed to work. Ned had smiled and wandered off, placated for now. I'd realised, as I'd walked away, that even his smile has little effect on me anymore.

By the time I get to the high street I'm rushing, my head a swirl of thoughts about Thomas and Ned and Lady Prunella who, only that morning, had announced again that she was sure Thomas was about to propose. Guilt surges through me whenever I think about it – guilt with a splash of jealousy, because he still might propose for all I know.

I almost miss Polly as she passes. She is wearing a long coat, even though the weather is far too hot for it, and I think it is because of this that I look at her again and realise who it is.

'Polly!' I call, delighted to have run into her. There are days up at Haverford when I miss her so much and long for someone to chat to as I'm getting ready for bed at night. Katy isn't much of a one for conversation, unless it's grumbling about Mr Prentice or talking about how handsome Mr Everard is and neither is a subject I particularly want to get into.

She doesn't turn and I call her name again, chasing after her and touching her arm when I catch up with her. She jumps out of her skin when she feels my hand.

'I'm sorry,' I say. 'I didn't mean to frighten you. It's only me.'

'Annie,' she says, smiling. Do I imagine the look of relief in her eyes. 'I thought it was…' she stops.

'Who?'

'It doesn't matter. It's good to see you. How are you? How's Haverford?'

I tell her that all is well, and very much the same as it ever was. I tell her that I miss her, that Katy is no conversationalist and seems rather bitter for someone so young, and I tell her about Thomas's parents arriving, and the party we will be having when they get here and how Mr Prentice is beside himself about it all. I don't tell her about Thomas and the bench in the kitchen garden. I don't tell her about the kiss.

As I said, I'm not sure I'd tell her that even if she were still at Haverford.

She smiles again when I talk about Mr Prentice, but otherwise she doesn't really seem to be listening. Her eyes are constantly flicking left and right as though she is looking for someone or something, and she pulls the brim of her hat down.

'Polly, are you all right?' I ask, remembering how she had been when she came to Haverford a few weeks ago and the black eye she had. She'd talked about 'accidents' and Mrs Derbyshire hadn't believed her. She wasn't all right though – I could see that.

'What's happening, Polly?' I continue, my voice low. 'Is it your husband? Has he…'

'No,' she interrupts, her voice a hiss. She turns her head to me quickly and it is then that I notice. She turns her head then and I see the bruise – blue and green and yellow – across her cheekbone and the scabs on her lips as though she has bitten them until they bleed. 'Everything is fine, Annie,' she says as she sees my eyes on her injuries. 'I'm just clumsy that's all.' She turns her face from me.

'Polly, you can talk to me you know, anytime. Or Mrs Derbyshire.'

'I have to go,' she says, turning away and walking back up the high street.

'Come to see us at Haverford,' I call after her, but she pretends that she hasn't heard.

When I get back to the house later that afternoon I wonder if I should tell Mrs Derbyshire what I have seen. Will she be able to help? Will she be able to talk to Polly? I know she thinks that Polly's injuries are her husband's doing, just as I do now – but what can we, two servants, possibly do to help Polly?

I hesitate outside the door to Mrs Derbyshire's parlour, my hand raised to knock. But as I stand there the bell to the sitting room rings and I know it is time to take the girls their tea.

Later that evening, when I meet Thomas in the kitchen garden, I want to tell him about Polly but I am still so unsure of our friendship – if friendship is what it is – and I don't want to betray any trust Polly might have had in me. She probably wouldn't want Mrs Derbyshire to know what I'd seen.

'How are you, Annie?' Thomas asks, but I don't know how to answer and he interprets my silence as regret.

'You're angry about that kiss, aren't you?' he says. 'As you should be. I forgot myself last night and I am very sorry.'

'It's not the kiss,' I reply. 'I'm certainly not angry about the kiss.' I hesitate. I don't want to sound too forward, but I want to know what he wants and why he is here. How do I ask that?

'Then what's troubling you?' he asks. His voice is so kind I take a breath and say the things that are on my mind.

'I don't understand why we keep meeting like this,' I say. 'We talk about books and you tell me about acting and America but... well... why?'

He blows air out of his lips and sits back on the bench, looking somewhat dejected. I wonder then if I have upset him somehow.

'I know how this must look,' he says. 'The glamorous, rich stranger trying to take advantage of Lord Haverford's hospitality by seducing the servants, but it's really not like that. Although after my behaviour last night I know that won't ring particularly true.'

'You know that His Lordship has invited you here in the hope that you'll marry one of his daughters, don't you? And that your father's money will save the estate which, between you and me and the garden wall, is on the brink of bankruptcy.'

He laughs then, briefly. 'How do you know all this?' he asks.

'Servants know everything,' I reply. 'The family forget we're there half the time or think that we're not really people. I don't know exactly but they say things in front of us that we shouldn't really hear, forgetting I think that we all have ears and brains and that we talk and gossip as much as anyone else.'

He nods. 'I hope you don't think of me like that,' he says. 'I hope you don't think I treat you as not really a person.'

'Americans are different,' I say. 'We haven't had many Americans staying at Haverford and you didn't even bring a valet. That caused quite a stir.'

'Really?'

'Mr Prentice expects people to act a certain way I suppose.'

'I'd noticed.' He smiles. 'But I can dress myself.'

'Anyway, all I was trying to say,' I continue, trying to move away from the idea of Thomas getting dressed, which makes me feel uncomfortably hot, 'is that His Lordship is expecting you to propose and, well you may as well know it, Lady Prunella is expecting you to propose too.'

He looks at me in a horrified sort of way. 'Is she?' he says. 'I'm not stupid, Annie, I figured Lord Haverford wanted me to marry one of the girls but I had no idea either of them were interested.'

'Well Lady Cecily isn't.'

'No, I did work that much out. She's very happy with just Hannah Rivington for company.' He pauses. 'I had no idea about Prunella though.'

'So you're not about to propose?'

'No I… honestly I shouldn't have stayed here at Haverford so long, but I thought it would be impolite to leave before my parents arrived and we were all having so much fun with the play and then I met you…' He trails off.

When I look up at the sky I realise that it is completely dark.

'I have to go,' I say.

'I know,' he replies sadly. 'But I need to ask you something before you do. I really like you, Annie, and I've really enjoyed working on the play with you and our evenings here among the vegetables.'

'So have I,' I say, my voice a whisper.

'And I want you to know that I expect nothing from you, nothing at all.'

I swallow, my mouth dry. I can't work out what he is about to say.

'But you are wasted here at Haverford. You could do so much more – you could write for a living just like you want to.'

'Not in Cranmere I couldn't,' I say, trying to bring some lightness to the conversation, which suddenly seems so heavy and loaded.

'No,' he agrees. 'Not in Cranmere. But in America you could.'

'I can't go to…'

'Yes, Annie, you could. I'm offering to take you there and help you find the life I know you really want.'

And then I do leave the kitchen garden. As fast as I can.

'This proposal is a very long time coming,' Lady Cecily says as she wanders into her sister's bedroom one morning later that week as I'm helping Lady Prunella dress. 'We're all on such tenterhooks.'

'Don't be so unpleasant, Cecily,' Prunella snaps. 'He's waiting until his parents get here and we can put on this play once and for all.' She sighs. 'I'll be glad of it to be honest. I'm bored of the stupid play. I can't wait for it to be over.'

Conversely, I'm dreading it being over and having to go back to the drudgery of my life in the servants' hall. Because whatever Thomas might think about taking me to America, he's living in Cloud Cuckoo Land like Lady Prunella. I can't possibly go with him – it's a ridiculous notion. What would my mother say? What would Mr Prentice and Mrs Derbyshire say? And how could I leave my mother alone in Cranmere anyway? I shake my head to push away the thoughts.

'Is everything all right this morning, Annie?' Prunella asks.

'Oh yes, my lady,' I reply even though everything is not all right. I'm consumed by guilt at this talk of the proposal, which I now know will never happen.

Prunella looks at me for a moment and then turns back to the mirror. 'Can we put a bit more of a curl in my hair do you think?' she asks me.

I nod and get on with my duties, as though the last few weeks have never happened and as I do so I make a decision.

I haven't been to the kitchen garden for a few evenings. I haven't spoken to Thomas about it and have avoided him as much as I can at rehearsals, pretending I need to rush away as Mrs Derbyshire is calling, when she isn't at all and has been very good about letting me enjoy the play. 'Things like this don't happen often at Haverford,' she says. 'Enjoy yourself while you can.' But today I seek him out.

'Annie,' he says. Whenever he says my name it makes my heart turn over. 'Where have you been? When can we...'

'Tonight,' I reply, interrupting him rudely. 'In the usual place.'

I arrive at the kitchen garden before Thomas that evening. I hadn't meant to snap at him earlier at the rehearsal. It's not my place to talk to people like that and I think of my mother telling me that I'm getting ideas above my station. I've had a lot of ideas above my station over the last few days but it took Lady Prunella's firm belief that Thomas will propose to really bring my feet back to the earth. Young women like me don't go to America. Our duties are here and, if there is another war as Andrews predicts, we will need to be here for the country and for each other.

At least this is what I tell myself – ludicrous stories about duty that I don't believe for a moment. I don't really believe that it's my duty to serve Lord Haverford and his daughters and I really don't want to think about another war, but it is easier than admitting the truth to myself.

America is a place full of opportunities – at least that's how Thomas makes it sound and, on the few occasions I've brought up America in the servants' hall, both Andrews and James have agreed that there is something for everyone just the other side of the Atlantic. We are always stopped in our discussions by Mr Prentice, who seems to disapprove of America as much as he does of electricity, telephones, gramophones and the wireless, and who reminds us ceaselessly of what happened to the *Titanic*. I think Mr Prentice would like it to be 1912 again.

Thomas's offer plays on my mind for days. I imagine

myself in New York sitting at a typewriter, writing novels or working for a magazine. I've never sat at a typewriter so I've no idea how they really work but in my dreams I can type fast and ceaselessly. I imagine the Empire State Building, which I've only seen in photographs, and the wide straight streets.

But when I imagine it all I can't really see myself there.

Because how could I leave my mother behind?

That was why, when Lady Prunella had spoken about Thomas at her dressing table as her sister had teased her about a proposal that would never happen, I'd known I had to tell Thomas I couldn't go.

When Thomas arrives on our bench – I think of it only as our bench now and never think of Mac and Ned sitting here at lunchtimes – he begins to talk at once, telling me how he knows that he sprung the idea of America, of New York, on me so quickly as though it came from nowhere and would I give him a chance to explain, to tell me about what could happen if I gave up my life of drudgery.

They are the words he uses – *a life of drudgery*.

And I know he's right. It isn't the life of duty that Mr Prentice still pretends it is. It is no longer 1912 and houses like Haverford are closing all over the country. A life of drudgery it may be, and a life of uncertainty, but it is the life I have to choose for now.

'I can't do it, Thomas,' I say. 'I can't come to America. This is all a dream, a nice dream but a dream nonetheless.'

'Anything is possible, Annie.'

'No it isn't,' I say, pulling away from him, knowing that this will be the last time I meet him here in the kitchen garden. 'I can't leave my mother in Cranmere alone. I want to see the world, of course I do. Or at least more of this country. But for now I have to stay here with my mother.'

He doesn't say anything. He knows too this is the last time.

After a few moments he stands up, with his back to me. 'I'll be travelling back to New York with my parents in September,' he says. 'If you change your mind, just tell me.'

I want to tell him I won't change my mind, that I can't change my mind. But he is still so kind, keeping the opportunity open for me, so I say nothing.

It isn't until he walks away that I start to cry, realising then that I've fallen in love with him, the one thing I promised myself I wouldn't do.

What fool I am.

What fools women are over men.

As I dry my tears and prepare to return to the house, I hear footsteps behind me. At first I think it is Thomas coming back but then the footsteps stop and I hear a chuckle that I recognise immediately.

'Well, well, Annie Bishop,' Ned says, his voice sounding sinister in the half-light. 'This is where you've been hiding.'

I turn on the bench to look at him but his face is shaded by the brim of his hat. I wonder how long he's been here in the kitchen garden.

'I come here sometimes to read,' I say holding up my copy of *David Copperfield* that I've been carrying around unread for half the summer, using it as an excuse to meet Thomas.

'Bit dark for reading,' Ned says, lighting a cigarette. The flare of the match lights up his face just for a moment but I can't make out his expression. He blows out a stream of smoke. 'What would Lady Pru say if she knew how much time you've been spending with her fiancé?' he asks.

'He's not her…' I stop, knowing that is not the big issue right now. 'Tonight was the last time,' I say instead. 'Please don't say anything, Ned.'

He steps towards me then, crouching so our faces are level.

'And I thought you had eyes only for me,' he says. He is no longer smiling.

## 20

Haverford House, Yorkshire – July 2003

The Haverford Shakespeare Festival opened to a full house at the end of July. It was an unusual crowd this year, a lot more teenagers and young women in the audience than in previous years – as successful as the festival had always been it tended to appeal to older people – and Viola suspected that might have a lot to do with her brother. She heard people whispering about him even before the first play began, and she heard the gasps and ripple of applause when he first took to the stage. She watched her brother lap up the attention, playing to the crowd, gently making everyone feel included. Sometimes it was hard to believe that he was her twin, her Sebastian, the man who had always preferred his own company to anyone else's.

They opened with *Twelfth Night*, fun and humour and, of course, a play that meant so much to Viola. On that first night, she sat quietly with Seraphina on a blanket at the back of the crowd sharing a bottle of wine, disappearing as usual into the background so her brother could have the stage. But she saw him look for her in the audience right at the start, watched him wink at her as he talked about music being the food of love and felt the eyes of every girl in the crowd turn to look for whoever it was he was winking at. How disappointed they would be to find out it was simply his unglamorous sister, still wearing her Haverford House polo shirt.

It was a magnificent night, a wonderful performance, and as it ended Viola looked towards the local newspaper reporters to see their reactions. They, like the rest of the crowd, were giving the cast a standing ovation.

Not that it mattered if this was going to be the last festival that Haverford ever put on. Who knew what would be happening on these grounds this time next year.

But she wasn't going to let herself think about that tonight. She turned back to the stage, applauding the cast once again. If this was going to be the last festival then several weeks of completely sold out performances and cheering crowds like this was definitely the way to go.

Afterwards Seraphina invited Viola and Sebastian to the dower house to share a late supper with her.

'I'd love to,' Sebastian replied. 'Just let me wash the make-up off and get changed. I don't really fancy eating supper in a doublet and hose.' Viola suspected he didn't much want to eat supper at all. She knew he liked time to decompress after stage performances and she could see the crowd of girls forming behind him waiting for his autograph. 'I might be a while,' he said, nodding towards the girls.

'That's all right,' Seraphina said. 'We'll wait for you.'

As she walked away Viola turned to her brother. 'It's OK,' she said, you don't have to come if you don't want to. I know you'll prefer to be alone.'

'It's fine, Vi.' He smiled at her. 'I'd like to come. I've got this feeling that something is about to happen and that you're going to be staying here when I leave so I'd like to spend as much time with you as I can.'

He turned away from her then, towards his adoring fans, and as she watched him she wondered what he meant.

He'd often told her he'd had a feeling about things before – a feeling she'd get into Oxford, a feeling something great was about to happen. Unlike her he was one of life's eternal optimists, something she suspected was necessary when you were trying to carve a career as an actor, and she was just Viola – not a pessimist exactly, but certainly a realist.

And at this stage she couldn't imagine anything that could happen that was going to save Haverford. Even Viola was almost at the point of giving up.

Seraphina spent most of the meal gushing and fussing over Sebastian, telling him how wonderful he was, listing the films she'd seen him in and going into minute detail about *Sunset Bay* on which she seemed to be a surprise expert. Viola watched as Sebastian lapped it all up, smiling benignly. She couldn't understand why he wasn't annoyed by it all. He must know all those details inside out himself, and whenever she, his own sister, had tried to talk to him about his career, he'd clammed up and had told her how boring it all was.

'She's quite the fan,' he whispered to Viola as Seraphina was in the kitchen making coffee.

'And you're quite the smooth operator when you want to be, aren't you?' she replied rolling her eyes at him.

'It's hard to believe she is a dowager countess,' Sebastian replied, ignoring her comment.

'What do you think dowager countesses look like?' Viola asked. 'They don't wear crinolines and sit about drinking tea anymore. They have estates to manage while the men fly off to America and are generally unhelpful.' She didn't tell him how much Seraphina had surprised her when she'd first arrived at Haverford, dashing her own preconceptions of what a dowager countess might be like.

'You're really pissed with this David guy, aren't you?' But Viola didn't have time to tell her brother exactly how angry and upset she was with the earl because Seraphina came back into the dining room.

It was over coffee that Sebastian mentioned seeing Chase Matthews by the boathouse. Viola could have kicked him, as she'd decided not to mention it, decided it would just cause more worry and upset, especially as she hadn't seen him again, despite keeping an eye out. And she was only looking for him to make sure he wasn't up to anything, not for any other reason.

Definitely not for any other reason.

'What do you mean, he's back?' Seraphina asked, looking annoyed and frustrated. 'Did you know about this, Viola?'

'Well… I…' She glared at her brother who shrugged. He hadn't known he wasn't supposed to mention it. He probably thought Seraphina already knew. 'We did see him briefly up by the old boathouse but I haven't seen him since.'

'Was that why you were asking about the boathouse and the lake the other day?' Seraphina asked.

Viola nodded.

'You should have told me.' She stirred her coffee and sighed.

'I didn't want to worry you.'

'No, I understand that.'

'I have been looking out for him and I'm sure he's not been back.'

Sebastian chuckled. 'For someone you claim not to like you sure do talk about him a lot,' he said.

Viola felt herself blushing from the very roots of her hair. When she looked over at her brother he was grinning at her in that way he always did when he knew he was winding her up. Having him here for so long was amazing, but she had forgotten how annoying he could be.

'Well, he did seem very keen on her until that unfortunate incident with the hotel and my son,' Seraphina said.

'It's a shame he didn't tell my sister who he really was before he took her out,' Sebastian replied.

'I'm right here you know,' Viola interrupted, sick of being talked about as though she weren't.

'If he did come back and apologise would you give him another chance, do you think?' Seraphina asked.

'I really don't know.'

'Did he give you his phone number by any chance? You could call him and...'

'I don't want to talk about Chase Matthews anymore, if that's OK with you both.'

Viola changed the subject back to the Shakespeare Festival then, telling Seraphina how they'd taken more money than any year before.

'It's not going to be enough you know,' Seraphina answered quietly. 'However much we take.'

But Viola already knew that and was already preparing herself for the worst.

'I'm thinking of going back to Australia after the summer,' Viola said. 'If we really can't save the house.' Saying the words out loud made it feel more real. She really was thinking of going back. If Sebastian was going to move back permanently it made sense.

But it didn't feel right and she thought about what Sebastian had said, his feeling that she would stay here.

'You are?' Sebastian and Seraphina said at the same time.

'Well at least that way I'll get two back-to-back summers,' Viola replied. She didn't mention to Seraphina about Sebastian returning to *Sunset Bay*. She thought it was still probably top-secret information and Seraphina was not the most secretive of people.

'I hate this,' the dowager countess said. 'I hate feeling as though I'm pushing you out of your home and chasing you away.'

'Australia is my home,' Viola said with more conviction than she felt.

Despite everything, Viola found herself unable to stop thinking about Chase after the conversation the night before. Of course having a walk around the lake didn't mean that he was still intending to buy Haverford or that he was up to anything at all. But at the same time he had said that he needed to return to America fairly quickly. She didn't want to think about him quite so much; she felt upset and embarrassed when she did. He was the first man she'd so much as looked at since she'd left London and, even though she'd known he wouldn't be in Cranmere for long, she had enjoyed being with him.

He had given her the mobile number of the phone he was using in England and she thought about calling him, if he was still in the country. Maybe they could talk again about what happened now that things had calmed down. Because Seraphina was right – he had seemed keen before the unfortunate business with the hotel, and Viola had to admit to herself that she had felt the same way.

In the end though she didn't need to call him as, on the morning after the opening night of the festival, Chase appeared as if from nowhere. As if he knew she'd been thinking about him.

He turned up on the first house tour of the morning, arriving just as the group left its meeting point in the grand hall and set off towards the ballroom, and from there towards the back of the house and the servants' staircase. He lurked at the back of the crowd – a big group this morning including ten tourists in matching yellow T-shirts – and she didn't get a chance to say anything to him. Whenever she did look over at him he just grinned at her, his eyes sparkling. He looked as handsome as ever and Viola was very aware of him the whole way through the tour, a tour he actually stayed on this time, not even wandering off as the group examined the dollhouses in the nursery.

'Which one was Lady Haverford's dollhouse?' he asked, even though he must already know the answer from his extensive research of Haverford. The whole episode was giving Viola flashbacks to the very first time she'd met Chase, on this same tour.

'This one,' she said, showing Lady Haverford's dollhouse to the group. 'It's an exact replica of Montagu House in London, the house in which Lord and Lady…'

'Is that Lord Albert, the fifth earl and his wife Arabella?' one of the yellow-shirted group asked.

'Yes, that's right. Lord Haverford.' Viola paused and smiled at the woman who'd asked the question. 'Albert had it custom-made for his wife as a wedding present. The couple spent the first year of their marriage in Montagu House, which is in Bloomsbury in London.'

'Can we visit Montagu House?' the woman asked.

'Unfortunately not. The Montagus sold it several years ago and it's privately owned now, but you can of course walk past it and see it from the outside whenever you're in London.'

As Viola started to usher the group out of the nursery, explaining to the woman exactly where the house was that had once been the London home of the Montagu family, she looked over her shoulder at Chase, but he just smiled back at her. What was he up to? Because he was certainly up to something – that much Viola was sure of.

As the tour drew to a close and Viola directed the tour group to the tearooms and gardens, Chase sidled up to her.

'Chase,' she said coldly. 'Or is it Charles? Who knows with you. I wasn't expecting to see you again.' Her words couldn't disguise the fizzing feeling she felt in her stomach whenever he seemed to draw near.

'I know and once again I'm very sorry about…' he paused, waving his hand vaguely in the air '…all that. And I prefer it if my friends call me Chase.'

Viola raised an eyebrow. 'Friends?' she questioned.

'Well I'm hoping that we'll be friends when I tell you what I've found.'

'Found where?'

'On the estate, out by the lake.'

'So you were up there looking for something that afternoon,' Viola said. 'I was surprised to see you show your face again to be honest.'

'I paid my entrance fee and...' He paused and rubbed a hand over his face. 'Look, Viola, can we talk? Are you free?'

She felt herself soften then. Was she really going to give the man who'd humiliated her in front of her brother and her boss a second chance?

Not necessarily. But she was going to hear him out. After all she needed to know what he was doing here.

'I've got an hour now.'

'Will you walk to the old boathouse with me?'

They walked in silence for a while and Viola led the way through the rose garden – the long way round – where she knew it would be quiet. The garden tour would be nearly finished and the actors would all be asleep or going over their lines for tonight if her brother was anything to go by. She remembered the last time they'd come up here together, how different things had seemed, how she'd thought Chase was going to kiss her.

'I want to apologise again,' Chase said after a while. 'About lying to you, about not telling you who I was, about the hotel—'

'I think the less said about Montgomery Hotels the better,' Viola interrupted.

'You know, Viola, if it makes any difference at all I thought it was a terrible idea.'

She turned to look at him. 'So you said, but is that really true?'

'Yeah, you can't force a hotel, you know, and this place isn't right. The building is so old and the grounds are so big and...' He paused, looking around him. 'It's too beautiful for a hotel, too steeped in history.'

'I'm surprised to hear you say that,' Viola said, softening to him a little more.

'I'm not my father, and your story about Annie Bishop really got me thinking. Real people lived here; real lives played out right here. That's worth preserving in my book. Annie Bishop, wherever she is and whatever happened to her, deserves more than just a plaque on the wall of an American chain hotel. This whole house deserves more.'

'Annie Bishop's story did that to you!'

'Well it might have had something to do with the person who told me the story.'

He held her gaze then for just a moment too long and Viola could feel herself going red yet again and she looked away first.

'I thought you were going back to America to talk to your father,' she said, trying to change the subject away from the still-obvious attraction that sat there between the two of them.

'I couldn't face him in the end,' Chase replied. 'I told him about Haverford over the phone.'

'What did he say?'

'He told me to take some time off to think about what I'd done.'

'Seriously?'

'Seriously. To my father I'm still eight years old.' He paused and looked away. 'That's the reason I decided I wanted to do this Haverford deal when David called me. We were at Oxford together you know.'

'No I didn't know,' Viola said, simply to fill the sudden silence. That meant that she and David had been at Oxford together too. She'd not really thought about it before, preferring not to think about that part of her life at all.

Chase sighed. 'Yeah, he made it sound like an easy deal, as though everyone was on side and I thought if I could pull it off my father might start taking me seriously. What a cliché it all is.'

'But then you got here and nobody was on side except David.'

'It was more than that though,' Chase said, turning to her again. 'When I went on that house tour, when you told that story of Annie Bishop, I knew then that this wasn't going to work out. This place deserves to be so much more than a hotel. I should have walked away then.'

'I'm kind of glad you didn't,' Viola admitted softly, without meeting his eye. They were approaching the old boathouse and she could only hope that whatever Chase had brought her here to show her would appear soon and diminish this embarrassing situation.

'David mentioned that you'd been trying to get the Conservation Trust interested in Haverford.'

Viola was surprised that the earl had mentioned that. He was, after all, rather against the idea as there wasn't enough money to be made from it. 'It's no good though,' she said. 'They aren't interested in us. We're just not special enough.'

She sighed. 'It's fair enough. They can't save every old house in the country.'

'Well that's exactly why I want to show you this,' Chase said, crouching down by the side of the lake and beckoning her to join him.

'What?' she asked, her voice sounding loud in the hot summer air.

'Shhh, or they might not come out.'

'What might…'

But Chase touched her arm and pressed his index finger to his lips. 'Just wait,' he said.

Viola was getting pins and needles in her foot and wondering how much longer she was expected to loiter here in the grass for, when Chase pointed across the lake towards the boathouse.

'Look,' he said.

'What at?' she asked following his finger. 'Is it… it's a frog isn't it?'

'It's a toad,' Chase replied.

'Frog, toad, what's the difference?'

'Quite a lot actually. Toads don't have webbed feet for a start and don't need to live near water although they quite like…' He trailed off. 'But that doesn't matter right now.'

'How do you know so much about it?' Viola asked. This was a wholly new and unexpected layer to Chase Matthews.

'Don't laugh at me OK but I was obsessed with amphibians as a kid. I used to collect newts.'

'Oh my God like Gussie Fink-Nottle!' Viola laughed.

'Who?'

'He's a friend of Bertie Wooster's – you know from the PG Wodehouse books?'

Chase shook his head. 'Anyway you said you wouldn't laugh at me.'

'I'm sorry,' Viola said. 'Now, why am I looking at these toads?'

'Because these toads are going to save Haverford House,' Chase declared dramatically.

'They are?'

'These are smooth-bellied toads,' Chase went on knowledgeably. 'You can't really see properly from here without binoculars but you have to trust me on that. Smooth-bellied toads are a protected species. There's a few breeding grounds in Scotland but, to my knowledge – until I saw them here – none in England.'

Viola was speechless, staring from Chase to the toads.

'I noticed them when I was up here with you that afternoon,' Chase explained. 'I didn't get a chance to have a good look so I came back. That's what I was doing when you and your brother saw me here.'

'And that means that the Conservation Trust will be very interested to hear from you now.'

'Oh my…' Viola stared at the toads again, squinting to try to see what was so special about them.

'I've looked into this Conservation Trust of yours and while they do indeed save a lot of old historical houses and gardens, they are also interested in preserving British wildlife.'

'I know,' Viola said. She'd read their guidelines so often that she knew them off by heart. And while the toads didn't look like much to her right now, she also knew, if Chase was telling the truth, that this was exactly the sort of thing the trust would be interested in. 'And you're absolutely sure that they are these smooth whatevers?'

'Smooth-bellied toads? Yes, absolutely sure.'

'Oh my God, I could kiss you!'

'Well, I probably wouldn't say no.'

## 21

At the end of July Lady Prunella announces that she'd like to go to London.

'Whatever for?' Lady Cecily asks in a bored voice. 'London is so tedious with everyone down for the season.'

'Another season stuck up here at Haverford,' Prunella replies sadly. 'Thank God for Thomas and the play and for a handful of friends nearby.' I know that she hates this life she has. I know she feels trapped at Haverford, unable to live the life she was supposed to live because of one stupid mistake in a jazz club and her father's dwindling funds. She would do anything to escape and she is pinning all her hopes on Thomas. 'Anyway,' she says, brightening a little. 'I just wanted a little shopping trip, to buy some new clothes before Thomas's parents get here. You'll come won't you, Cecily?'

'No, I shan't. I really don't need to go shopping. You'll have to go alone. I'm sure Papa will let you use Montagu House.' Montagu House was the family home in London that, these days, remained shut up for great parts of the year.

'Well, I won't be alone,' Lady Prunella says, turning back to the mirror so I could continue with her hair. 'Annie will be coming with me, won't you, Annie?'

'Yes, my lady, of course,' I reply, glad really to be getting away from Haverford for a few days, away from Thomas, away from any chance of bumping into Polly again, and most importantly away from Ned who I absolutely do not want to see right now. He frightened me in the kitchen garden the other night and now I have met Thomas I don't know how I ever thought Ned was attractive. Not that Thomas will ever be mine either. All of it feels a little too much, too confusing, and the chance to escape for a few days with Lady Prunella seems too good an opportunity to miss.

'We'll leave first thing tomorrow. Can you get everything ready by then, Annie?'

'Yes, my lady,' I reply, wondering what would happen at tomorrow's play rehearsal without Prunella. I also wonder why she wants to leave so quickly.

'And while I'm shopping you can have some time to yourself, Annie,' Prunella goes on. 'Is there anything special you'd like to do?'

'Well,' I say quietly. 'I've always wanted to go the British Museum.'

'Then you shall.' Prunella claps her hands together gleefully. 'I'll arrange it all for you.'

I don't say any more but I've always wanted to see the Rosetta Stone. I don't know why particularly but ever since I read about it in one of the old newspapers in His

Lordship's library I've wanted to see it. Every summer when I've gone to London with the girls I've thought about it, but until now haven't had an opportunity to visit. I smile to myself. Without knowing it Lady Prunella has done me two small favours.

That evening, before we go to London, I decide that I must speak to Mrs Derbyshire about Polly. I know it will be the last thing that Polly will want, but then I remember that she did come here mysteriously that afternoon – was that a cry for help? I know I need to do something. So much in my life feels, suddenly and ridiculously, out of my control. Lady Prunella, the play, Thomas, his parents, Polly, my mother. At least talking about Polly with someone else will ease my load a little. A problem shared and all that, or so they say. Not that I'm doing this for only selfish reasons to lighten my own load – I am worried about Polly and there must be something we can do.

That doesn't mean I'm not nervous about seeing Mrs Derbyshire. There is something about standing outside the door to her parlour that always makes me nervous and reminds me of the time when I was new here and she asked to see me and I was sure I was going to be sent away. It turned out she was just wanting to know how I was getting on, but that feeling has never truly left me. I knock hesitantly.

'Come in,' she calls from behind the door. As I open it, she looks up, sees that it is only me and smiles. 'Oh, Annie, come and sit down. I thought it would be Mr Prentice fussing about this party again.'

I smile too as I sit. The butler has still not calmed down from the impending staffing disaster that the party next month will, according to him at least, inevitably bring.

'Would you like some tea?' Mrs Derbyshire asks.

I shake my head. 'I need to talk to you about something.'

'About London tomorrow?'

'No, no, that's all organised.' It's the first time I'll be going to London alone with just one of the girls. Usually in the summer we travel in a pack but, presumably because of Thomas's arrival, the household did not go to London this year. 'It's just that I saw Polly in the village the other day.'

'I see.' Mrs Derbyshire sits back in her chair and gives me all of her attention. I can see the shift in her. 'And how is she?'

'Not good,' I reply.

'Did she say something?'

'Nothing specific, but she was wearing a coat on a warm summer's afternoon, as though she was trying to cover up something and when I touched her arm she nearly jumped out of her skin and...' I falter. Should I be telling the housekeeper any of this?

'And?' Mrs Derbyshire prompts.

I lower my voice as though imparting a dark secret. 'She had another bruise along her cheekbone.' I run my finger along my own cheek to show her where.

The housekeeper nods slowly.

'I don't know what to do,' I say.

'I'm not sure there is much we can do, Annie. I didn't say as much when she came to visit, but you and I both know that Polly was not a clumsy girl prone to accidents about the house as she claimed. To put it bluntly I think the bruises are from her husband's fists.'

I say nothing; my mouth feels dry. I'd worked out that was what Mrs Derbyshire thought but hearing her say it out loud shocks me. I know it shouldn't and I know this sort of thing goes on – there are men in the village who, when I was growing up, we all knew were all too handy with their fists after too many drinks, but nobody speaks of it, not out loud.

'I've shocked you I can see,' Mrs Derbyshire says.

'No,' I say, finding my voice. 'I knew what you meant last time, when she came for tea but... well... nobody really talks about this sort of thing do they?'

'No, more's the pity.' She tightens her lips and looks away from me. 'I've seen this sort of thing too many times before, but mercifully never here at Haverford. I didn't expect this at all. How did she seem in herself?'

'Jumpy, as though she didn't want to see me, didn't want to stop and talk. She seemed scared.'

'You're worried about her aren't you?'

'I knew things would change after she got married. I knew I would never really see her again, but I thought at least she'd be happy.'

'As I said, I'm not sure there is much we can do until Polly herself asks us for help. People don't talk about this sort of thing and in general what happens behind closed doors is considered to be very private.'

'You don't think that, do you?' I ask.

'Not in circumstances like this,' she replies. 'But I'm limited in what I can do. Mr Prentice would tell me not to interfere but I will go and pay her a visit if I can. I'll have to think of a reason.'

'Thank you,' I say, really meaning it. 'It's been playing on my mind.'

'Now go and get a good night's sleep,' Mrs Derbyshire

says, smiling again. 'Forget about everything for a few days and enjoy yourself in London.'

That is exactly what I intend to do, to immerse myself in the busy capital and forget about Haverford for a few days. However, fate has other ideas for me. When Lady Prunella and I arrive at Montagu House the next afternoon, there is a telegram waiting for us, a telegram full of devastating news summoning us straight back to Yorkshire.

'Is there anything I can do Annie?' Lady Prunella asks for the fourth time since we boarded the train, and for the fourth time I shake my head. I can't speak. I haven't been able to eat anything since I heard the news – I forced down a small cup of tea this morning on Prunella's insistence – but all I want to do is get back to Yorkshire, to understand what has happened and, hopefully, for it all to turn out to be a terrible mistake.

But I know deep down that the news is true, that there has been no mistake.

My mother is dead.

I feel as though a carpet has been pulled from under my feet, but instead of crashing down to earth I am floating above it, untethered. I have felt like that since Lady Prunella read the telegram last night, summoned strong tea and sat me down in the sitting room. It felt strange to sit on that high-backed chair in a room I rarely had need to go into. It felt as though I had got above my station. But I can't think of that without thinking of my mother.

Lady Prunella had telephoned Haverford, just as the telegram had asked her to do. She spoke to her father, who told her that my mother had been found dead in her chair by the baker's boy who'd peered through the window when nobody had responded to his knock. The doctor had been told and His Lordship informed. Mother has no family other than me so it was to Haverford that everybody went when they wanted to find me. His Lordship, having been fond of my mother – that was after all the reason I got the job in the first place – took over from there.

'Do you want to talk to him?' Lady Prunella had whispered to me, her hand over the mouthpiece of the telephone.

I'd shaken my head. I could barely string a sentence together in front of Prunella. Of course I couldn't talk to His Lordship on the telephone. I've never spoken on a telephone in my life.

'The doctor thinks she had a heart attack,' Lady Prunella had told me when she'd ended the telephone call. 'Papa said to tell you that the doctor told him that she would have passed peacefully. He hopes that will be of some consolation.'

It was of no consolation at all either yesterday evening or now as I sit on the train, which seems to be moving much more slowly than it had when it was going in the other direction the day before. It doesn't matter to me how my mother died and there is nothing anybody can do, although obviously I don't tell Lady Prunella any of this. What matters to me is this. Yesterday was Wednesday. On Wednesdays I always take my afternoon off and go to see my mother.. But this week, instead of taking that half-day, or even questioning it at all, I had jumped at the chance to escape the confines of Haverford for a few days in London.

Lured by Lady Prunella's promise of a trip to the British Museum and desperate to escape the eyes of Thomas and Ned and my constant nagging doubts about Polly and my future, I hadn't given my afternoon with my mother a second thought. I'd simply sent her a note to tell her I wouldn't be there.

All I can think about now is that maybe, if I'd gone to see her yesterday afternoon, I'd have been with her when she took ill and I might have been able to do something, anything, to help her. At the very least she wouldn't have died alone to be found, later, by the baker's boy. I curse my selfishness the whole way back to Yorkshire.

Andrews meets us from the station and I sit next to him up front as usual for the journey back to Haverford. We are halfway back before he quietly asked me if I'm all right and if there is anything that he can do. Once again I shake my head.

It is Mrs Derbyshire's sympathy that finally breaks me, that finally allows me to cry the tears that have somehow been blocked inside me since Lady Prunella first read the telegram. She can see, as soon as I arrive back at Haverford, that I am uncomfortable with the fuss everyone is making of me and I am relieved when she takes me into her parlour for a warm drink. The tea she gives me smells distinctly of Mr Prentice's brandy.

'I thought you would need a pick-me-up,' she says.

And that's when the tears start to flow.

Mrs Derbyshire sits with me as I cry, her hand quietly resting on my back – supportive without being intrusive. She always knows the right way to be, the right way to behave in any situation and I know, as I sit there, that in years to come I will gauge my own behaviour on Mrs Derbyshire's and that she will be a person, much like my own mother, who will be with me long after she has gone.

'She was the only family I had,' I say once I find my breath and my voice. 'It had always been just me and her. I don't really remember my father.'

'We were so fond of her here,' Mrs Derbyshire says. 'We all loved her, even His Lordship, and Her Ladyship – God rest her soul – always called for your mother when she wanted mending doing.'

I smile sadly. 'She was incredible with a needle and thread.' I have always been rather embarrassed that I didn't inherit her sewing skills and I think, briefly, of Lady Prunella in her mother's wedding dress wondering if I can let it out. This makes me sad all over again.

We talk for a few moments about my mother's time at Haverford and Mrs Derbyshire tells me about how she met my father at the back door and their strange courtship. It's a story I know well but one I never tire of hearing. I remember when I first came to Haverford how I wondered if I would meet my future husband there just as my mother had done. I dreamed of what it would be like. Perhaps that is why I spent so much time with Ned at first, wanting to believe that I would have a story like my mother's. But instead I fell in love with Thomas Everard. I should never have allowed that to happen, just as I should never have led Ned along for such a time.

'Katy and I will take over your duties until the funeral,' Mrs Derbyshire says. 'To give you some time to grieve and settle.'

'The funeral!' I blurt out. 'What do I need to do? Where do I...'

'Now now, don't you go worrying about that. His Lordship has everything in hand.'

And doesn't he just.

His Lordship must have had a bigger soft spot for my mother than I realised as five days later Haverford closes for the morning as the entire household makes their way to the village church, the same one that Polly married in, for my mother's funeral service. I walk down arm in arm in with Mrs Derbyshire.

'How are you feeling?' she asks.

'I'll be glad when today is over,' I reply. But in truth I don't know how I feel. Still untethered and unable to see a future without my mother, without my Wednesday afternoons spent with her. When I wake in the mornings, I wonder how I can go on without her, but here I am already one week after her death, carrying on. I suppose it is just what people do.

To my surprise Polly is at the church when I get there. She presses my hand when I arrive and sits at the front with me. The church is packed to the rafters – the whole of the village is here along with everyone from Haverford and all the shops have closed for the morning.

'Quite the turnout,' Polly whispers.

'I'm so glad you're here,' I reply.

But she rushes off again after the funeral service, not staying for the burial or the wake that His Lordship has paid for at the pub.

'I'm sorry, Annie,' she says. 'I have to get back.'

I scan her face for fresh bruises but can't see any. Perhaps things are settling down. Perhaps I don't have to worry.

Later, after the burial, when everyone has either returned

to Haverford or gone to the pub for sherry and sandwiches, His Lordship finds me standing by my mother's fresh grave. It is the closest he has ever stood to me.

'I just wanted to pass on my condolences,' he says stiffly. 'Your mother was very popular at Haverford and a great favourite of my wife's...' He trails off as he talks about his late wife before turning around and walking away.

I understand a little then about why he is like he is.

Loss changes everything.


'Please don't think this insensitive, Annie,' Lady Prunella says two days later. 'But how do you feel about coming back to rehearsals as our prompt?'

I look at her in the mirror and catch sight of my own reflection, pale and hollow-eyed. This is my first day back at work since we rushed home from London and neither Prunella nor Cecily have mentioned my mother at all. It's uncomfortable for them I suppose. I am after all just a servant, and no doubt the situation has brought back memories of their own mother.

I remember standing here before we went to London, looking at Prunella in the mirror, and making an important decision. I had vowed to stop seeing Thomas in the kitchen garden, to stop daydreaming of America, and to accept my lot in life until I could work out what I wanted to do next. The decision had been based on my mother, my inability to leave her here in Cranmere when she had always been there for me.

Except my mother isn't there for me anymore. I'm entirely on my own.

'I'll be there,' I say to Prunella now. 'I've missed rehearsals. It'll be nice to get back into it.'

'The quicker we get back to normal after tragedy the better, I've always found,' Cecily says quietly from the corner where she is sitting. I don't respond; I don't acknowledge. I don't want to talk about my mother with anybody.

Prunella starts to tell me about rehearsals, about how much better they all are, but I barely listen. Instead I think about seeing Thomas again. I haven't seen him since the night I told him it was over, that I couldn't go on, that I couldn't go to America. This afternoon at rehearsal I will stand next to him again, catch his eye.

At least I hope I will, because there is something I want to talk to him about.

When I arrive at rehearsal that afternoon, a little late and flustered after helping Mrs Derbyshire with some starched tablecloths, he is the first person I see. The only person I see. My breath catches in my throat for a moment as he stands in front of the cast, jacket discarded and shirt sleeves rolled up in the heat, talking to them about the play, about how important each scene is. He is so passionate about it, but he has lost most of the cast members who are sleepy and far away on this hot afternoon. The only person hanging on to his every word is Lady Prunella. Poor Prunella, is she still holding out hope of a proposal?

When he looks at me, I can feel my heart beat faster. Ridiculous I know, like a breathless heroine in a terrible novel. He smiles then, and he is even more devastatingly handsome than I remember – not that I've been allowing myself to remember him. It hurts too much.

'I'm so sorry about your mother,' he says to me quietly

as the cast of the play begin to find their places in a rather chaotic way that makes me think that they haven't improved as much as Lady Prunella thinks they have. 'And I'm so sorry that I haven't been able to say that to you before. I haven't seen you – perhaps you've been avoiding me.'

'I've had some time off,' I reply.

'Well, it's lovely to have you back.'

I feel nervous suddenly, as though I don't want to say anything else. Perhaps I should leave things as they are, keep Thomas Everard at a distance, get on with my own life, my own job.

But I know now that I cannot do that. And I know that Thomas's family arrive in just two days' time. I might not get another chance.

'Can we meet?' I ask. The words come out fast and breathless. 'This evening, in the usual place.'

'But I thought...'

'Please,' I interrupt, almost desperately.

He says nothing, turning back towards the cast, back to directing the play. I can only hope that he will be there.


The evenings do not stay as light for as long now we are in early August and I stumble a little on my way to the kitchen garden. I am still clutching His Lordship's copy of *David Copperfield* – not that I've had much chance to read any of it this summer and not that I could see to read it anymore if I did. I wonder if the other staff notice that I've gone, if they wonder what I am doing. I've always had a tendency to spend time alone, to disappear with a book whenever I can. That has worked in my favour now.

I am sick with nerves, have been all afternoon and was unable to eat any of my tea.

'You must eat, Annie,' Mrs Derbyshire had said. 'I know it's hard.'

She thinks that my lack of appetite is down to grief.

The nerves don't go away as I walk as fast as I can to the kitchen garden. I have no idea if he will be there, or if what I said to him last time we were here has changed his mind about me completely. Alternatively, what I'm about to say might change his mind too – it leaves me looking fickle, unable to make a decision.

But my whole life has changed since we last spoke. Everything is different now.

He is there when I arrive, leaning against the shed blowing smoke rings into the gloomy, sticky air. I watch him for a moment before I say his name.

'Thomas.'

He turns immediately, dropping his cigarette and standing on it. Ned will know we've been here I think to myself, when he sees that stubbed-out cigarette. I realise that I no longer care. I have nothing left to lose.

He walks towards me and stands as close as he can without touching.

'I've changed my mind,' I say, my voice a rushed whisper. 'I want to come to America.'

He doesn't say anything for a moment and the air stills as though fate itself is making a decision.

And then I feel his hands on my arms, his lips on mine.

He tastes of cigarettes and champagne.

He tastes of my future.

## 22

Haverford House, Yorkshire – August 2003

'So you just happened to find these frogs,' Sebastian said.

'Toads,' Chase corrected.

Sebastian turned and glowered at him. He could be quite intimidating when he put his mind to it but Viola knew he was just playing another part tonight. The part of the concerned brother, growling and threatening anyone who approached his sister. This wasn't really about frogs or toads, although the toads were about to change Viola's life. At least, she hoped they were.

Viola hadn't been sure whether to trust Chase at first. He had lied to her by omission back in June and she couldn't be sure whether or not there was some other, more suspicious reason why Chase was so interested in these toads. After all, he seemed the least likely newt-fancier she had ever seen. But he'd met her by the lake every afternoon and they'd watched the toads together as he'd told her more about how rare they were, how they'd only been found in Scotland for the last forty years and what a big deal this could be for Haverford – a make-or-break deal.

She hadn't told anyone about the toads at first, wanting to do her own research and be one hundred per cent sure of Chase before she broke the news to Seraphina. She couldn't find any holes in his story at all. She'd gone into Harrogate to look up 'smooth-bellied toads' at the library and spent so long reading about them the librarian looked at her as though she was going mad. She'd even phoned up a local conservation group to ask their opinion. Not knowing who she was and thinking she was talking about toads in a backyard pond, the chair of the group had tried his hardest not to laugh at her, telling her that it was extremely unlikely she had found smooth-bellied toads anywhere in England.

The discovery of the toads had thrown a new light on Chase as well, and Viola was beginning to see him as the person he wanted to be rather than the person he thought his father wanted him to be. He talked less and listened more, answered her amphibian-related questions patiently and smiled a lot more than he had done before his newt-loving secret was out, especially when they were down by the lake. She might not have kissed him immediately after having seen the toads for the first time, but she did kiss him three days later by the lake, the toads croaking in the background.

Two weeks had passed since Chase had first shown Viola the miracle that might save Haverford and, now she was sure of everything, she was going to tell Seraphina all about it the next morning. She had no idea how David would take it as the toads would likely mean that the property couldn't be sold and developed after all, but she was sure the dowager countess would be delighted. But first she had to tell her brother everything.

Which is how they came to be sitting in a row on Viola's tiny sofa in her small sitting room at Haverford, looking as though they were waiting for a bus. Sebastian sat in between Chase and Viola and grilled Chase about amphibious wildlife for a surprisingly long time considering that he couldn't tell the difference between a frog and a toad.

'So you're absolutely genuine?' he asked after a while, sounding a little bit calmer. It was understandable he hadn't trusted Chase at first – after all, neither had Viola.

'Absolutely,' Chase replied. 'I have no idea if the Conservation Trust will help or if this really will save Haverford from developers but I do know that it's definitely worth a try and I would be very surprised if they weren't interested.'

'Hmmmm,' Sebastian grumbled. 'And what about my sister?'

'My intentions with your sister are entirely honourable,' Chase jumped in before Viola had a chance to say anything. 'I messed up last time and I've explained and apologised about…'

'I'm right here,' Viola interrupted. 'And none of this is your business, Sebastian. I'm just keeping you in the loop.'

Sebastian glowered at both of them a little bit more in an affected sort of way as though even he was tired of playing the part of protective brother.

'I don't quiz you on every girl you're photographed with after all,' Viola went on. 'Now tomorrow, I suggest we go and see Seraphina and we tell her everything.'

'And I'll take her down to the lake and show her the toads,' Chase said, his eyes lighting up at the prospect, which made Viola smile. 'You should come too, Sebastian.'

'Maybe,' Sebastian replied. But Viola knew he'd be there. He was invested now, she could tell.

'Toads?' Seraphina said for about the fifteenth time. 'Toads are going to save Haverford?'

'That's the plan,' Viola replied.

'Come and see them,' Chase said, enthusiastically.

They stood – Sebastian, Viola, Chase and Seraphina herself – in the living room of the dower house, too excited to sit, too unsettled to make tea or talk around a table. To an outsider it was a bizarre ensemble – the movie star, the dowager countess, the heir to a hotel magnate (although after this toad escapade he may well be written out of his father's will), and Viola in her Haverford House polo shirt.

'Yes, let's go and see them,' Seraphina said, turning to Viola. 'David is not going to like this,' she went on, but her smile betrayed the fact that she was delighted that maybe Haverford would be saved, that it might not be sold.

They walked up to the old boathouse two by two, Chase and Viola leading the way, hand in hand, and Seraphina and Sebastian bringing up the rear.

What was happening between her and Chase? Viola wasn't sure for now. She was sailing on a cloud of positivity brought on by the idea that she might not have to leave Haverford, coupled with Chase's frequent kisses. Once things with the Conservation Trust were certain, once everything was in writing, then she would talk to Chase and ask what was going on. Until then she was just living day to day, hour to hour, relishing a sense of joy she hadn't known for a very long time.

When they arrived at the lake, Chase took Seraphina to one side to show her the toads and explain their importance once again (although he certainly didn't seem to mind talking about his favourite subject).

Viola stood with her brother as the others peered at toads through binoculars. Pleased as she was about the toads she was in no hurry to look at the ugly things again.

'Can we really trust him?' Sebastian said.

'I think we have to. I mean how likely is it that he's winding us up about these toads? And if he is won't the Conservation Trust just nip it in the bud and then we'll know?'

Sebastian nodded. 'And what about you and him? I'm not interfering,' he said. 'Honestly. I just don't want you to get hurt.'

Viola sighed. 'Oh, Seb, I'm thirty-three years old. I can take my own risks, you know.'

'I know it's just... well... he lied to you before...'

'Omitted to tell me something important as encouraged by David,' Viola interrupted. 'And David can be rather ruthless.'

'OK.' Sebastian shrugged, reluctance in his voice. 'But how can you be sure?'

'I'm not sure.' Viola smiled. 'How can any one of us be sure? How can he be sure about me? Chase and I have only just met and we'd be mad to be sure or trusting each other already. I do really like him – you were right about that – but for now it's just a bit of fun.'

'I'm sorry. I know you don't need your brother here telling you what to do,' Sebastian said.

'But it is good to have you here during this momentous toad-related occasion.'

He smiled then. 'I haven't seen you for so long, Vi,' he went on. 'It's years since we spent any proper time together and I know that's my fault. I'd just hoped we'd spend this summer together.'

Viola reached out then, taking her brother's hand in hers. 'And we will, I promise. There's still quite a lot of summer left you know.'

'And I'd hoped, when I made the decision about *Sunset Bay* that you'd come back to Australia too but now we've found these damn toads...' He paused, looked away. 'I know I'm being ridiculous.'

'Seb, if we can save Haverford then I'll stay because this is the nearest thing I've had to a home since I was eighteen. But I promise that I won't let things slip back into how they have been. Even if we live half a world away from each other we won't go years without seeing each other again. I don't think it's good for either of us. But it cuts both ways.'

Sebastian looked at her then. 'I know,' he said. 'I know.'

The fact that Viola and Sebastian had drifted apart hadn't happened on purpose; it wasn't anybody's fault. It had just been the result of two people running away from their own feelings when they should have been talking to each other. And now they were here, and talking – Viola wasn't going to let that go again.

'Come and look at these toads properly,' Viola said then, pulling her brother towards the lake. 'Look at them through binoculars and let Chase bore you to death about them. You never know, maybe he is winding us up about them and then you'll get your way and I'll come back to Australia.'

Chase wasn't winding them up about the toads. The Conservation Trust confirmed their presence just a week later, three weeks to the day since Chase had first shown them to Viola.

A group of three men and a woman arrived one morning, laden down with equipment. It was extremely early, not long past dawn, but Viola and Chase were ready and waiting for them. Sebastian, who had promised to be up and ready, was nowhere to be seen and Viola wasn't surprised. He'd never been a morning person and he'd been up late the night before after the performance of *Macbeth*. The Shakespeare Festival seemed to be running itself this year without much interference from her, which was just as well because her mind was full of toads.

There was a sentence she never thought she'd say to herself.

'I hardly slept last night,' Viola admitted as she clutched Chase's arm as though her life depended on it. 'I'm so nervous, this is make or break.'

Chase ducked to kiss the top of her head. 'It's make,' he said. 'I promise.'

'Hi, I'm Michelle,' the woman said as the Conservation Trust team piled out of their van. She shook Viola's hand vigorously. 'I'm one of the amphibian experts at the trust.' She turned then to her team. 'This is Nick, Dale and Jason.'

Viola nodded, smiling at the men, not really sure who was who.

'Shall we go and see the toads then?'

Chase led the way, talking to Michelle the whole time about amphibians of various kinds while Viola brought up the rear, desperately trying to quell the increasing nausea she felt as they got nearer to the old boathouse. When they arrived she hung back, not wanting to hear what was going on. She had convinced herself that the toads in the lake were common-or-garden toads, not smooth-bellied ones at all. She was about to make a complete fool of herself in front of the Conservation Trust and that would be the end of Haverford forever.

She looked out across the lake. It was the most beautiful morning and the boathouse was shrouded in early morning mist, making it look ethereal. The sun was already warm and Viola felt suddenly tired as though she wanted to just lie down here in the sun and sleep for days. So much seemed to have happened this summer.

Chase interrupted her thoughts. 'Come on,' he said, taking her hand and leading her toward the lake just as she had with Sebastian a week before. 'This is your moment. You don't want to miss it.'

'But what if they're not...

'They are,' Chase interrupted quietly. 'Stop worrying.'

'It's incredible,' Michelle said as Viola approached. She was looking intently towards the toads through powerful binoculars as Nick, Dale and Jason were measuring various things with complicated-looking equipment down by the edge of the lake. 'I've never seen smooth-bellied toads so far south before.' Michelle took the binoculars away from her face and grinned at Viola. 'I cannot tell you what a joy this is to see,' she said. 'These little guys are incredibly rare and for them to have a breeding ground in Yorkshire is…' She paused and rubbed a hand across her face. 'It's unbelievable really.'

'So they are definitely smooth-bellied toads?' Viola asked nervously.

'Definitely,' Michelle replied. 'Congratulations, Viola, I can't believe you found them!'

'It wasn't me who found them,' she said, finally starting to believe that Chase's toads were going to save Haverford. 'If it hadn't been for my friend we'd never have known they were here.'

'Well, whoever found them, I am absolutely delighted,' Michelle went on. 'The Conservation Trust will want to preserve and improve the habitat for the toads, which means we will probably want to acquire the whole estate.'

'What about the house and gardens?' Viola asked.

'Well, we'll need them to keep running to bring money into the estate. The trust will want to continue to run the estate as a business. Or rather help the Montagu family run the estate. From the family's point of view things will remain much the same. We'll be on hand to help financially and in any other ways that are needed. While the toads live quite some way from the house itself, we won't want anything to change significantly. It'll be too disruptive to the habitat, especially in the early days.'

Viola felt the relief flowing through her body. She would be able to stay at Haverford. The Conservation Trust would help preserve the house, her job and Seraphina's home. Despite having spent the summer desperate to find some way of saving the house and grounds, she hadn't really expected to, not in the end.

'How busy does it get in this part of the estate?' Michelle asked.

'Oh not very busy at all. This area isn't really open to the public. We don't close it off exactly but we don't encourage walks around here.'

'Good because we are going to have to close it off, for a while at least. The situation here isn't ideal. The pH of the water is all wrong and that boathouse is slowly rotting into the lake. We'll have to dismantle it and have it removed before the water becomes detrimental to the health of the wildlife. Then we'll have to work on growing various plants and encouraging various wildlife to make the perfect ecosystem for the toads.'

'I see,' Viola said slowly. 'The boathouse would have to go.'

'Is that a problem?'

Viola thought about this part of the lake and the boathouse, the place where David's grandmother and her siblings had swum as children. What would Seraphina say? Would this change things? Surely not? At the end of the day it was just a boathouse made of rotting wood. Sacrificing that to save Haverford had to be worth it.

'I'm not the owner, so I can't really say one way or the other…' Viola began.

'No, sorry, I do realise that.' Michelle smiled but she seemed to be starting to get impatient now, as though she was ready to tear down the boathouse with her bare hands. 'Is it possible to speak to the owner?'

'Well David… um, I mean the Earl of Haverford, is in America right now but his mother is meant to be meeting

us here.' Viola looked at her watch. Seraphina was late –
another person who wasn't great in the mornings.

'Perhaps you could call her?' Michelle asked.

'Of course.'

Michelle went back to the lake and Viola walked over to
a place where she knew there was a better phone signal. She
flipped open her phone to dial, but in the end didn't need to
as she spotted Seraphina walking towards her.

'So sorry I'm late,' she said. 'I was on the phone to David
– it's about midnight over there. What's the verdict?' She
nodded towards where the Conservation Trust team and
Chase stood at the side of the lake.

'They are definitely smooth-bellied toads and the trust
will almost definitely help us keep Haverford open.'

'Oh thank God,' Seraphina said, letting go of a huge
breath. 'I've been so anxious. I mean after what Chase
Matthews did I had no idea if we could trust him, although
I suspect that was more David's fault than Chase's.'

'What did the earl say when you spoke to him?' Viola
asked.

'Oh he's in the most terrible rage. Absolutely furious that
it looks like he won't be able to sell the estate. He's flying
home on the first available flight.'

'Is this going to be a problem?'

'Of course not. Leave David to me.'

'And your daughter – Belinda?'

'I've spoken to her as well and while she pretends not to
care either way and tries not to take sides between David
and me, I think she was relieved when I told her, to be
honest. All's well that ends well I guess.'

'Perhaps,' Viola said quietly.

'There's a problem isn't there?'

'Maybe…' Viola looked back towards the lake. 'The trust say that the lake is not in an ideal condition for the toads. They want to make some changes.'

'Well, that is to be expected I suppose. What sort of changes?'

'They want to pull down the boathouse.'

'Oh,' Seraphina said with a smile. 'Is that all?'

'I thought it might be a problem, what with the family connection and everything.'

'That's all sentimental nonsense really, me hanging on to my husband's memory.' She sighed. 'If it's a choice between the boathouse and the whole estate, well, quite frankly, the boathouse can go.'

'Really?'

'Really. In fact let's get the damn thing torn down before David gets back and starts pretending he's interested in the memory of Daniel Montagu just to annoy us all!'

The team started work on the lake almost immediately and a few days later Viola received a letter that she felt she had been waiting years for – a letter confirming the terms of the acquisition and a five-year preservation grant from the Conservation Trust to the Haverford estate. Her job, and her life here, secured for the next five years with one piece of paper.

'Let's celebrate,' Chase said when she showed him the letter. 'All of us. You, me, Sebastian, Seraphina. We can go anywhere you like. My treat.' Despite everything he was still trying to prove himself to her brother and to the dowager countess, even though they had both accepted that he had been misled about the hotel situation by David.

As for David, his rage seemed to have dissipated somewhere over the Atlantic and by the time he had returned to Haverford, like a modern-day prodigal son, he too had learned the art of acceptance.

'It's a bloody shame I can't make any money out of it all,' he'd said ruefully, 'but at least I won't be losing money anymore with the Conservation Trust plugging up the gaps.' He'd stayed overnight, simply to keep his mother happy, and then disappeared back to London to make more of the money that he loved so much.

'I'd rather celebrate alone with you,' Viola said now, taking the letter back off Chase and wrapping her arms around his neck, kissing him rather chastely on the cheek but they were standing in the hallway of the house where anyone could see them – the hallway where, just a few weeks ago, Viola had first found out that Chase was the son of Reese Montgomery. So much had happened since then and she and Chase still hadn't had a chance to talk about where their relationship was going. She wondered if he wanted to go back to America at the end of the summer and how she would feel about that if he did. She should just ask him, but there was something she had to do first.

'Just the two of us it is,' he said. 'Besides I have something I want to tell you.'

Viola felt her stomach flip at that, wondering what it could be. But she pushed it aside for now.

'I need to go and find Sebastian,' she said. 'Show him the letter.' She waved the piece of paper in the air.

'He won't be happy,' Chase replied. 'This means you won't be going back to Australia with him.'

'He'll live.' She turned away from Chase then, towards the visitor' entrance to see if she could find her brother before rehearsals started. She met Michelle coming the other way, breathless and red in the face.

'Michelle?' Viola asked. 'Is everything all right?'

Michelle looked at Viola and then at Chase standing behind her. 'No,' she said. 'I don't think it is. We started to dismantle the boathouse this morning and we've found something. I...' She stopped and took a breath. 'I'm afraid we're going to have to call the police.'

Part Four

# DEPARTURE

The Connaught Hotel, Mayfair, London – September 2003

*E*mily *is having the time of her life. As she tells the writer
about her day – a day of museums and art galleries,
of cocktails at the Ritz and oysters in Borough Market –
the writer sits back in her chair and smiles to herself. She
is happy she has been able to give Emily this experience,
happy that she can make something good happen out of a
trip that might just break her own heart.*

*'And have you seen all of London that you wish to see?'
the writer asks.*

*'I don't think you could ever see all of London could
you?' Emily replies. 'I think Dr Johnson was right about
that. How could anyone ever tire of this city? But I've seen
what I wanted to see for this trip if that's what you mean.
I'm ready to help you with the next stage.'*

*'Yes,' the writer says slowly. 'The next stage.'*

*'I've reserved first-class tickets on the train to York the
day after tomorrow and I've booked us into a hotel near
York Minster.'*

*'Oh, you'll love the Minster,' the writer says, even though*

she has never actually seen it herself. The writer had wanted to stay in Harrogate, which was much nearer to Haverford, but the train journey was difficult, with several changes and Emily did not want to drive too much on what she called 'the wrong side of the road' so in the end the writer had conceded that York would be just fine.

'But this part of the trip isn't about me. This is about you.'

Emily knows the whole story now, everything about the writer's life before she became a writer. Before New York, before her first husband even. Everything. The writer has never told anyone everything before.

'We will drive from York to Haverford if that's all right with you. There used to be a branch line, back when I lived at Haverford, just outside Cranmere. None of those little village train stations exist anymore.' She wonders what it will be like to be back in Cranmere and how it will have changed.

'It's not too far,' Emily says.

'Not too far,' the writer repeats.

The writer hears somebody calling her name. 'Elizabeth Smithson?' the voice asks and she jumps for a moment. Nobody should know who she is here.

And then she remembers. Of course people know who she is.

'I'm such a fan of your books,' the woman gushes. 'I don't want to bother you or anything; I just wanted to tell you how much I love your work.'

'Thank you,' the writer replies, relieved that the fan didn't want a picture or an autograph.

'Have you let them know you're coming, Ms Smithson?'

*Emily asks, as the fan walks away, whispering to her companion.*

'Who?'

'The people at Haverford House.'

*Elizabeth Smithson shakes her head. 'Not yet, dear,' she says. It has been harder for her to make that phone call than she'd thought it would be. 'I thought I would call from York.'*

# 23

Haverford House, Yorkshire – August 1933

The house is a whirl of activity as we prepare for the arrival of the Everards and the party that will welcome them, not to mention the grand debut of *Twelfth Night* of course. Meanwhile my head and stomach are also in a constant whirl. I'm unable to eat, unable to concentrate, unable to think of anything but Thomas and America.

We meet in the kitchen garden whenever we can both get away which, with the party looming ever closer, is becoming increasingly less frequent. I seem to be constantly busy, helping in all areas of the house when the girls don't need me, and Thomas is wanted by the family all the time as his parents' visit gets nearer. But none of that has stopped him making the plan he promised. True to his word he is planning my escape, and he is coming with me.

He wants us to leave on the night of the party.

'There's a ship that sets sail from Liverpool the next day,' he says. 'It's the perfect opportunity.'

'How can I leave everyone in the lurch on the busiest night Haverford has known for years?' I ask. 'I can't do it.'

'The house will be chaos though,' he goes on. 'It will be full of temporary staff and all the maids and valets that come with the guests. Nobody will notice you're gone until we're miles away.'

I know he's right, but I am awash with guilt and whenever Mrs Derbyshire asks me if I'm all right I feel that I can't do it; I can't leave. But I know I have to. I've come too far to stay now.

I am to travel as Thomas's wife, which fills me with a mixture of horror and excitement. 'Annie Everard,' I say to myself.

'No,' he replies. 'We should probably get rid of the "Annie" while we have a chance. So you can disappear.'

I hadn't realised I was disappearing. Do I want to disappear?

'A fresh start,' he corrects himself. 'Do you have a middle name?'

A fresh start I can get behind. I tell him my middle name.

'And when we get to New York we can get married for real,' he says, kissing me gently. 'That is, if you want to. This offer of taking you to America still comes with no conditions at all. You are your own woman, Annie Bishop. You can do as you like.'

'Are you asking me to marry you?'

He nods, a shy and hopeful look on his face.

'Then the answer is yes,' I say. Of course it is yes! As if I'd have said anything else. All those weeks of waiting for Thomas to propose, wondering if it would ever happen, and when it did it was over in heartbeat.

And he proposed to me.

How could I say no, and yet how could I not feel guilty at the prospect when I know full well Prunella is still expecting something, still expecting him to say those words to her.

My head is full of plans, full of fear that I'll back out at the last minute, fear that we'll get caught, fear that we'll hurt people. But there is something else. Too late I remember that I'm not as free as I thought I was. My mother may not be in Cranmere anymore but Polly still is. How can I leave her?

Mrs Derbyshire has been to see her, but Polly told her that nothing was wrong, that she was happy in her marriage.

'She didn't ask me to come inside the house though,' Mrs Derbyshire had told me. 'She opened the door herself, which was strange as I'm sure her mother-in-law has a maid, and she hovered in the dark hallway as though she didn't want to be seen.'

But if Polly didn't want our help what could we do? I would have to leave her behind and carry that guilt with me as well.

The girls are caught up in what they are going to wear for both the arrival of the Everards and the party. Well, Lady Prunella is caught up in all that at least. Lady Cecily claims not to care and spends most of her time with Hannah Rivington. Prunella talks about the coming weeks a lot. Thomas's parents will be here in a couple of days and then the party is to take place a week from then. In less than two weeks I will be packing my few belongings in my box again and leaving Haverford forever. I am worried about my lack of clothing but Thomas assures me he has sorted that out.

We are to travel second class as well. He doesn't want to bump into anyone who might know him or his parents. Not until we are in New York and married and it is too late for anyone to object.

'I suppose he is delaying his proposal until his parents arrive,' Lady Prunella says one night as I help prepare her for bed. I hadn't really been listening, thinking instead about that day in the not-too-distant future when I would never have to prepare anyone but myself for bed, and her statement feels as though it has come out of nowhere. She hasn't mentioned Thomas or his imminent proposal for several days and part of me had thought she had given up on him. At least that what I'd hoped. Anything to allay the guilt.

'My lady?' I ask in a non-committal way, not really sure how to respond.

'When Thomas proposes,' she says, turning around to look at me. 'Weren't you listening to a word I said? I must say, Annie, you seem to be in dreamland most of the time these days. Are you all right?'

I cannot bear everyone asking me if I'm all right. *Of course I'm not*, I want to scream, *my mother has died and I'm about to run away to America. Would you be all right in those circumstances?*

'I'm fine,' is all I say out loud. 'It's just quite stressful downstairs what with the Everards arriving and this party coming up and Mr Prentice training the temporary staff.'

'I'll bet,' Prunella says with a smile. 'But the sooner his parents get here the sooner he'll finally propose.'

'I suppose so, my lady.' I think it's the lying I hate the most. I'll be glad when I don't have to lie anymore.

'He'll need to ask Papa's permission too, of course,' Prunella rattles on. 'But I suppose that has already been done. After all let's not kid ourselves, why else would he stay all summer other than to marry one of us – and Cec is hardly going to marry him.' She gives me a wry look, one eyebrow raised.

'Do you love him?' I ask. The question is wildly inappropriate for a lady's maid to ask but I suddenly need to know. Am I going to be breaking her heart with what I am about to do?

'Oh no,' she says breezily, getting into bed and settling back against the pillows. 'But I imagine I will grow to love him. He is incredibly handsome after all. It's hard to marry for love when you are the daughter of an earl. You either marry for connection or, as is the case with us, for money. Lots of the bloody stuff. It's all Papa cares about.'

I am relieved to hear she doesn't love him.

'All that love stuff doesn't really matter you know, Annie,' Prunella says, sounding unusually cynical. 'Not in the grand scheme of life. You'd do well to remember that.'

But it matters to Thomas, I think to myself. I know him and I know it matters to him.

And I also know that I love him desperately and that Prunella is wrong.

Love does matter. It matters tremendously. And that's why I have to try to do something about Polly before I leave.

As it turns out Polly comes to us for help in the end.

The Everards arrive on a Friday evening. We, the staff – including the temporary staff Mr Prentice had hired to boost numbers – greet them in the formal manner on the steps of the house and we therefore hear their complaining right from the start. Thomas had told me they were difficult people, but I'd just put that down to the normal arguments between parents and children, and the fact that they hated his acting career.

They complain relentlessly – Mrs Everard has a headache from the 'dreadful British weather'. It is too hot and stuffy and, according to her, British hotels have no idea how to look after their guests. She's hated all the food she's eaten so far and takes immediately to her bed upon arrival at Haverford. Mr Everard Senior complains about the roads, the pollution, the state of the British people, the chaos.

'You wouldn't get this sort of thing in Germany,' he says, as he shakes His Lordship's hand vigorously. 'That Mr Hitler has everything back in order it seems. A great man.' I watch His Lordship's mouth tighten and hear Mr Prentice sniff beside me. Neither of them is a fan of Mr Hitler and what he is doing in Germany. Mr Prentice, who rarely offers an opinion about anything, will not have him spoken about below stairs. Mr Everard Senior will need to keep those opinions to himself if he hopes to get along with everyone over the next few weeks and I make a mental note to say something to Thomas when and if I can.

Like their son, neither of the Everards have brought any staff with them. Unlike Thomas, however, they do expect to have everything done for them so it is up to me and James to act as their lady's maid and valet respectively. James is not happy about it, but I haven't got time to listen to his whining as I'm now busier than ever, looking after Mrs Everard as well as the girls and performing all the other duties necessary as we prepare for a house party in a very understaffed house.

On that first evening I help Mrs Everard to bed. She has brought a box of American medications, which all have long, complicated names that mean nothing to me. When she asks me to prepare her 'headache tincture' I have no idea what she's talking about.

'You British girls are hopeless,' she says, snatching the medicine box from me and preparing a complicated tonic herself. 'I do hope my Thomas doesn't end up marrying one of you, no matter what Teddy might think.' Teddy is her husband, Theodore. I already know that he is keen for Thomas to marry into the British aristocracy. That's what his visit to Haverford has been about all along. Mrs Everard (her name is Marjory, but I don't think she wants anyone to know that) is less keen it seems.

The next morning Lady Prunella is full of questions about Marjory Everard, the woman she thinks will become her future mother-in-law.

'Did she mention the wedding at all?' she asks.

'No, my lady,' I lie. 'She wasn't at all well last night and went straight to bed with some American medicine.'

'American medicine? How intriguing. Illegal drugs do you suppose?' Lady Prunella has always had an eye towards the salacious.

'I couldn't possibly say, my lady.'

'Hmmm.' Lady Prunella seems disappointed by this. 'Hopefully she'll be well enough for the play this afternoon.'

The play! I'd almost forgotten that the one and only performance of *Twelfth Night* is to take place this afternoon.

'I'm sure she will, my lady,' I say.

But Mrs Everard doesn't want to see any play at all.

'This headache still bangs like a drum behind my eyes,' she tells me when I arrive to take her breakfast tray away and help her dress. 'And now Thomas wants me to watch some goddam play.' She looks up at me, eyes narrowed. 'Are you in it?' she asks.

'No, my lady,' I reply.

'Now tell me, Annie,' she goes on, still glowering at me. 'Why do they call you Annie? As a lady's maid shouldn't you be called by your last name whatever that is? I've been reading up on all this British etiquette but what's the point if you can't stick to it.'

'I started as a housemaid, my lady,' I say. 'Lady Cecily and Lady Prunella always called me Annie then and it stuck.'

'I shall call you by your last name,' she proclaims. 'What is it?'

I think about the paperwork Thomas is putting together for the ship to America and how my name on that will be 'Elizabeth Everard'. I don't know how or where he is getting this paperwork from and I don't ask. I have this feeling that asking will get somebody in trouble, somebody who is not Thomas.

'Bishop,' I reply.

'Bishop,' she repeats and begins to bellow her orders.


The play goes badly, which is no real surprise. Nerves have hit and if only some of the cast knew their lines in rehearsals, none of them seem to remember anything at all today, not even Hannah Rivington. The only person who knows their lines is Thomas and he knew them all before. His Lordship has insisted that all the staff are to watch the play from the edges of the garden and this means that I cannot be there to prompt the actors. Unfortunately they have become too reliant on me and fall apart completely. Mr Everard Senior stands up during the second act and storms off.

'Complete waste of my time,' he says as he leaves. Mrs Everard clutches her temples, her headache clearly still bothering her, and I wonder if I should fetch her medicine box.

Thomas breaks for an interval early and I manage to catch his eye before he goes off to find his father. His face is a mask of despair. I remember how the play was supposed to be fun, something to while away the long hot summer. But none of it seems fun anymore and the summer has become too hot, too oppressive. Mrs Everard isn't the only one with a headache.

It is as I am helping to serve afternoon tea to everybody that I notice Ned standing at the edge of the garden in the shadow of one of the bushes. I haven't seen him properly since the night he approached me in the kitchen garden, before my mother died, back when I had decided not to go to America. I wonder how much he knows now.

He beckons me over and I try to ignore him and carry on with the tea service. Mr Prentice already disapproves of how distracted the play has made me – the play has become a handy foil for what is really on my mind – and he will not appreciate me breaking for a liaison with the gardener's boy. Everyone stands or sits about, drinking tea and eating the tiny, delicious cakes that Cook has baked, wondering what is going on. The interval came early and now Thomas has disappeared. The actors mill around, waiting for instructions.

When everyone seems suitably distracted I slip across the garden to Ned.

'What do you want?' I hiss. 'I'm working.'

'You've got a visitor,' he says.

'What visitor?' I ask. 'I can't see anyone right now.'

'I know you're still seeing Mr Everard in the kitchen garden,' he says, changing the subject and making me wonder if there is a visitor at all.

'Please, Ned,' I beg. 'Not now. You can't say anything now it's…'

'America,' Ned says. He knows and that means I'm in trouble.

'Do I have a visitor or are you just trying to distract me?'

'Come with me,' he says.

I look over my shoulder, hoping that nobody can see me, as he leads me away. I follow Ned towards a small copse between the garden and the near side of the lake and I see that somebody is there waiting in the shadows.

Ned turns to me. 'I don't know what trouble you've got yourself into, Annie,' he says. 'But I do know when I need to keep my mouth shut and I will if you want me to.'

'I need you to,' I say, peering at the figure in the trees. 'Please.'

He shakes his head. 'I'd have given you a good life you know, Annie. Don't forget that.' And with that cryptic statement he walks away just as I realise the person in the trees is Polly.

She turns to me as I approach and I gasp when I see her. She has two black eyes today and a cut on her lip that is still bleeding a little. There is blood on the front of her blouse.

'You have to help me,' she whispers.

# 24

Haverford House, Yorkshire – August to September 2003

'It's Annie Bishop isn't it,' Viola said. 'It has to be. I knew she'd never left the estate. Oh God, how awful. I wonder what happened to her?'

'We don't know that yet,' Seraphina replied. 'We don't know anything. I can't believe the police still won't tell us what's going on.'

'We know what's going on,' Sebastian said, his voice dull with boredom. 'They've found human remains in the old boathouse and…'

'I don't mean that,' Seraphina snapped. 'I mean they won't tell us whose skeleton it is or when we can reopen.'

Sebastian didn't reply; he just pressed the bridge of his nose with his forefinger and thumb. Viola could tell he was going out of his mind. He never could sit still and do nothing.

'I'm sorry,' Seraphina said more quietly. 'I shouldn't have snapped at you, Sebastian. None of this is your fault. It's just extremely stressful.'

Sebastian nodded. He understood; they all understood.

The four of them – Viola, her brother, the dowager countess and Chase – were all sitting in Seraphina's living room in the dower house. This is where they had spent most of their waking hours since the Conservation Trust had broken the news about what they had found.

A skeleton, in the mud under the disintegrating wood of the boathouse structure. A human skeleton. Human remains, as Sebastian had said.

Human remains. Whenever Viola heard those words she felt sick to her stomach. She'd been down to the boathouse with Seraphina after the Conservation Trust made their gruesome discovery, but neither of them had been able to look. It hadn't felt right to do so.

She felt as though she was living inside one of the crime novels her brother loved so much. How could this be happening here at Haverford?

'It does look to be fairly old,' Michelle had told Viola when she'd first broken the horrible news. 'But we are still obligated to let the police know. I believe that if the body is over fifty years old it will be considered archaeological remains, which means that there probably won't be an investigation, but…' She trailed off, shrugged. Viola, whose stomach was at a rolling boil by that point, had wondered how Michelle could stay so calm. Perhaps this wasn't the first time she'd found something horrible during the course of her work.

The first thing that had come into Viola's head, once she had got the contents of her stomach under control, had been Annie Bishop. She hadn't been able to stop thinking about her since. She should be worrying about the fact that Haverford was closed, the Shakespeare Festival on hold and that there was no money coming in. But as usual her mind was with a lady's maid who had disappeared seventy years before.

Almost exactly seventy years before.

It had been over a week now since the skeleton had been unearthed and August was about to give way to September. The light had changed. The days were shortening as the shadows lengthened. The weather in the day remained hot and humid but the evenings betrayed more than a hint of autumn and a sense of the ending of things. The ideal time for outdoor theatre had been and gone and still Haverford was left in a kind of limbo.

The police had arrived almost immediately after they were called but, after their initial investigations and questions, they realised how old the remains were and seemed to lose interest.

'It's probably somewhere between sixty and a hundred years old,' the detective inspector had told them. 'At a rough guess anyway. Not a recent crime anyway, if it was a crime at all. When it comes to archaeological remains like this it's very hard to ever find out what happened.'

'So you don't know?' Viola had asked.

The detective inspector had shaken his head. 'No idea. We've had the cadaver dogs in as you know, and they didn't find anything else.' Viola remembered their arrival as they leapt out of the back of a van and ran towards the lake. 'Obviously human remains are always a serious business but it's not our department given the age of it really. We deal with current crime.' He had said that last with an air of superiority as though current crime was more important, as though people from the distant past didn't deserve justice. 'This one's for the cold case lot.'

'And when will they be here?'

The detective had sucked air through his teeth and coughed. 'Not for a week at least. Their Chief is on annual leave isn't he? Canaries I think, lucky bugger. They'll be here when he gets back.'

'In a week's time,' Viola repeated.

'That's right.'

'So what happens to the area? Will it be sealed off and then we can reopen?'

'Afraid not, sorry to say.' Although he hadn't look sorry at all. He'd looked as though he wanted to leave. 'You'll have to stay closed. We can't risk anyone tramping about on it.'

'We have to close for another week?' Viola had been horrified. 'This is our busiest time of year.

The detective had held his hands up. 'Nothing we can do about that but I believe that's what insurance is for.' He'd smiled a smarmy sort of smile and Viola had loathed him even more.

'So we just have to wait here twiddling our thumbs until this cold case squad deign to grace us with their presence?'

'That's about the size of it.' The detective had looked over his shoulder where his sergeant was signalling to him. 'There'll be police on site keeping an eye on things, protecting the area from gawpers.'

'Gawpers!' Viola had exclaimed. 'How will people even know about it?'

'It'll be in the papers tomorrow – you mark my words.'

Viola wanted to punch this smug detective. 'Place is crawling with press already but we'll keep them at bay – don't you worry. Now...' he'd sucked air in again '...I must be off.'

And off he'd gone. Viola hadn't seen him again and now, over a week later, couldn't even remember his name.

David had turned up again briefly not long after that, furious about everything. He stayed just long enough to complain endlessly about the amount of money they were losing and to tell everyone that should the Conservation Trust pull out after all this bother, then he would be selling the house to the highest bidder and would not be talked out of it.

'Remember who's the damn earl,' he'd said before returning to London and leaving everyone else to do the work. Not that there was much that could be done other than keeping the house and gardens in immaculate order for when the public could return.

What police presence there was, and mostly it was fairly low, could not be drawn into saying a word. They hadn't been very good at keeping away the 'gawpers' either. Viola had chased several people with cameras out of the estate over the last few days and the story had been all over the press.

At first it had been the local news only – a few column inches that just reinforced what everybody in Cranmere had already been talking about. Annie Bishop had finally been found – it was strange how everyone had suddenly changed their opinion about what happened to her when the press came asking questions. People who had laughed kindly at Viola and told her that Annie had left for a better life were now in the local paper claiming they always knew she'd never made it out of the estate that night.

It was infuriating but it was only the local press. However, it being August, a slow news month when parliament was closed and everyone, like the cold case squad, was on summer holidays, the national press needed to fill their pages too. Unfortunately for everyone, they chose to fill them with the grim discovery at Haverford House and endless, often factually incorrect, stories about Annie Bishop and Thomas Everard. The story was everywhere but Seraphina had insisted that nobody – none of the staff, none of the actors who were still hanging around, not Chase nor even David – could talk to them under any circumstances after the initial press release.

'Perhaps it will all blow over,' she'd said, without conviction.

Viola thought they could work the whole thing to their advantage, once they were allowed to open again, but she didn't voice that opinion out loud just yet. It was too soon.

Everyone was even more on edge than usual this morning because the cold case squad had finally turned up. Led by Detective Superintendent Fintan Boyle, they had arrived in two huge black cars and a van. Their vehicles had driven down the gravel drive far too fast and then the cold case squad themselves had swept out of the vehicles like they were film stars.

'For God's sake,' Seraphina had muttered as they watched from the dower house window.

They had all gone straight to the lake, ignoring everyone else. Viola had been told that the superintendent would be down to talk to them later that morning. So once again they waited in the dower house hoping for news, hoping that today would be the day they could finally reopen.

'There's a good chance it is Annie Bishop though,' Chase said to break the uncomfortable silence after Seraphina had snapped at Sebastian. 'The age of the skeleton fits and who else could it be?'

'Exactly,' Viola replied leaning back into Chase's arms. 'Who else could it be?'

Chase had been a rock since the discovery. He'd stayed on at Haverford – Viola had made up one of the empty rooms for him so that he didn't have to keep staying at the pub in the village – and he'd tried to be as helpful as he could during a very difficult time. Viola had been happy he was there and even Sebastian was warming to him.

'If you're happy then I'm happy,' her brother had said.

They hadn't been able to have the celebration they'd planned when the Conservation Trust grant was confirmed – they weren't even sure that they would still keep the grant now, but they had been able to spend time together, to get to know one another, and Chase had been able to tell Viola his news.

'I've decided to leave my father's business,' he'd said. 'I've been working in a job I hate for far too long. I'm going back to school.'

'You are?' Viola had replied, worried that this meant his return to America would be imminent.

'Zoology, specialising in herpetology.'

'Herpe-pardon?'

'Herpetology is the study of amphibians and reptiles.' Chase had looked slightly embarrassed as he said it.

Viola had laughed. 'Of course it is! That's fantastic, Chase. I'm so pleased for you. When will you start?'

'October.'

Viola had tried to hide her disappointment. 'So you'll be going back to America soon?'

He'd taken her hand then. 'I'm not going back to America,' he'd said. 'This is something I want to do on my own and I've always had a bit of a longing to live in the UK again, ever since I was at Oxford. I've been thinking about it for ages, filling out the forms and then not sending them off, but when I first spotted the smooth-bellied toads I knew I was kidding myself. I had to give this a go and I've been in England a while now, since my father sent me here.' He'd looked up at her and smiled then. 'It's beginning to feel like home.'

'So where will you be studying?'

'Sheffield,' he'd replied.

'That's going to be a culture shock after a lifetime in New York and a year in Oxford,' Viola had said.

'But it's a culture shock I'm happy to take,' he'd replied.


There was a loud knock on the dower house door that made all of them jump.

'A policeman's knock,' Sebastian said as he got up to answer the door.

Viola heard voices in the hall and then Sebastian came back in, the police trailing behind.

'Detective Superintendent Fintan Boyle apparently,' Sebastian said.

'I do usually do my own introductions,' Boyle said, holding his police badge out in front of him. 'And this is Sergeant Caroline Lewisham.' The blonde woman standing next to Boyle smiled and took out a notebook. 'Would you mind if we asked a few questions?'

'Not at all, Superintendent,' Seraphina said. 'Would you like a tea or coffee?'

'It's a bit hot for that,' Boyle replied. 'But an iced water would be lovely. One for my sergeant as well please.'

While Seraphina was in the kitchen, Viola made cursory introductions. She wanted to ask Boyle if he'd had a nice time in the Canary Islands while they were all waiting to find out what would happen to the estate, but didn't really dare.

'So you're Viola Hendricks,' Boyle said. 'We'll start with you I think. You're the manager here.'

'Yes.' Viola's mouth went dry and she became unusually monosyllabic. The last time she'd sat in a living room talking to a policeman had been the night her mother had died.

'How long have you worked here?' Boyle asked.

'Um, since 1998,' she replied.

Sergeant Lewisham wrote something down in her notebook.

'So you know all about the legends of Haverford?'

'You mean the disappearance of Annie Bishop, don't you?' Viola said, finally finding her voice.

Boyle nodded slowly and smiled. His smile reminded her of a snake.

'Everyone round here knows some version or other of that story,' she said.

'But it is more than just a legend or story, isn't it,' Boyle went on as Seraphina handed him his glass of water. He stopped to take a long drink. 'Annie Bishop did disappear one night in August 1933 during a party and Thomas Everard, our American actor, returned to the house with blood on his shirt claiming he couldn't find her.'

'And the case was closed,' Sebastian said from where he was standing in the corner of the room.

'The case was indeed closed,' Boyle replied. 'But it was closed without evidence or conclusion and now human remains that may date back to that night in 1933 have been discovered. And that's why I'm here.'

'So the skeleton is Annie Bishop?' Viola blurted out, unable to help herself. She felt Chase's hand on the small of her back and she sat back in her chair. 'Sorry,' she said.

'That's quite all right,' Boyle went on. 'Now did any of you know that Annie Bishop wasn't the only person to disappear that night?'

'Edward Callow and Polly Mather also went missing,' Sebastian said.

'Well you have all been doing your homework, haven't you?' Boyle replied. Viola couldn't work out his tone of voice. Were they in trouble in some way? 'Tell me, Mrs Montagu,' he went on, turning to Seraphina.

'I'm usually addressed as Lady Haverford,' Seraphina interrupted in her most penetratingly posh voice.

'My apologies.' Boyle ducked his head to hide his smile. 'I am unfamiliar with aristocratic traditions.' He looked up again. 'Lady Haverford, the Conservation Trust tell me the boathouse where the body was found had been unused for years. Do you know why?'

'Superintendent,' Seraphina said then, authoritatively. 'Are we being formally questioned in a murder case?'

Boyle softened then, smiled. 'No, of course not,' he replied. 'I'm not even sure there has been a murder. I just wanted to ask you what you knew about the events of that night in August 1933 and why the boathouse was such a secret.'

'Probably no more than you,' Seraphina sniffed.

'Humour me,' Boyle said.

So Seraphina told him about the boathouse and how her husband's mother and aunt had closed it up after the First World War and how it would have been closed for fourteen years by the time Annie disappeared. Viola went on to tell him everything she'd ever known about Annie Bishop, both truth and legend, and Sebastian admitted to asking his researcher to do a little bit of digging.

'As far as I was aware,' Seraphina said, 'nobody has ever really known the truth about what happened to Annie Bishop that night. Although I believe the police pinned the blame on Edward Callow in the end, as nobody could find him. Either he'd run off with Annie or...' She trailed off.

'Something more nefarious,' Boyle finished for her, looking at his sergeant who was scribbling in her notebook.

'Could it be Annie's body?' Viola asked quietly.

'We don't know very much more than you do,' Boyle replied. 'But I can tell you that the remains are not those of Annie Bishop.'

'They're not?'

'No, my pathologist reliably informs me that the remains are of a male.'

There was a palpable silence in the room then, and Viola

didn't understand why Boyle couldn't have told them it wasn't Annie right from the start. He seemed to be enjoying himself and she became inexplicably angry with him until he told her, in the next breath, that she could open Haverford to the public again.

'The day after tomorrow,' he said. 'We need to move the remains and work with the Conservation Trust to make the area safe again.'

After much effusive thanks and a great sense of relief, Boyle and Lewisham left and everyone started talking at once. Viola was about to ask them all to be quiet when her mobile started to ring. She took it into the kitchen where it was quieter and flipped it open.

'Hello?'

'Is that Viola Hendricks?' a woman's voice asked.

'That's right.'

'I was given your number by the main switchboard at Haverford House. They said it would be all right to call.'

'Who is this?' Viola asked.

'My name is Elizabeth Smithson,' the woman replied.

'Like the novelist? Sorry people must say that all the time.'

The woman chuckled gently. 'I am the novelist,' she said.

*Great, just what we need*, Viola thought. *A detective novelist wanting to write a book about Haverford.*

'But I am not telephoning in my capacity as a novelist,' the woman went on.

'How can I help you?' Viola asked.

'I read about the discovery at Haverford House in the *New York Times*. I grew up in Cranmere and I used to work at Haverford in the 1930s.'

'You did?' Viola felt herself grip her phone tightly. She couldn't believe that the story had made it into American papers.

'I was a lady's maid,' Elizabeth Smithson went on. 'I've changed a lot since then as you can imagine. I'm ninety-one years old now, but I have never forgotten what happened in 1933 and I think it's time to set the record straight.'

She paused then and Viola didn't know what to do. She felt that if she asked the wrong question then Elizabeth Smithson, novelist and ex-lady's maid, might hang up.

'I went by a different name then of course,' Elizabeth continued eventually. 'I used to be called Annie Bishop.'

# 25

The play fizzles out after Polly's arrival, not that anyone other than Ned knows yet that Polly has arrived. Thomas is still missing after the impromptu interval – according to James he is locked in the library having a heated discussion with his father – and I don't much feel like chivvying the actors on now. It's a shame after all their hard work but really no amount of rehearsing could make this group put on a successful play so perhaps it is a blessing in disguise. We were fools to think that anyone would want to see our little play, however much joy it had brought us over the summer.

I ask Ned to take Polly to the servants' hall and to tell Mrs Derbyshire to meet me there. Surprisingly, he does as I say without asking questions. Perhaps he has worked out what is going on, perhaps he is as appalled as I am. Maybe she has even told him. I don't have time to think about that though.

Instead I help clear up the teacups and make sure

Prunella's guests are all right. Lady Prunella herself looks sad and subdued – no wonder really, the play has been a disaster and now Thomas and his father have disappeared. The guests start to disperse, calling greetings to each other and saying they would see each other again at His Lordship's party next week.

Next week.

My mouth is suddenly dry at the thought that a week from today I will be on my way to America.

And that's when the idea comes to me.

'She can come to America with me,' I say. Hearing the words come out of my mouth for the first time feels like a shock, but not as much of a shock as the one I have given Mrs Derbyshire, who looks horrified.

'America! What's America got to do with anything?'

'I'm leaving,' I confess. 'On the night of the party, next week. I'm leaving with Mr Everard, with Thomas.' I hate having to tell someone the secret. The more people who know, the harder it will be to escape on the night, but it's the only way I can think of to get Polly as far away from her husband as possible. She can't go on living like this, not now.

We sit in Mrs Derbyshire's parlour, Polly asleep in the armchair. We are trying to keep our voices low so as not to wake her, but Mrs Derbyshire's shock is hard to keep quiet and she takes a moment after my revelation to compose herself.

'I thought I could deal with him,' Polly had said before she fell asleep. 'I thought I could change him, calm him down, make him the man he was before we got married. But I couldn't. It's when he drinks you see, but now he drinks all the time and so...' She'd paused.

'When did this start?' I'd asked. 'Did you know he was like this when you married him?'

'No. It started on my wedding night,' she'd said. 'Of course I didn't know,' she'd snapped at me. 'Do you think I'd have married him if I knew?'

'I'm sorry,' I'd said. It was a stupid question.

'No, Annie,' Polly had replied, reaching for my hand but not meeting my eyes. 'I'm sorry. I shouldn't have snapped at you.'

I'd squeezed her hand back.

'It started on my wedding night,' she'd said, her head bowed as though she had something to feel guilty about. 'I was such a fool.'

'None of this is your fault,' I'd said.

'I'd thought it was so romantic, falling in love with a solicitor who I bumped into at the Easter fair. I never told you how we met but it was literally that. I bumped into him and stumbled. He helped me up and offered to buy me a lemonade. We started talking and he seemed so interested in me. He was so handsome and clever and funny and when he asked if we could meet again I said "yes" without thinking. It never crossed my mind why he would want to marry a maid, someone so far beneath his social class.'

I'd realised then that it had never occurred to me either and perhaps it should have done. Perhaps I would have been more wary of Thomas if I had thought more about Polly's situation. I'd looked over at Mrs Derbyshire and wondered what she had thought about Polly's marriage at the time. Whatever it was, she had kept her opinions close. I'd wondered then if she had regretted that.

'Of course it's obvious now why he wanted to marry me,' Polly had gone on, still not lifting her head. 'Me with no family or connections, nobody to ask awkward questions or keep an eye on me. He thought he could do what he wanted with me.'

'Well,' I'd replied, 'he didn't reckon on your family back at the house then did he? We're always here for you, always here for each other. You know that.'

'And what about his mother?' Mrs Derbyshire had asked. 'She lives with you. Does she know?'

Polly had smiled wryly. 'If she does she certainly doesn't let on.'

Nobody knows Polly is here yet. Ned had the good sense to install Polly in a quiet part of the servants' hall and then immediately went to fetch Mrs Derbyshire without telling anyone else or making any fuss. He is still loyal in a way. He hasn't told anyone what he knows and the thought makes me feel that slice of guilt all over again.

*I'd have given you a good life you know, Annie. Don't forget that.*

Am I making a terrible mistake? Am I getting those ideas above my station that my mother always warned me about? Will Thomas abandon me in New York or at some point on the journey? But the thought of staying in Cranmere and marrying Ned fills me with more fear than either of those options. I have to trust Thomas.

'And how are you getting to America?' Mrs Derbyshire asks me now, her voice measured and quiet again.

'By ship from Liverpool,' I reply.

'And Thomas Everard is paying for all this, is he?'

'It's not what you think…' I begin.

'But you have been meeting him in the kitchen garden every night, haven't you?'

'You know?'

'I didn't come down in the last shower, Annie,' she says, her voice resigned. 'I've seen more than one maid… well, you know.'

'I promise you it's not like that,' I say. 'Thomas isn't like that.'

'He hasn't taken advantage of you?'

I shake my head. 'No, not even a little.'

Mrs Derbyshire purses her lips and looks down at her hands in her lap.

'Does he love you?' she asks.

'He says so. I believe him.'

'And do you love him.'

'Yes.' I pause. 'Does everyone know?' I ask.

'No, just me.'

*Just you and Ned*, I think.

'I don't blame you,' she sighs. 'I don't blame you wanting other opportunities. You're an intelligent young woman, Annie, and you shouldn't be stuck in service for the rest of your life. You don't want to end up like me.'

I open my mouth to protest but she stops me by raising her hand.

'And you shouldn't be stuck here married to Ned either,' she goes on. 'That's no life for a woman like you. So I don't blame you to want to escape. But why the secrecy?'

'So as not to hurt anyone,' I say. 'Particularly Lady Prunella.'

'Ah yes, running off with His Lordship's daughter's fiancé. You're going to cause quite the scandal at Haverford, Annie Bishop,' she says, a smile twitching at the corners of her mouth.

'You're not going to stop me?' I ask. One of the risks of this plan of course was Mrs Derbyshire turning on the whole thing, telling Mr Prentice or even His Lordship and stopping it completely. But I have to get Polly away, quickly, and so I had to take the risk.

I had to tell Thomas that we'd need another ticket, more paperwork. I wasn't even sure if he could get it all in just a week.

It feels as though the plan is unravelling before my very eyes. But then I look over at Polly's sleeping form in the chair and I know I can't leave her behind to her fate at her husband's fists.

'I'm not going to stop you,' Mrs Derbyshire says. 'And I'm not going to tell anyone.'

'Thank you.'

'I'm not doing it for you,' she goes on. 'I'm doing it for Polly. If you can't take Polly with you for whatever reason you'll have to stay and help her some other way. She came to you. You can't abandon her.'

'I know.' I'd known from the moment Ned brought her to me that afternoon.

'So I suggest you speak to Mr Everard as soon as possible as he'll have to procure more papers for Polly.' She stopped then and looked at me. I couldn't read her expression. 'I'm assuming they are false papers that you're travelling on.'

I look away. It's something I'd tried not to think about. 'Well I'm travelling under a false name so yes. I assume so,' I say.

'I see. Well if Thomas loves you he'll be able to do the same for Polly.' She pauses for a moment. 'You should ask him where he's getting them from. We both know money can buy you anything and, as Mr Prentice puts it, the Everards are richer than Croesus, but you need to be able to trust each other. He should tell you the truth.'

I sit for a moment, not saying anything. She's right of course and a lot more switched on about everything in the world than any of us give her credit for.

'Well, you'd best get on,' she says. 'You've got a lot to do and the girls will want you soon. I'll look after Polly.'

Polly goes home that evening. We don't have any choice; her husband will be expecting her. I feel as though we are sending her into the lion's den but I know it's only temporary. I know Thomas will help us.

I'm sure he will.

Won't he?

I arrange to meet him at the top of Ringbury Hill. I wonder if he has ever climbed it, if he has gone there with the girls on one of their afternoons out. I try not to think about what he does when he is not with me. Ringbury is the highest hill in Cranmere – higher than the hill that Haverford House stands on – and the views from the top across the moors are spectacular. They make you feel as though nothing really matters. But I'm not meeting him here for the views; I'm meeting him here for privacy. I can't afford prying ears to overhear. If Ned hears my business that's one thing, but Polly deserves her privacy and I still don't know how much she told him when she arrived on the afternoon of the play.

I leave Thomas a note in the usual place, inside the front cover of a copy of Milton's *Paradise Lost* in His Lordship's library, and hope that he sees it in time.

The next afternoon I slip out of the kitchen door, that same kitchen door where my parents met all those years ago, and wonder how many more times I will walk across the yard, and down to the lake. Not many surely. And as I walk I think about my mother, about the little house in the village where she lived, where I grew up, and the grave where she is buried alone, because all we ever had to remember my father by was his name on the war memorial. I think again about the two young people who met at the kitchen door, and about who they became – the war that tore them apart. Is this my destiny too? Will there be another war as Andrews predicts? If so would it be safer to stay here, in the country, away from everything?

Safe.

I'm halfway up the hill when I turn and look back towards Haverford, which you can see from a completely different perspective up here. I think about everyone I have known there – James and Andrews, Mr Prentice and Mrs Derbyshire, Williams, Polly, Lucy, Cook. I will miss them all, just as I will miss Cecily and Prunella, and even His Lordship.

But I don't want to be safe. I don't want to be like Mrs Derbyshire.

I want something else.

And besides, I have to try to do this for Polly.

I take a breath and carry on climbing.

Thomas is there waiting for me when I get to the top.

'The view from here is incredible,' he breathes.

'Have you not come up here before?'

He shakes his head and holds out his hand, taking mine in his. 'I'm glad I'm here with you,' he says.

'Thomas,' I say quietly and I watch as a momentary look of concern crosses his face.

'You're having second thoughts, aren't you?' he asks.

'No, not at all.' And I realise I'm not. That my doubts have blown down the hill all the way back to Haverford. 'But will you tell me where you got the tickets and papers from? Because I'm assuming they're false.'

He looks away for a moment and then meets my eyes again. 'False name, false papers,' he says. 'I know people.'

'What people?'

'People who mostly use their skills for the good, for getting people out of Europe and into America.'

'Jewish people you mean?' I ask, thinking about what Mr Everard Senior's beloved Hitler is doing in Germany.

He nods once.

'You can't really talk about this, can you?'

'Not really. It's not that I don't trust you it's…'

'Can you get more papers,' I interrupt. 'For a friend of mine.'

'To travel with us?' he asks. He looks pale and tired. 'It's very short notice.'

I take both his hands in mine and, as we stand on the

top of Ringbury Hill with the sun beating down on us, I tell him everything – about Polly and her solicitor, about how sure she'd been, and about the bruises, the cuts, the 'accidents' she kept having. And I tell him about what happened on the afternoon of the play, while he was arguing with his father.

'And you've been carrying this around with you all summer?' he asks.

'I couldn't tell you,' I reply. 'Until she asked me for help, it wasn't my story to tell.'

'I understand.'

'Thomas, the thing is, I can't leave her behind to this awful fate. If she can't come with us, I'll have to stay until I can think of something else. I know it sounds like another excuse as to why I don't want to come with you but that's…'

'I understand,' he repeats. 'Leave it with me.'

We walk back down the hill hand in hand and I ask him what happened on the afternoon of the play, where he went and what he was talking about with his father.

'He wants me to stop acting, to join the family business.'

'What will you do?'

'As he says.'

'Really?' I'm surprised. I thought he would be back on the stage as soon as we arrived in New York.

'You see, he has also banned me from marrying any English girls, so if I am to marry you I need to please him in some other way or we will be penniless.'

I stop and turn to him. 'We're really getting married?' I ask. It still all seems unbelievable to me.

'Only if you want to, Annie. I've told you before, you

owe me nothing. I'm helping you get out of here but after that, the choice is yours.'

'And I've told you before,' I say. 'Of course I want to.'


I don't see Thomas again for two days. By the end of the second day I'm starting to worry. I can't tell Polly anything until we have the papers as I don't want to get her hopes up and I start to wonder what I can do if Thomas doesn't come back.

'Do we need an alternative plan do you think?' I ask Mrs Derbyshire.

'Give him time,' she replies. 'And try to calm down. Mr Prentice is starting to ask questions.'

'What about?'

'About why his most trusted, grounded member of staff is starting to act like a frightened bird.'

'I'm not...'

'Please, Annie, for Polly.'

She doesn't need to say any more and, thankfully, Thomas comes back the next day. I check *Paradise Lost* for messages and find a thick envelope tucked into the cover. I put it into my apron and at the first opportunity I hide in my room to read it.

He has Polly's papers and I feel myself exhale properly for the first time in days.

He hasn't let me down.


It is Mrs Derbyshire who explains the plan to Polly. I, apparently, have been going into the village far too often and

Mr Prentice is asking questions about my well-being – the housekeeper made the foolish mistake of telling him I had visited the doctor with 'women's problems', but Mr Prentice is not a man to be put off by something like that.

'I'm fine,' I find myself telling him with a fake smile every time I see him. It's obvious to everyone that I'm not fine, but Mr Prentice at least doesn't ask any more questions.

'What's going on with you?' James corners me in the servants' hall to ask me one afternoon.

For a fraction of a second I almost tell him, but he'll know the truth soon enough and I can't risk it. I feel as though too many people know already.

'Nothing really,' I say instead. 'I'm just nervous about this party. It's been a long time since Haverford had so many guests.'

'Tell me about it,' he replies and launches into a litany of moans and complaints about the amount of work expected of him, which I half-listen to only because it distracts him from asking about me.

On the afternoon of the day before the party the guests begin to arrive, bringing their servants with them who crowd the servants' hall with luggage and hats and bags and chattering voices. It feels almost too much, and I'm thankful that there is no spare bed in our room for one of them.

Katy and James are delighted by the distraction of all the visitors and an excuse to stop working for a while but Andrews gulps his tea and disappears back to the garage.

'There'll be cars arriving,' he says. 'I should be there.' But I know he hates crowds of people, and small talk. I'm not much in the mood for it myself.

'Where is Mrs Derbyshire?' Mr Prentice asks me as he tries to create order out of the chaos. 'She should be here.'

She should, but she is visiting Polly to discuss a scheme that seems less and less likely with each passing hour. I no longer believe that in a few days' time I will be somewhere on the Atlantic Ocean. It doesn't seem real. I can barely think about it and I've packed nothing. I should go and do that now while Katy is otherwise engaged.

'I'll go and look for her,' I tell Mr Prentice as I rush up the stairs.

I feel sick by the time I reach my room, but I know now is the best time to put those things that are precious to me into my box, the box I arrived at Haverford with five years ago.

What a lot has happened in that five years.

I pack a few clothes – Thomas says I won't need much and he will have some clothes for us that are suitable on board the ship – and my father's copy of Shakespeare's *Complete Works*, wrapped in the blanket I brought it in. I look at my meagre possessions. It's not much to show for five years.

But what I do have is my savings and they are much less meagre than my possessions. I tuck them away inside a woollen stocking because if Thomas lets us down, that is all we will have. At least I have our papers – the ones that Thomas left in the copy of *Paradise Lost*. I tuck them inside my Shakespeare, but I'm not sure whether I will be able to go through with this on my own if Thomas doesn't turn up for any reason.

There is one thing left to do. This isn't something that is part of the plan; it isn't something that I've discussed with Thomas. But it is important to me. I must write to Lady Prunella. Leaving with the person she still believes is going to ask her to marry him without saying anything feels wrong. Perhaps writing the letter is wrong as well but Prunella will be hurt either way. The least I can do is to tell her how sorry I am.

I don't have much time and the letter is shorter than I want it to be, but it says what I need it to say – that Thomas and I fell in love, that it took us both by surprise and that he has offered to help me move to America. I tell her how sorry I am, how much I have enjoyed working for her and how I know that she will find her own happiness one day too. I don't tell her anything about Polly. That is nobody else's business.

About half an hour later Mrs Derbyshire comes into the room without knocking. I have just put the letter into an envelope, which I stuff into my apron pocket. I just need to find the right time to leave it for Prunella where she will not find it until after I am gone.

'Polly will meet you by the disused boathouse at half past ten tomorrow night,' the housekeeper says.

'The boathouse where the girls used to swim with Daniel?'

'What other disused boathouse do you know?' she snaps. She's had enough of all of this; I can tell. 'I suggest you tell your Mr Everard to meet you there as well.' She pauses and looks at me. 'And that, my girl, is all I'm having to do with this. It's in your hands now.' She turns to go.

'Mrs Derbyshire,' I say tentatively.

She turns back to me.

'Thank you,' I say. 'Not just for this but for everything.'

She nods. 'You make sure you look after yourself and Polly. And write to me, won't you, once you're settled. Let me know how you get on.'

The day of the party goes by interminably slowly. There is much to do but I find myself unable to concentrate on any of it and instead seem to get in everyone's way. I have no idea which of the visiting servants belong to which of the visiting guests so I smile and nod and try to disappear out of Mr Prentice's line of sight as much as I can. Mrs Derbyshire finds me jobs to do that will keep me busy but out of everyone's way. She knows how nervous I am by now.

'Am I doing the right thing?' I ask her quietly.

She squeezes my arm gently. 'It's a little late to think about that,' she says. 'Focus on what's ahead, Annie. Don't be driven by fear.'

And so I imagine New York harbour, the Statue of Liberty and the life that I could live when I get there. That image gets me through the afternoon.

As I help the girls get ready for the party they both ask, more than once, if I'm all right.

'You seem very distant, Annie,' Lady Cecily says. 'It's as though you're miles away.'

'I'm sorry, my lady,' I reply. 'The last few weeks have been quite exhausting in the servants' hall. Mr Prentice has been so worried about this party.' Not to mention the fact that my mother has died and I've fallen head over heels in love with someone I shouldn't have done.

They both smile then, thinking that they understand, knowing what Mr Prentice can be like.

After they are dressed and ready, after I have tidied their rooms and prepared the beds and fires for later, my work for the evening is done. I take my time, trying to fill the hours as best I can as the sounds of the guests arriving and the beginnings of the party drift up the stairs. I can hear Mr Everard Senior holding forth in the hallway and I wonder where Thomas is, what he is doing. Is he ready to leave? Is he too watching the hands of the clocks move towards half past ten?

Eventually I go down to the servants' hall and sit with the other valets and lady's maids who are playing cards around the big table. They all know they have a long night ahead of them, waiting for the party to end and their employers to need them again. I join in the card game and laugh along at the jokes but my mind is elsewhere.

At ten o'clock I slip away quietly. I don't think anybody notices. I creep back up the stairs to Lady Prunella's room and take the now-crumpled envelope out of my apron pocket and prop it up on the dressing table next to her hairbrush. I think about how she will have to get herself ready for bed tonight. I wonder how she will feel, how she will react. And then I wonder if she will come up here early and see the letter before Thomas has left the house and I snatch it up again. For a moment I think about getting rid of it altogether, of burning it in the kitchen stove, but in the end I leave it on her pillow, under her eiderdown, where she won't see it until she goes to bed.

Then I slip up the servants' staircase to my room, change quickly out of my uniform and into the clothes I wear on my day off. I take up my box and take one last look out of the window. It is dark now but I can see the glint of the lake in the moonlight. I have to move quickly, before I lose my nerve.

Back downstairs I go, tiptoeing through the corridors by the kitchen so that nobody in the servants' hall sees me and calls out to me. I walk out into the yard, where Thomas Everard first came to see me as I read *David Copperfield*, a book I never did finish. As soon as I am away from the house and yard I start running. My breath comes in gasps as I near the lake and turn towards the old boathouse. It's dark and the ground is uneven. I throw up a prayer of thanks for the moonlight that lights my way and hope that I don't trip.

I am the first one to arrive and presume I'm early. I have no real way of telling the time though so I put my box down and I sit on the wall to wait.

After a few moments I hear a footstep behind me and I turn, expecting to see Thomas. But it is Ned who stands behind me.

'What are you doing here?' I whisper.

I see him smile in the gloom.

'I knew it would be tonight,' he said. 'I knew you'd run away while everyone was distracted by the party.' He slurs his words and I wonder if he is drunk.

'Ned, I'm not…'

He sighs. 'I know you think I'm stupid, Annie, but I've got eyes and ears and the ability to work things out. You'd be surprised by all the things I know.'

'Have you told anyone?' I ask, my heart beating hard in my chest now. Where is Thomas? Where is Polly?

'It doesn't really matter who I've told or not told, because you're going to stay here with me. Live that good life you know I can give you.'

'Oh, Ned,' I reply. 'I can't stay here with you. It would suffocate me. I couldn't love you like you deserved. I wouldn't be the wife you deserved and you'd resent me.' I think about what Mrs Derbyshire told me, how I wouldn't be happy staying in Cranmere.

'I'll be the judge of that,' he replies. 'Let Polly go with Everard. God knows she needs to escape.'

'She told you?'

'She did. We're old friends me and Polly. I tell you what, Annie, I'd make a better husband than that bloody solicitor she married.'

'I know you would, Ned,' I say, trying to keep my voice calm. 'You'll be a great husband one day.'

I turn to look over my shoulder then, searching the darkness for Thomas and Polly. Something about that makes Ned angry.

'Stop looking for them!' he shouts, grabbing my upper arms tightly so I can't move them. I can feel his fingers digging into my flesh and know they will leave bruises. 'Look at me!' he shouts into my face. I can smell the beer on his breath. You could set fire to it he's that drunk. I don't know if it's the shouting, his hands on me or the smell of alcohol that does it but suddenly I'm very afraid of him. I have no idea what to do, or what to say but then I hear footsteps, running.

'Get your hands off of her,' a voice shouts, breathless. It's Thomas. He's still wearing his evening suit and doesn't seem to have any luggage with him, which makes me think something has gone horribly wrong.

'Thomas,' I whisper.

'Don't even say his name,' Ned shouts, but his grip on my arms has loosened as he turns to look at Thomas, and I am able to wiggle free. Thomas catches my eye and looks as though he is about to speak when he is struck in the side of the face by Ned's fist. The drink doesn't seem to have harmed his aim. I watch as Thomas's nose explodes and blood drips down his evening shirt.

'Don't come any nearer,' Ned hisses at him and Thomas holds up his hands. I want to rush up to him, see if he's all right, try to stem the bleeding, but I also don't want to upset Ned any more than I have to.

It is then that I hear more footsteps, more running.

'Ned, what are you doing?' Polly asks. She is standing beside me holding a box very similar to mine. I wonder if it is the box she first arrived at Haverford with. It is all she has. Everything else was Stephen Mather's.

Ned turns to her. 'You go with him,' he shouts, gesticulating wildly. 'You go to America with him and leave Annie here with me.'

Polly opens her mouth to say something but Thomas gets there first.

'I'm not going anywhere without Annie,' he says. The words are firm but simple and something inside me unravels then. Despite the chaos and the noise, despite the fact that we will alert somebody in the house if we carry on like this, I know then that Thomas will always have my back.

But the words have antagonised Ned even further and he turns to Thomas.

'Fight me for her,' he snarls.

'I'm not going to fight you for her,' Thomas replies calmly.

How can he stay so calm with blood streaming down his face? I feel Polly's hand slip into mine and I squeeze it.

'It's going to be all right,' I whisper to her, even though I have no idea if that's true.

'What I will do,' Thomas goes on, 'is set you up in whatever business you want. Gardening yes? And enough money for a house of your own and…'

'No,' Ned shouts at him. 'How dare you try and buy me off, how dare you…' He starts to make his way towards Thomas, stumbling now as the drink starts to slow him down. He swings a fist wildly, ready to land another punch.

What happens next changes all our lives forever and plays out before my eyes as though in slow motion. Ned is caught off balance, and as he tries to right himself, the heel of his boot catches on the edge of the one of the boathouse steps. We watch as he loses his footing and falls backwards. It looks as though it happens slowly but at the same time I don't think any of us can help him. We can't get to him quickly enough. As he lands I hear the crack of his skull hitting the wall and then there is nothing as he lies there completely still. The silence that surrounds us is the loudest thing I've ever heard.

After a few moments, Polly starts to cry quietly beside me. Her hand is still in mine but I feel frozen as though I can't move. I certainly can't speak.

'I was late,' Thomas says into the dark silence. 'I'm sorry. This is my fault. I should have been here before you got here. I should never have let that happen.'

I find my voice. 'You're still in evening dress,' I say inexplicably, as though that is the biggest problem we have.

'I couldn't get away,' Thomas replies. His voice has a

strange faraway note to it. 'Everything we need is already packed and on board the ship. I've told you that.'

I watch then as Thomas runs down the steps towards Ned's inert body. His fingers feel for something on Ned's neck and after a moment he pulls away.

'No pulse,' he says quietly.

'What happened?' Polly says between sobs. 'What are we going to do?'

'He was waiting for me I think,' I say, my voice sounding slow and croaky. 'He knew about tonight, about us leaving for America. He wanted me to stay. He wanted me to marry him and…' I pause. I can still feel the throbbing in my upper arms where his hands had been. He said he wouldn't be like Polly's husband but I wonder if that was true. He'd hurt me when he'd grabbed me. He'd terrified me when he shouted in my face. Are they all like that? Will Thomas turn out to be violent in the end?

'We can't leave him here,' Thomas says and I watch him for a moment as he works out what to do.

'We have to go,' Polly says. She is trying to pull herself together, but I can hear the fear in her voice. 'Stephen will get home from the pub. He'll see I'm not there and come looking for me.' She pauses. 'We have to go,' she says again more loudly.

'You already have all the papers you and Polly need to get on the ship and to travel to America, don't you?' Thomas asks.

I nod, glancing towards my box, which is still by the wall.

'Take Polly,' Thomas goes on, 'and walk into the village to the war memorial. My friend is there with a car. His name is Clark. Tell him that I'm all right but there's been an accident and I'll be delayed. He'll take you to Liverpool and tell you what you need to do when you get there.'

'And what about you?' I ask. I can't keep the fear from my voice anymore.

'I'm going to get rid of a dead body,' he says. How is he so calm?

'And you'll meet us in Liverpool?'

He turns to me then and walks slowly back up the boathouse steps. He holds my arms and his fingers are in exactly the same place that Ned's had been only a few minutes ago but Thomas's feel soft and gentle. I don't flinch from him.

'No, Annie, I'm not going to make the ship. I'll meet you in New York.'

'But…' I begin. How can I go without him? How will Polly and I survive alone?

'Do you trust me?' he asks.

I nod. I have no choice not to.

'Then go, quickly. I'll send word somehow, I promise. I'll send someone to meet you in New York. Everything is going to be all right.'

He kisses me then and, as he slowly pulls away he turns to Polly.

'Will you be all right?' he asks.

'As long as I get away from the man I made the mistake of marrying I'll be fine,' she replies. She pulls herself up to her full height and I realise that, however scared I am, I have to do this for Polly. If she can do it after everything she's been through, so can I.

But I know that what has happened tonight changes everything.

I had wanted the lying to stop and thought that once I left Haverford the pretence would all be over. But as Polly and I run towards the village clutching our cardboard suitcases I realise that after tonight I will be lying for the rest of my life.

## 26

Haverford House, Yorkshire – September 2003

Viola had been feeling jumpy for days – ever since the visit from Superintendent Boyle and the phone call from Elizabeth Smithson claiming to be Annie Bishop.

'Do you think it's true?' Seraphina had asked when Viola told them about the phone call from Elizabeth Smithson.

'It smells like bullshit to me,' Sebastian had said. He was getting more restless the longer he was forced to stay in England, as though now he had made his decision he could barely contain himself in a country so small. But Viola knew he would keep his promise and see the festival through to the end. Reopening Haverford had settled him a little. At least everyone had something to do now.

Seraphina and Viola went back to running the house and gardens with their staff. Once Boyle had told them they could open up again it felt as though a weight had been lifted from everyone. All the staff and volunteers suddenly had a new lease of life, not least because Seraphina had celebrated by hosting an evening buffet of cheese and wine to keep morale up. Who knew how they were all feeling after everything that had happened?

'We'll have to think of new things to do next summer,' Seraphina said to Viola now. 'Especially if it does turn out Annie Bishop is alive and well and living in New York.'

'Nature walks,' Chase suggested. He'd been spending a lot of time with the Conservation Trust while Viola went back to work. 'I know you two think the toads are rather boring but, trust me, lots of people are going to be interested once we're able to reopen that whole boathouse area.'

'Any clue as to when that will be?' Viola asked.

'Probably not until next spring but it'll be worth the wait.' He grinned.

Boyle had contacted them a couple of times since the police had cleared out from the lake, taking the remains of whoever had died in the boathouse with them, and eventually had paid them another visit – without his entourage this time.

'The deceased was definitely male,' he'd told them. 'So not your missing lady's maid I'm afraid. He was around five-ten and probably in his early to mid-twenties judging by his teeth.'

'Any idea what happened to him?' Viola had asked.

'Sharp blow to the back of the head,' Boyle replied without any emotion. He was probably used to talking about blows to the head.

'So it was murder?'

'Impossible to say. It could quite easily have been an accident, although that poses the question as to why he was shut up in an old unused boathouse. I doubt he closed the door himself after he'd died.' Boyle's expression was inscrutable.

'And are you able to tell when this man died?' Viola asked, her heart in her mouth. She was lying by omission to Boyle by not telling him that Annie Bishop may still be alive. May, at that very moment, be on her way to Haverford House.

'Well now, that's a funny story,' Boyle said, smiling slowly at each of them from where he stood in the middle of the dower house kitchen. 'Because from what my forensics department seem to have discovered it looks as though he died around the same time your lady's maid went missing.'

'In the 1930s?' Viola's mouth felt dry.

'In, as you say, the 1930s,' Boyle went on, tapping his top lip with his index finger. 'Now the obvious conclusion is that the body in the boathouse is that of Edward Callow, the gardener's boy who went missing on the same night as Annie Bishop and Polly Mather, but how he died will probably remain a mystery.'

'Will you investigate?' Seraphina asked.

'I'm not sure there's anything to investigate really. Edward Callow left no relatives, not even a distant cousin so far as our records show and nobody from that time at Haverford House is still alive. There is nobody to question.' He paused and looked up at Seraphina and Viola. 'Unless you can think of anyone.'

'No,' Seraphina said, almost too quickly. 'All of the Montagu family who lived at Haverford have passed away now, and my father-in-law never lived at Haverford at all, never even visited as far as I'm aware.'

'What about staff?' Boyle asked. Viola's heart was beating

so loudly now she was surprised the detective couldn't hear it.

'Not so far as I know,' Seraphina replied. 'I mean, it's very unlikely.'

'I spoke with your children,' Boyle said.

'I hope they were helpful?'

'Not really.' Boyle smiled. 'But I didn't expect them to be. It's a very old case and, as I said, unlikely to be solved.'

'So what happens now?' Viola asked.

'We keep the body of our unidentified person who may or may not be Edward Callow for a few weeks and, if we have nothing else then, we will cremate the remains.'

'And that'll be that?'

'That will be that,' Boyle said. 'We can all get on with our lives.'

Nobody said it but Viola could sense they all thought it. Edward Callow was never able to get on with his life and none of them would probably ever know why.

Unless what Elizabeth Smithson had told her on the phone was true. If it was then she would know what happened that night. Viola swallowed. She felt guilty to even think about that phone call in front of the police superintendent.

Boyle left not long after that but not before telling them exactly what they and the staff had to say to any prying journalists. 'We can't stop people gossiping,' he said. 'But if you could keep it to a minimum for the next month or so.'

'And after that?'

But Boyle didn't answer.

'We have to tell him you know,' Seraphina said after he'd left. 'About Elizabeth Smithson.'

'Not until we've spoken to her ourselves,' Viola said. 'I promised her that on the phone. After all it might be nothing. She might be fooling us into believing she's Annie Bishop so she can get as much information as she needs to write a book about it.'

'Do you really believe that?'

Viola sighed. 'No,' she said. 'I don't.'

Elizabeth Smithson finally arrived on the last night of the Shakespeare Festival. The long, hot summer had broken and Viola wondered if this last performance of *Twelfth Night* was such a good idea after all. The evenings were chilly now and if this rain persisted she would have to call it off.

The mystery author from New York had called early that morning. She had already cancelled her visit to Haverford House twice and Viola had begun to think she was never going to come and that the mystery of Annie Bishop would never be solved.

'We are on our way,' Ms Smithson had said. 'On the road, as they say. I'm calling from my assistant's cell phone. I don't have one of my own. We'll be with you in a half hour.'

Viola sat in her office and waited. She was too nervous to do any work and, besides, her phone beeped every few minutes – messages from Seraphina, Sebastian and Chase asking if she'd heard anything, if Elizabeth Smithson had arrived.

Ms Smithson had been very specific in her instructions. She wanted to speak with Viola alone at first.

'Once I've told you everything,' she'd said, 'then we will discuss what to do next.'

Eventually Viola's phone rang – a number she didn't recognise.

'Viola Hendricks speaking,' she said.

'Viola,' a young American voice replied. 'My name is Emily and I'm Ms Smithson's assistant. I'm just phoning to tell you that we've arrived and we've parked in the disabled car park.'

'That's great,' Viola said. 'I'll come and get you. I'll be there in five minutes.'

Viola took the buggy that was used to get around the estate more easily and to assist older and disabled people and drove it down to the car park. It was still quite damp and school holidays were almost over so the estate was quiet. Emily and Ms Smithson were the only people in the small disabled car park. As Viola drew near she felt incredibly nervous. Was she really about to find out what had happened to Annie Bishop? Or was she, as a rather cynical Sebastian seemed to think, about to get conned?

She smiled as she parked the buggy and got out.

'Hello,' she said. 'I'm Viola Hendricks. It's so lovely to meet you both.'

She held out her hand and Elizabeth's assistant took it. 'It's great to be here,' she said. 'And this is Elizabeth Smithson.'

The mystery writer seemed quite sprightly for ninety-one – she held herself upright and used no walking aid. She was immaculately dressed and, when she took Viola's proffered hand, her grip was warm and strong.

'Viola,' she said. 'It's wonderful to meet you at last. I'm so sorry I had to cancel before. I'm afraid my nerves got the better of me.' Her voice was soft and there was no trace of the Yorkshire girl in it. She was all New York now.

'Not a problem,' Viola replied. 'It's lovely to have you here. My brother is a big fan of your books.'

'But not you?' Elizabeth asked with a smile.

'I'm afraid I'm more of a romance fan.'

'Nothing to apologise for there. And your brother is Seb McKay of course.'

'You've done your homework.' Viola laughed. 'Yes, that's my twin brother although he's always just been Sebastian Hendricks to me.'

'I must say I was always a fan of his when he was in *Sunset Bay.*'

'Really?' Viola was unable to hide her surprise. Elizabeth Smithson watched *Sunset Bay*?

'Oh yes, very much,' Elizabeth said.

'Well, if you stay until this evening it's the last night of the Shakespeare Festival and you can meet Sebastian for yourself.' Viola smiled, but Ms Smithson's face changed then.

'Well, we'll see,' she said. 'We'll see how you feel when I've told you what I've come to say.'

It was then that Viola properly realised that this wasn't just Elizabeth Smithson, famous and reclusive mystery writer, standing in front of her. This was also Annie Bishop, the lady's maid who went missing just over seventy years before. And she had come to lay a mystery to rest.

'I think Ms Smithson would like to talk to you alone,' Emily said then into what had become a rather uncomfortably prolonged silence. 'So I'm going to explore the gardens if that's OK with you?'

'Of course,' Viola said, pointing her in the direction of the information stall for a map and the coffee stand for a caffeine fix. As she walked away Viola turned back to her other visitor.

'Shall we go up to the house, Ms Smithson?' Viola asked, biting back the urge to call her Annie. 'We can go up to my apartment and talk there. We'll be left alone.'

'Yes, thank you.' Ms Smithson paused for a moment. 'And you must call me Elizabeth.'

Viola wondered why she was Elizabeth now and how long she'd been known by that name. The question must have shown in her face because she saw Ms Smithson smile.

'You're wondering why I changed my name, aren't you?'

'I... well, yes. I mean it's understandable but I suppose I'm wondering why you chose Elizabeth Smithson.'

Elizabeth climbed carefully into the buggy as Viola started it up and slowly manoeuvred it back into the direction of Haverford House.

'I travelled to America as Thomas Everard's wife,' Elizabeth began. 'We weren't married at that point but it seemed easier. Elizabeth was my middle name and we used that name from the moment we left Haverford. Nobody has called me Annie Bishop in seventy years and the only people who ever knew I even was the missing lady's maid were Thomas and his family and another woman who travelled with me.'

'Polly Mather,' Viola said.

'Ah, so I'm not the only person who has done their homework.'

'No,' Viola replied. 'We also know that Edward Callow disappeared on the same night.' She didn't mention what Superintendent Boyle had said about the body in the boathouse probably being that of Callow.

'Ned,' Elizabeth said softly and Viola wondered if she imagined the shake in the older woman's voice. 'Anyway,' she went on, seemingly changing the subject. 'I was Elizabeth Everard from the moment I left Haverford. Thomas and I married in America and then, after he died, I kept the name until I married a man named Sylvester Myers. This was several months before my first book was published and I chose to write under the pen name Elizabeth Smithson. Smithson was Sylvester's mother's maiden name. After my second husband died I changed my name to Smithson by deed poll.'

They were nearing Haverford House now and Viola glanced at Elizabeth to see her reaction.

'It hasn't changed a bit,' the writer said softly as if to herself.

'How does it feel to be back?' Viola asked.

'I honestly don't know. At the moment everything feels a little like a dream, as though my life then and my life now are suddenly merging. I've never allowed my two lives to cross paths before, you know. Even my second husband didn't know that I used to be Annie Bishop.'

Viola didn't say anything. She just parked the buggy near the house and listened.

'So many coincidences,' Elizabeth went on. 'You and your brother being called Sebastian and Viola, your brother performing in *Twelfth Night* right here in the Haverford grounds.' She turned to look at Viola then. 'You know we put on a play in the summer of 1933 here in the grounds?'

'I'd heard that Thomas directed *Twelfth Night* that summer. It's one of the reasons I began the Shakespeare Festival.'

'Thomas directed it and played Orsino who I believe your brother is playing?'

Viola nodded.

'The servants were not allowed to perform in the play. Lord Haverford put his foot down about that, but I was the prompt because *Twelfth Night* has always been one of my favourite plays and I knew it so well. Our housekeeper gave me some time off for that. It's how Thomas and I met and fell in love.' She stopped then, suddenly, as though lost in memory. Just as Viola was about to ask if she was all right, Elizabeth spoke again, her voice more business-like.

'Shall we get on?' she said. 'I have much to tell you.'

## 27

Haverford House, Yorkshire – September 2003

'Writing that letter to Lady Prunella was my first mistake of course. I should never have done that. It ended up causing a lot of trouble but at the time I'd assumed both Thomas and I would be well away from Haverford before anybody read it.'

Viola and Elizabeth sat together on the sofa in Viola's small flat. It had taken Elizabeth some time to climb the stairs but she'd insisted on doing it. She'd wanted to see the view from Viola's flat – a similar view across the lake to the one she'd had from her own room at Haverford all those years ago. 'My room was much higher up of course,' she'd said.

'We can go up to the servants' rooms if you like,' Viola had replied, but Elizbeth had shaken her head.

'I'm not sure I'd make it all the way up those stairs now, dear,' she'd said. And then she'd sat down, accepted the cup of coffee that Viola had made for her and began to tell the story of Haverford House in the summer of 1933 and the disappearance of Annie Bishop.

'If it hadn't been for that letter you see,' Elizabeth went on, 'Thomas could have made up a story about why there was blood on his shirt, about where I had gone and about why he needed to leave for America immediately. Because of that letter though, the whole family already knew that Thomas was meant to be leaving with me and when he appeared in the house with blood down his front, Lady Prunella, who I presume was already dreadfully upset, somehow managed to convince her father that Thomas had killed me. She may have really believed that or she may have been exacting some sort of revenge. I suppose we'll never know.'

Viola stared at the woman who used to be Annie Bishop, slowly unravelling the story she had just been told. It sounded like one of Elizabeth Smithson's novels but there was so much truth in it, so many details about Haverford and Cranmere, and it was told with such passion, such sympathy, such regret, that Viola knew what she was hearing was true. She already knew about the letter Annie had written to Lady Prunella, a letter Lady Cecily had held on to after Prunella's death. Seraphina had once told her that Jeremy had seen it as a child. Nobody seemed to know where it was now.

'I made the mistake, you see, of thinking that Prunella cared about what happened to me. I knew we weren't friends; I wasn't a fool. The daughter of an earl and her lady's maid could never be friends, but we did have confidences of course; we did speak to each other about certain things. She didn't care though. I was just a servant to her.'

'I'm sure that...' Viola began.

'No, dear, I'm old enough now to know that was how things stood. Life was very different seventy years ago and I imagine that it's hard for somebody your age, who grew up in a different country where the class system isn't entrenched, to understand. But I wrote the letter because I cared about Prunella, about hurting her feelings, and I mistakenly thought she cared about me. But as I said, the letter caused more trouble for us all.'

Viola thought about Elizabeth's words. She too worked for a member of the minor aristocracy – not as a servant admittedly, but Seraphina and David were still in charge. She had often thought of Seraphina as a friend but was she kidding herself?

On that melancholy thought she decided to change the subject.

'So,' she said tentatively. 'The body that was discovered in the boathouse was Edward Callow?'

'Yes, that was Ned,' Elizabeth replied, a tear running down her cheek. 'When I read in *The New York Times* about a body being discovered here at Haverford I knew I had to come back and tell the truth for the first time in my life. My second mistake, and the only one that really matters of course, was walking away that night. I should have stayed. I shouldn't have left Thomas to hide Ned's body, to go through all that suspicion on his own. And he never told anyone the truth. He was so loyal to me, so loyal to Polly.'

'It was an accident though ultimately,' Viola replied, pushing her cold cup of coffee away from her. 'He was threatening you and he was the one who was drunk; he was the one who hit Thomas.'

Elizabeth turned to her and looked Viola straight in the eye. 'But Ned was the one who died, and I've kept his death quiet for all these years. He had no mother or father, or anybody to really grieve for him except me. I know he acted badly that night, that he scared me and hurt me, but he still deserved so much better than being left, literally, for dead. And I shouldn't have left Thomas alone to his fate either.' Her eyes flicked away from Viola then, looking back towards the window, towards the lake. 'They let him go in the end of course; there was no proof and no body. He told them he'd walked into a tree while looking for me and broken his nose, that he'd been frantic when I hadn't shown up at the meeting place. He had to think on his feet I suppose. Later, when it was discovered that Ned had disappeared, he told the police that I must have run off with him.'

Viola sat dry-mouthed, unable to think what to say. The whole thing was shocking, far beyond anything she had imagined. To hide a death like that, even if it was accidental, seemed so callous. To pretend that the dead man had run away. But at the same time Thomas was protecting the woman he loved and Elizabeth had been protecting Polly. She had needed to get her away from her husband. Who was Viola to judge?

'Thomas lied to the police,' Elizabeth went on. 'But he did it for me and, most importantly, he did it for Polly. It was an accident as you say, but if we'd gone back to the house, if we'd told the truth, then Polly would never have escaped her husband. We had one chance to get her away.' She paused and drew a shaky breath. 'I hope,' she continued, 'that if it hadn't been for Polly I would have stayed and faced the consequences. But I had to get her away before her husband noticed she was missing.' She paused and shook her head.

'But I'm here now,' she said. 'And it's time for me to tell the truth to the police.'

Viola's breath caught in her throat. Of course Elizabeth was here to tell the police. She could hardly tell all this to Viola and not expect her to go to Boyle. It was better coming directly from Elizabeth. But she also felt there was so much still unanswered.

'Can I ask some questions before you do?' Viola said.

Elizabeth took a handkerchief out of her handbag and dabbed her eyes. 'Ask away,' she said.

'What happened when you and Polly got to America?'

'We were so relieved to finally be there. The crossing took six weeks back then and it had been a terrible six weeks. I had no idea what I was meant to be doing or how to behave and Polly, who had been brave and strong on the journey to the ship, fell apart once we set sail. Leaving a husband, however badly he treated you, was not the done thing in those days and she felt as though she had shamed herself and me and both our futures. She never quite seemed to understand that nobody need ever know. She travelled as my sister you see – Thomas had ways and means of getting false papers, because money could buy you anything back then.'

'I don't think that's changed much,' Viola interjected.

'No, perhaps not.' Elizbeth nodded. 'So we arrived in New York as two sisters who had come to America to live with my new husband, to start our lives. It was a believable enough story. Plenty of people were emigrating out of Europe at that time for various reasons.'

'I suppose that's why false papers were easy enough to get if you knew were to get them.'

'I'm not sure it was easy,' Elizabeth replied. 'And it was certainly expensive, but a lot of people were fleeing for their lives and continued to do so throughout the thirties and forties. At the time I felt that Polly was fleeing for her life. I sometimes think that the only reason I got through that journey without Thomas was for Polly. I couldn't have done it on my own. And we had no idea what was happening at home, no idea where Thomas was or if he was on his way back to New York as well. We didn't know anything until we arrived.'

'So what happened then?' Viola asked again. She watched as Elizabeth closed her eyes for a moment as though this wasn't what she wanted to talk about.

'The police investigation at Haverford had fizzled out within a couple of weeks as you know. Both Lord Haverford and Thomas's father were extremely influential people after all, but sadly the damage had been done to the Haverford name and you know already that the house was shut up for many years. Once the police had left Thomas alone he organised for us to be met when the ship arrived in New York. We didn't know that at the time of course. I don't think either Polly or I had thought much beyond landing in America if I'm honest. Luckily for us Thomas's uncle met us and helped us get through customs on our false papers. He'd always been close to Thomas, so he told us, and would do anything to help him out. I later found out that this particular uncle had helped Thomas when he'd wanted to be an actor and also had something to do with the groups that were helping people to get out of Europe. In other words,' she said, looking up at Viola with a knowing smile. 'He was quite used to dealing with false papers.

'He assured us that Thomas and his parents were safe and were on their way home. After that we were taken to an apartment in Manhattan – a huge apartment, the like of which I'd never seen before. It was so different to Haverford and it was rather a wake-up call for us both that we had walked into alien territory. We were looked after in the apartment by a maid and a cook and Thomas's uncle took us out to Central Park and so on, but basically at first we just sat in the apartment and waited for Thomas.'

'When did he get there?'

'About four weeks after us. His parents had just about got used to the idea that he was going to marry me by the time they arrived. But they swore they would never go to England again. It took them months to stop talking about the cold houses and the ignorant people and the useless police.' She paused for a moment. 'They never did go back and neither did I, until now. Thomas returned to England of course, for his training during the war but...'

Elizabeth stopped then and looked down at her empty coffee cup, which she moved slightly to the right.

'We never spoke about it you know,' she said in a soft voice, almost a whisper. 'After our initial conversation when he told me what had happened in the aftermath, Thomas and I never spoke again about what happened on that last night at Haverford. We never talked about Ned. We thought, perhaps, that if we ignored it, the whole episode would go away. But these things never go away and it sat there between us throughout our short marriage like a heavy weight that stopped either of us being happy. I loved Thomas very much. He was the only man I ever truly loved but because of what happened that night, because we tried to hide what we'd done, we could never enjoy what we had. We should never have walked away. You say that what happened was an accident, and yes it was in the moment. But it stopped being that as soon as I walked away. That is when it became a crime. One that haunted me for the rest of my life.'

Viola didn't know what to say to that. She tried to imagine herself in the same situation, but failed miserably. Would she ever be able to walk away? Can any of us know until we are in that situation?

'You were helping Polly,' she said.

'I told myself that for many years but it isn't enough; it isn't an excuse. By treating Ned badly for months, by dismissing him and ignoring him, I brought this on all of us, even Polly. She spent the rest of her life looking over her shoulder, convinced that her husband was looking for her, and I often wonder if it wasn't for the memory of Ned's death that hung over us, if she would have got over that feeling eventually.'

'What happened to her husband after Polly left?' Viola asked. 'I don't suppose you know, do you?'

'I do as a matter of fact. Another rather sad story I'm afraid.' Elizabeth stopped and dabbed her eyes again. 'Stephen Mather did exactly what Polly had predicted and turned up at Haverford that night after the pubs had closed. He was drunk of course, so Thomas told me, even more drunk than Ned had been. He started shouting and demanding that the staff stop hiding his wife and bring her out to him.'

'Thomas was there when this happened?'

'Yes, so was the whole family, all the party guests and staff and most of Cranmere's rather small police station.'

Viola tried to picture the scene but again it felt as though it was something from one of Elizabeth Smithson's novels.

'Mrs Derbyshire stood up to him apparently.' Elizabeth shook her head. 'I'd loved to have seen that. She told him exactly what she thought of him, of how she knew he'd been abusing Polly and how, when this current mess was cleared up, she'd be talking to the police about him.'

'Did she?' Viola asked. 'Talk to the police later on?'

'No, she didn't. Before Thomas had left for America Stephen Mather was dead." Elizabeth paused. "He killed himself.'

Viola's stomach dropped again. The knock-on effects of that terrible night in 1933 seemed to reach all over the village. 'He killed himself?' she repeated.

'Hanged himself,' Elizabeth replied. 'In the bedroom he had shared with Polly. I suspect it was the shame of what Mrs Derbyshire had said and in front of all those people. I've always wondered what Mrs Derbyshire thought, if she regretted what she'd said. Knowing her I expect she did.'

'You didn't keep in touch with her?' Viola asked.

'How could I after everything that had happened?' Elizabeth replied. 'I had wanted to keep in touch with a few people from Cranmere but how could I write to them, when by then they would have been under the impression that I'd either run away with Ned or something terrible had happened to me? Although I have wondered over the years whether or not whether Mrs Derbyshire worked out the truth. She was nobody's fool.'

'Thomas died in the war I understand,' Viola said, steering the conversation back to something that felt more neutral. When Seraphina had told her that she would, eventually have to tell Superintendent Boyle about the visit from Elizabeth Smithson, she hadn't been expecting this. What would happen when Elizabeth finally spoke to Boyle?

'Thomas joined the air force,' Elizabeth went on. 'He was shot down over Dresden in 1944. I never got over his death; I never got over any of it, truth be told. It was my writing that saved me. It had always been a dream of mine, a dream I had never dared imagine would become a reality. When I'd first arrived in New York I'd written a column for a magazine about being an Englishwoman in New York. Thomas fixed that up for me; his father owned the magazine company. I couldn't talk about where I'd come from of course, or who I really was, so I suppose I was writing fiction from the start. It was a popular column, even through the war, but after Thomas died, after I got the telegram, I never wrote the column again. I knew that part of my life was over.' She leaned forward and moved her empty coffee cup.

'Can I get you another drink?' Viola asked, but Elizabeth didn't answer the question.

'I thought that perhaps after Thomas died, Ned's death wouldn't weigh so heavily but it became worse without Thomas there to help bear the weight. And then Polly became ill and my life revolved around her for a year until she died in 1950.'

'I'm so sorry,' Viola said, and she genuinely was. Of all the people who deserved a second chance in this story, a happy ending, it was surely Polly.

'Breast cancer,' Elizabeth said, her voice choked with emotion. 'With her and Thomas gone I didn't know what to do with myself. I had nobody. Thomas's family stayed in touch – we'd grown fond of each other by then, united in grief I suppose – and I had some friends, but I felt lost and alone. I considered going back to England but what would I have done there? And then, suddenly when I was least expecting it, I met my second husband.'

Viola knew from Sebastian, who was genuinely a fan of her books, that she had remarried in 1952 and had her first mystery novel published not long after that. Her books had been an immediate success, making her a household name.

Elizabeth slowly closed her eyes and pressed a hand to her chest.

'Are you OK?' Viola asked.

Elizabeth nodded, carried on. 'I heard about the family, Lord Haverford's family, from Mrs Everard, Thomas's mother. I don't know how she knew so much; she seemed to know everything about everybody. It was from her I heard about His Lordship locking up the house, and from her I heard about Prunella's death. I was surprised when she told me about Cecily's marriage.' She turned to me again. 'Lady Cecily was in love with a woman called Hannah Rivington whom she met at Cambridge. Hannah was there that summer too; she performed in *Twelfth Night*. So I was surprised that she married, that she'd had a son.'

That son had been Jeremy, Seraphina's late husband, and mercifully he had been born before Lady Cecily's father died so the title continued down the line as it was meant to.

'I suppose that she felt she was doing her duty to the family,' Elizabeth mused. 'I wonder what happened to Hannah Rivington.'

Another mystery.

'One last question,' Viola said, and Elizabeth inclined her head in response. 'Why me? Why did you choose to tell your story to me and not to Lady Haverford?'

'Two reasons,' she replied. 'Firstly, it was your name in the newspaper article; it was you who had given the statement to the press about the boathouse. Secondly, none of this affects you directly.'

'How do you mean?' Viola asked. She felt it affected her very deeply, but of course Elizabeth didn't know how invested she had become in the story.

'If I'd told Lady Haverford or the current earl what I'd done it would be their family I would have been talking about, their history. Imagine how that would feel. It seemed more practical to talk to you.'

Viola nodded; she could see the logic in that.

'Now, Viola,' Elizabeth said, her voice suddenly stern. 'It has been lovely talking to you but I am here for one reason only. I'm here to admit what I did seventy years ago. And not just to you. I need to talk to the police.'

Viola had known this was coming and had realised from the start of Elizabeth's story that eventually Boyle would have to know everything, but did he have to know today?

'I believe there was a policeman assigned to the case,' Elizabeth went on. 'I saw his picture in one of the papers.

Would you be able to tell me how to contact him. It's time, I think.'

Viola paused for a moment. There was a lot at stake here. As soon as the story came out Haverford would be crawling with reporters again – Seraphina needed to know, to be prepared.

'It would have been nice though,' Elizbeth continued softly, 'to have seen *Twelfth Night* one last time.'

And it was then that Viola had an idea.

# 28

Viola persuaded Elizabeth Smithson and her assistant to stay at Haverford for just one night, to watch the last performance of the Shakespeare Festival, to see *Twelfth Night* once again, and to go to speak to Superintendent Boyle in the morning.

'Everything always feels a bit more manageable in the mornings,' Elizabeth agreed, and Viola felt herself release a little.

'I'm going to have to tell the dowager countess everything that you've told me,' Viola said. 'Before the story gets out.'

Elizbeth nodded. 'I understand. Will you tell her perhaps tomorrow, while I speak to your policeman?' she asked, as though Boyle belonged entirely to Haverford House and had no other cases to work on. Viola agreed. If they were going to put off telling Boyle until tomorrow, they could put off telling everyone.

'Your friends, your brother, will they not ask questions?' Elizbeth said.

'Not if I ask them not to,' Viola replied.

They went then to find Emily, to get rooms made up for them both. Emily said she would drive back to York and collect their things while Elizabeth rested. She'd be back in time for the final night of the festival.

'Wouldn't want to miss seeing Seb McKay in tights after all,' she said. Viola smiled tightly. She hated it when people clearly lusted after her brother.

When Emily had gone and Elizabeth had settled in, Viola sent the same text message to Seraphina, to Chase and to Sebastian.

*Elizabeth is staying for the play. Please don't ask any questions tonight. We'll tell you everything in the morning.*

Seraphina's text came back first.

*I'm desperate to know*, she wrote. *But I'll keep my big mouth closed for one night only.*


The atmosphere was electric at the Shakespeare Festival that night. The very air itself felt charged as though everyone knew something was going to happen. Something big. Something that would change everything. To Viola tonight didn't feel so much like the end of something, but rather a beginning.

They sat together on fold-up chairs towards the back of the crowd – Viola, Chase, Seraphina, Elizabeth and Emily – and ate the picnic Seraphina had prepared. They opened champagne and Emily, in particular, cheered very loudly as Sebastian took to the stage. In the interval they talked to Elizabeth about New York, about her trip over and, mostly, about her books. Nobody spoke about who she really was, even though they all knew.

'As a child I wanted to be a writer,' Seraphina said. 'My parents were big readers, had shelves and shelves of books and I liked to imagine that one day my name would be on one of the spines – Seraphina Reynolds as I was then. But the future had other plans for me I suppose.'

'It's never too late to start,' Elizabeth replied. 'I was nearly forty when I wrote my first book. It's not something you have to retire from after all.' She paused and smiled. 'It seems to me that Viola has everything in hand on the estate and thanks to Chase you have the Conservation Trust grant to keep you going. Now, I must know more about these toads.'

As Chase talked to Elizabeth about the smooth-bellied toads they'd found in the lake, carefully avoiding talking about what else had been found, Viola thought about the Conservation Trust grant. Tomorrow, when she took Elizabeth to see Superintendent Boyle, when she told Seraphina the truth about Elizabeth, about what she had done, what would happen then? They couldn't keep it quiet; there was already so much speculation about the discovery in the boathouse and, now, why Elizabeth Smithson was visiting Haverford. There were stories they could concoct and lies they could tell, and no doubt Boyle would have his own ideas about what the press should and shouldn't know, but ultimately the truth would come out as it always had a tendency to do, and what would the Conservation Trust do then? Would they take the grant away?

Then she felt Chase's hand on her back, warm and comforting, and she leaned into him reminding herself that there was nothing she could do. She couldn't control everything. For now Haverford was safe, and so was her job and all she could do was enjoy the moment and look forward to the future.

'I'm sorry I can't tell you yet what Elizabeth has shared with me,' she said to Chase.

'It's OK. I'm dying to know of course but I understand. Your loyalty to Haverford knows no bounds, does it?' He smiled.

'It's the only place I've ever lived since my mother died that truly feels like home.'

'Even now? Even after everything that has happened?'

'Even now.'

'So I'm not going to lose you to the bright lights of Kiama?'

Viola laughed. What kind of place did he imagine Kiama was?

'No, I'll definitely be back and you won't be far away.'

'I hope I'll never be far away,' he said, kissing her gently.

In ten days' time Chase would leave for Sheffield to begin his course. Two days after that Viola and Sebastian were flying to Sydney so that Sebastian could find out his schedule for the new season of *Sunset Bay* and from there the drive up the coast to Kiama. Viola was nervous. It had been fifteen years since she'd left and she'd never really imagined going back. But it also felt right – going home with Sebastian was exactly what she needed and it would give her the closure she wanted. She needed this, just as she needed her brother. Even though they would be living on opposite sides of the world, she felt they had made a breakthrough this summer. They had both stopped running. They had both found things that captured their hearts and, from now on, they would both know where the other one was. There was something very comforting in that.

Seraphina would look after things while Viola was away, as everything wound down for the end of the season. And when Viola was back, through the dark days of winter when the house was closed to the public, she would work out where they would go from here. They could hardly live off the legend of Annie Bishop anymore, not once everyone knew she was alive and living in New York. But perhaps that was just as well. Perhaps Haverford had leeched off Annie Bishop's sadness for long enough.

As the second half of the performance began, as Seraphina handed around glasses of champagne and Chase threaded his fingers through hers, Viola allowed herself to relax. Whatever happened tomorrow, however things went with Elizabeth and Boyle and people's reactions to the truth, she had so much to look forward to.

# Epilogue

'A heart attack,' the doctor confirmed. 'In her sleep. She probably wouldn't have felt anything.'

Viola stood in the living room of her own apartment at Haverford as she absorbed the doctor's words.

'I've called for an ambulance,' the doctor went on. 'It's on its way.'

Elizabeth Smithson, the woman who used to be known as Annie Bishop, was dead and with her passing everything had changed.

Emily cried quietly into a tissue, and Viola went to comfort her. Hopefully she would be even more comforted when she found out that Elizabeth had left her almost everything.

The previous night, after Emily had taken Elizabeth up to her room and settled her, the mystery writer had put her affairs in order, so far as Viola could see. It was almost as though she knew what was going to happen.

'She'd enjoyed the play so much,' Emily sniffed. 'I'm glad she got to do something special on her last night. There

347

was a run of *Twelfth Night* in Central Park last summer but she wouldn't go – she hardly went anywhere. I'm glad that article she read about Haverford and the body in the boathouse made her get out and do something again. It wasn't good for her to be cooped up like that.'

'How long had she been like that?' Viola asked.

'About four years,' Emily replied. 'She used to say that as she got older the past started to become clearer and she wanted to be alone with her memories. I thought she meant her first husband; she never really got over him. But then she told me everything…' She paused and looked at the letter and thick notebook that Viola held in her hand. 'Did she tell you?'

Viola nodded. 'She told me yesterday. She wanted to go to the police and tell them too, but I persuaded her to stay and see the play. I thought that after all these years what did one more day matter?'

'I didn't think any less of her when she told me,' Emily said. 'I admired her bravery – standing up for her friend like that, crossing the Atlantic on her own on fake papers to basically save Polly's life. I know what she did was a crime, not reporting a death, knowing a body had been hidden but…' She stopped, sniffed again. 'She was defending herself from that gardener and she was helping her friend defend herself from her violent husband.'

'Male violence seems to be something women have lived with since time began,' Viola said, biting back her own tears.

'And nothing has changed,' Emily replied. 'Nothing ever changes.'

Viola looked down at the notebook she was holding once again. It had been sitting on Elizabeth's nightstand this morning when Emily had found her, along with a letter addressed to Viola. In the letter Elizabeth explained that she was leaving the majority of her estate to Emily but there would be a yearly trust to be spent on Haverford, to preserve it and keep it open. 'Just in case,' the letter said. *In case of what?* Viola wondered. In case the Conservation Trust withdrew their grant when the truth came out?

'She wrote it all down,' Viola said to Emily as she tapped the cover of the notebook – it was thick and leather-bound, every page covered in small, neat script. 'Everything that happened at Haverford. It's all here.'

'I knew she was writing something,' Emily said. 'And I knew it wasn't another novel. Usually she dictates her books these days, since she stopped using a typewriter, and then I type them up. She was writing her confession.'

'It certainly looks like it.'

'What are you going to do with it?'

Viola sighed. 'I honestly don't know. I should take it to Superintendent Boyle. It was what Elizabeth would have wanted.' But part of Viola didn't want to do that, didn't want to live with the consequences.

'We don't have to, do we?' Emily asked. 'We could keep it just between ourselves.'

Viola thought of Seraphina, who was in the dower house waiting for news, waiting to hear Annie Bishop's story. She thought of Chase who had carefully removed himself from Haverford first thing that morning when Emily had found Elizabeth, so as not to be in the way. And she thought of Sebastian, who didn't know anything yet, who was still asleep in his trailer after the final-night party the evening before.

All of these people were invested in the story of Annie Bishop and all of them deserved to know the truth. Most importantly Annie herself, or Elizabeth Smithson as she was now known, had wanted the truth to be known and had left her confession in Viola's hands.

'You know we can't do that,' she said to Emily now. 'You know I have to go and see Superintendent Boyle. This is Elizabeth's confession after all. You and I owe her that last request for closure, that last chance to tell the truth.'

Emily sniffed again and blew her nose. 'You're right,' she said. 'Can I come with you to the police?'

'I wouldn't have it any other way.' Viola smiled.

# Author's Note

Haverford House does not exist but is based on several large houses in the north of England, as well as a house that exists only in my head. The grounds and lake at Haverford, however, are based upon the estate at Nostell Priory near Wakefield in West Yorkshire. There has never been a mystery of a missing lady's maid at Nostell so far as I know, but there was a scandal over some unpaid-for Chippendale furniture.

The smooth-bellied toad, like the blue-crested hoopoe in *Midsomer Murders*, is entirely make-believe.

# The Haverford House Playlist

1. 'A Heart in New York' – Art Garfunkel
2. 'I Walk on Gilded Splinters' – Paul Weller
3. 'Be Still My Beating Heart' – Sting
4. 'When We Was Fab' – George Harrison
5. 'There She Goes' – The La's
6. 'Sweet Jane' – Cowboy Junkies
7. 'Dream Now' – All About Eve
8. 'You've Got to Hide Your Love Away' – The Beatles
9. 'Cornflake Girl' – Tori Amos
10. 'The Whole of the Moon' – The Waterboys
11. 'Solsbury Hill' – Peter Gabriel
12. 'Mandinka' – Sinéad O'Connor
13. 'Running Up That Hill' – Kate Bush
14. 'Mr Writer' – Stereophonics
15. 'Walking on Broken Glass' – Annie Lennox
16. 'Good Morning Britain' – Aztec Camera
17. 'Love is Stronger than Death' – The The
18. 'Charlotte Sometimes' – The Cure

# Acknowledgements

First, as always, a huge thank you to my agent, Lina Langlee, for getting me through another book and listening to the usual complaining and whining that accompanies every first draft, this time with added Long Covid (mine not hers). Always grateful for you, Lina.

Also, everyone at the North Literary Agency for all their hard work, especially the foreign rights agents who sell my books all over the place, including countries I have to look up on a map!

Thank you to everyone at Aria/Head of Zeus for another beautiful book package, but especially my editor Martina Arzu, Helena Newton who has copy-edited most of my books (not too many mistakes this time, I must be learning) proof-reader Jane Howard, and Leah Jacobs-Gordon who designed the cover.

This was one of the most fun books I've ever written and incorporated many of my favourite things – old houses, unsolved mysteries, sibling relationships, social class, and my favourite Shakespeare play. Like Viola, I first saw *Twelfth*

*Night* when I was fourteen and have never forgotten it. My dad took me to the Barbican where Richard Briers was playing Malvolio, and it was perfect. A lifelong love of the playwright began on that Saturday afternoon and I am ever grateful to my dad for that.

The ideas that shaped Haverford House came from a lifetime of love for old houses but the books that helped me make it seem real include: *The Long Weekend* by Adrian Tinniswood, *1930s Britain* by Robert Pearce, *The Story of the Country House* by Clive Aslet, and *English Country Houses* by Vita Sackville-West.

Thanks as always to my husband – my beta reader, proofreader, harshest critic and greatest support. Nine books now! On to the tenth.

Finally, a huge hug to my little brother to whom this book is dedicated. He is the Linus to my Lucy and I couldn't have written Sebastian and Viola without him.

# About the Author

RACHEL BURTON has been making up stories for as long as she can remember and always dreamed of being a writer until life somehow got in the way. After reading for a degree in Classics and another in English Literature she accidentally fell into a career in law, but eventually managed to write her first book on her lunch breaks. She loves words, Shakespeare, tea, The Beatles, dresses with pockets and very tall romantic heroes (not necessarily in that order) and lives with her husband in Yorkshire.

Find her on Instagram and Twitter @RachelBWriter.